Pandora's Box 2

Pandora's Box 2

An Anthology of Erotic Writing by Women

edited by
KERRI SHARP

BLACK
lace

First published in 1997 by
Black Lace
332 Ladbroke Grove, London W10 5AH

Extracts from the following works:

Gothic Blue	© Portia Da Costa 1996
The Ninety Days of Genevieve	© Lucinda Carrington 1996
Lord Wraxall's Fancy	© Anna Lieff Saxby 1996
The Black Orchid Hotel	© Roxanne Carr 1996
Dream Lover	© Katrina Vincenzi 1995
The Big Class	© Angel Strand 1996
Ace of Hearts	© Lisette Allen 1996
The Houseshare	© Pat O'Brien 1996

Short Stories

A Very Lucky Young Man	© Mercedes Kelly 1997
The Bridal Gift	© Jan Smith 1997
The Sins of the Flesh	© Cleo Cordell 1997
Celia's System	© Meredith Sears 1997

Illustrations © Insa Heiss 1997

Typeset by CentraCet, Cambridge
Printed and bound by Mackays of Chatham PLC

ISBN 0 352 33151 8

Contents

Introduction

Pandora's Box 2 comes four years after the launch of Black Lace erotic fiction by and for women. Like its predecessor, the anthology is a mixture of extracts from books with contemporary and historical settings plus four new short stories. The first *Pandora's Box* anthology proved to be very popular. We have since published two subsequent anthologies – *Modern Love* and *Past Passions* – and a collection of entirely new short stories is being put together for publication in December. The imprint is still receiving media attention. With a number of women's magazines now printing erotic short stories as a regular feature, and Black Lace books now selling worldwide, female erotic writing is firmly on the map. Watch out for *Pandora's Box 3* plus other arousing new fiction over the coming year.

Kerri Sharp
Black Lace Editor
February 1997

A Very Lucky Young Man

Mercedes Kelly

The first of the original short stories in this anthology is by Mercedes Kelly, who has already written two books for Black Lace. *A Very Lucky Young Man* explores a type of love which still raises eyebrows – that between an older woman and a much younger man. It is said that a woman reaches her sexual peak in her thirties and men reach theirs in their late teens. In that case, the characters in the following story are very well matched.

The first of her Black Lace novels – *Île de Paradis* – is set on a tropical island at the early part of this century. The location is idyllic but it is not without dangers: the evil Jezebel, slave-mistress of nearby Dragon Island, has plans for the young English castaway who is betrothed to the Prince of Île de Paradis.

The Lion Lover – her second book – is set in the 1920s in Africa and features the intrepid Mathilde Valentine, a doctor who has been posted to a remote mission in Kenya. The dissolute missionary in charge of the post has sexual tastes which run contradictory to his chosen calling and both his former wives have disappeared in suspicious circumstances. Mathilde intends to find out the truth.

A Very Lucky Young Man

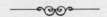

The old woman was alone in the house.

'Come in, dear. Sit down! Have you come to see Jane?' she asked. 'She's not home yet.' The white-haired lady made Laura comfortable in the sitting room and brought her a cup of tea. Laura hadn't come to see her neighbour, Jane, at all, but she didn't tell the old lady. She made polite conversation, which wasn't difficult, as she actually liked Jane's mother very much, but all the time she was in a state of tension, unable to concentrate, waiting for the gate to open and for him to walk in.

'Oh, there's Joseph arriving home,' said Jane's mother, rising from her seat and going to the kitchen to greet her grandson and pour him a mug of tea. He gave Laura a wide smile through the back window. He was covered in fine grey dust and his face was smeared and grimy. His teeth seemed incredibly white when he smiled. Laura stayed where she was, biting her fingernails in nervous anticipation.

He always showered as soon as he got home, and today was no exception. When he came downstairs he went into the living room and sat next to Laura on the only sofa.

'Hello, Joe!' she said warmly.

3

'Hello,' he said.

He was just three years older than Laura's own son and, at twenty, was a very lovely youth. He sat now, as was his habit, without shirt or vest, in jeans and bare feet. His fair curly hair was still damp from his shower. They sat in silence watching the television news – the old lady making clicking noises with her tongue at various shocking items and sighing to herself. Joseph's arms were folded over his smooth tanned chest. He worked all day with his shirt off in the sun and was as brown as a chestnut. Laura sat a few inches from him, aware all the time of his physical presence, wanting desperately to touch him.

Soon, Jane arrived home and Laura joined her in the kitchen for a glass of wine and a chat. Laura often dropped in on her friend at odd times, but now she contrived to be there when the young man was home from work. He had come back to live at his mother's house just a few months ago after an absence of three years at college, and had found work as a builder's labourer in Camden, North London. Laura remembered when she had first seen him three years before when he was still a shy young boy. Now, with the tough physical work he was doing he had blossomed into a well-developed, muscular young man with a pleasing open face and a winning smile. He also seemed to be a kind, helpful lad, always pleased to fetch and carry and do jobs around the house. In fact, he was proud of his strength and found satisfaction in showing and using it.

Laura found herself more and more under his physical spell. She lusted after him – wanted to feel his strong arms holding her down – wanted to stroke the hairless smooth chest and square shoulders. But she doubted her powers of seduction. She was, after all, eighteen years older than him. She tentatively asked Jane if Joe had a girlfriend. Yes, apparently there had been a long-standing relationship with a young girl in Leeds, a fellow agricultural student, but they had broken it off when he came back to London.

'So, is he a virgin?'

Jane didn't think so, but raised her eyebrows at the question. Laura laughed embarrassedly. 'It must be all this fresh air and sunshine,' she said, 'I'm not used to it.'

'Hmm!' Jane's sidelong glance at Laura's slender, tanned figure and glossy hair spoke volumes. For a while Laura contented herself with sitting near Joe on the sofa and, at weekends, when he had time off, lying in Jane's garden, displaying her neat, lightly-clad body to his innocent eyes.

Several days went by in this languorous way with a gradual build-up of tension as she realised he was becoming aware of her as a woman and not just a friend of his mother's. Then came the chance she had been waiting for. Jane was going away for a week or two to take her mother to her sister's house. Joseph was going to be left to his own devices.

'I'll live on fish and chips, I expect,' he said. 'I'm too whacked when I get home to bother with cooking.'

Laura's heart leapt and she seized her opportunity. 'I'll invite you to eat with me sometime, shall I?' she asked. 'Would you accept?'

A rosy blush spread over the young man's face and neck. 'That would be lovely,' he replied.

The food preparation had all been completed and Laura had closed the white curtains to keep out the light of the summer evening. She was wearing a simple summer dress of pale blue cotton, very low at the back and with a full skirt. Her hair was gleaming and her smooth skin glistened from a liberal application of baby oil. She smelled of summer – sea-breeze fresh – but with the heat of the day still on her body.

He arrived at the back door armed with a bottle of wine and a bunch of cornflowers. His dancing eyes were

5

almost the same blue. He wore clean blue jeans and a blindingly white cotton, collarless shirt open at the neck and with the cuffs undone and folded up to reveal strong thick arms. The hairs on his arms were sunbleached and the colour of his skin was like whisky or wild honey or glazed earthenware. She wanted to eat him. His big calloused hands were ingrained with hard-earned dirt and his spatulate fingers had nails that were clipped very short.

He saw her looking at them and said, 'I'm sorry, they won't come any cleaner.'

'I don't mind at all,' she said. 'I like them. I like your hands.'

A blush spread over his face.

Poor lad – he must feel even more embarrassed when he feels himself blushing, she thought. She poured wine for them both.

Joseph sat at the kitchen table and watched her while she put the flowers in water. Her back revealed her low-cut dress and her tanned, slim body. She broke off one of the blooms and, turning, placed it in the front of her dress at her bosom.

He looked huge on the bentwood chair. His arms bulged from the white shirt and she could see the muscles trembling through the fine cloth. She was hot from the thought of those muscles already.

She fed him magnificently, enjoying the obvious pleasure he took in eating, and basking in his compliments. After a few glasses of wine he looked totally relaxed in Laura's company. They moved to the sitting room and she put on some music.

'Would you like to see my drawings, Joe?' she asked. She showed him the pencil sketches and the ink and water-colour pieces she had produced that summer. They were mostly landscapes, but there were one or two of people – including a good head of his grandmother that Laura had done in the garden earlier that week. Joe admired it very much.

'It's yours! Keep it, please,' she said.

'No, I couldn't. You mustn't give away your best work,' he answered.

'I want you to have it, Joe, to remind you of me.'

'Thank you,' he muttered. He blushed again and smiled a wonderful warm smile that melted her and made her dizzy.

'What time is it, Joe?' asked Laura.

'Midnight.'

Laura steeled herself for what she was about to do, then took the plunge. 'Do you want to go home or will you come to bed with me?'

'Come to bed with you, please.'

She touched him for the first time, taking him by the hand and leading him upstairs, leaving the pile of pictures on the floor. She went immediately to the bathroom and when she entered the bedroom dressed in a white kimono, he was lying face down and naked across the bed. His back was beautiful. Every muscle was defined and moved like sun rippling on smooth water. His arms and shoulders were huge, strong, magnificent. She stared in pleasure at the gift of his body. His tight small buttocks were white and hairless and his strong calves and thighs were young and smooth.

She knelt over him on the bed and touched one arm, moving her hands to the shape of his biceps and gently stroking the same place over and over.

'You are a lovely young man, Joe,' she said.

'Thank you,' he answered.

'Shall I massage you?'

'Mmm, yes please.'

She took the baby-oil and dripped it over his shoulders. She began to languidly rub both hands over his lovely flesh, enjoying the sensation of the smooth youthful body under her touch. She moved across his arms, marvelling at their size and the thickness of his wrists. She lazily stroked his rough hands with the oil, working into the chips and scars of his battered flesh. He had such obvious strength in his smooth body. Her hands firmly moved down the length of his spine, the tips of her fingers pressing on each vertebra. He groaned with enjoyment. Laura playfully stroked the line at his waist where his tan finished and his white hips began.

She poured more oil on to his back and innocently moved her firm-fingered hands over his taut buttocks, circling them and digging her fingers into the flesh very slightly so they made faint pink tracelines on his white skin. She became almost hypnotised by the inflamed marks she drew on his buttocks; as they disappeared she sketched them again with her sharp little nails. She was very wet.

She could feel her moist sex vibrating in anticipation. She slipped her fingers between his thighs and they slid open slightly to allow her access. Her oiled fingers dug firmly into his sensitive inner thigh. He writhed on the bed, groaning in ever-increasing pleasure.

'Turn over,' she commanded quietly, and she knelt back on her heels so he could twist over on to his back. His face was flushed and his eyes dilated. She had a momentary glimpse of his short, stubby cock as it leapt up to her, before he grabbed her and pulled her roughly on top of him. She felt his small but very hard penis thrusting against her body through her thin cotton kimono, and his lips sought hers eagerly, then his tongue pushed into her mouth. She let him have this moment of passion before gently pushing him away, saying, 'Shh, shh,' as if to a hurt child. 'You must let me finish your massage.'

She poured the oil on to his lovely muscular chest that had no hairs to hide its beauty, and smoothed her little hands across his body, taking great delight in the hardness of his shoulders, the flatness of his stomach, the firmness of his thighs. His fat, stubby cock stood straight and proud, throbbing slightly; his hands were relaxed, palms upward; his arms apart. His eyes burned into her, seeing through the thin material and making her nipples hard on her swinging little breasts. She knelt up and placed his hands on her waist. He undid the bow that held the kimono together and slipped his calloused hands under the edges. Her tanned flesh tingled with anticipation. He delicately pushed the garment from her shoulders and let it drop, revealing the small brown body glistening with desire.

'You are so beautiful – I can't believe it,' he whispered.

She smiled at the artless flattery, arching her back so that her belly and breasts were pushed forward to meet his hands. They swept over her body slowly and with a gentleness that belied the strength behind them. Her nipples were little peaks of desire, as erect and thrusting as his penis. His rough hands felt marvellous on her smooth body, as if they were delicately scratching the fine skin made taut and tender by the hot sun. His stubby hands covered her breasts and let the nipples draw circles on his palms. She almost purred in appreciation.

'You'll have to show me how to please you,' he whispered humbly.

'You're doing wonderfully,' she smiled.

He let one hand wander down over her round little belly to stroke her dark mass of sex hair. Laura leant towards him and felt his hand slide between her legs. Her little body pressed his and writhed round, her breasts squashed against his hard young chest. She opened her legs so she was still kneeling over him but only supported by his body. He groaned and held her tightly, his penis pressed hard against her sex. One arm held her hard against him; the other was behind her and his hand came up between her damp thighs and stroked the engorged flesh. She was certain he was no virgin now – he was experienced in pleasing a woman. She moved her buttocks in circles to feel his fingers all over her sex lips and the plump little mound of flesh covered in curly hair. He grabbed her writhing buttocks and slammed his hips upwards, his penis finding her slit immediately and making her cry out in surprise and excitement. It might look relatively small on his sturdy, muscular body, but his penis had authority, purpose, passion. It was very hard and seemed almost sharp, touching her wetness with a force and intensity that was very exciting. She had to hold back her orgasm. She wanted to savour the first one longer than this, but Joe was having trouble making his love-making last, too. His face and chest had the strong flush of sexual arousal – his blue eyes were almost black – and sweat glistened between his breasts. She resolutely lifted herself off and away from his urgent cock and lay down by his side, all the time stroking his hair and face soothingly, licking his cheeks like a mother cat would her kitten. His chest rose and fell heavily and he groaned and put an arm across his face.

'What's the matter, lovely Joe?' she asked.

'Nothing. I just always have trouble, not coming too fast.'

'Don't worry, Joe, there's no problem, just enjoy yourself. If you want to come quickly, that's alright.'

'No, I don't want to come yet. I want to make you happy.' He opened his cornflower-blue eyes and looked at her. She was smiling, reassuringly.

'Let me make you come first,' he said.

She raised her arms in surrender and lay still, her eyes closed, her mouth slightly open. His mouth was on hers, tongue piercing her lips and searching her mouth. He was over her, his legs wide apart, his cock in one hand, his other hand stroking her thighs, holding her flesh and kneading it firmly.

'Touch me, Joe, please touch me,' she begged.

He released his cock and it sprang upwards to his belly. He pushed both hands between her legs and buried them in her moistness. His fingers found her outer lips and rubbed them, holding them open to explore inside, parting her inner lips and pushing into the juicy tunnel, which made sucking noises as he moved them in and out, leaving her gasping for more. She put her hands on his shoulders to feel his rippling young body, the clean muscular form bearing down on her. She almost swooned with delight at his eager, fumbling touch. He reached behind her to hold her rounded buttocks in one hand while he stroked the palm of the other roughened, pitted hand across her sex, and held her up from the bed by her buttocks. He levered her up from the bed and held her pressed against his cock so that her sex lips could feel it throbbing and hard at the entrance to her vagina. She began to orgasm as he carried on pressing against her, his palm rasping against her pubic hair and his hard little cock just at the entrance of her sex. His fingers rubbed slowly and firmly as the waves of orgasm rolled through her body, the walls of her vagina coming together in spasms that went on for many seconds. She fell back in a swoon of delight and sensuality.

'And you wanted to be shown what to do!' she murmured. 'Thank you, Joe.'

'Thank *you*,' he smiled widely.

They lay in a blissful state for half an hour, drifting in and out of sleep until, once more, Laura's desire got the better of her.

'Well now, what would you like me to do to you, Joe?' she said, coming awake.

He answered by lifting her on top of him.

'Do what you want, I'll like it all.'

She began to lick his face, his nose, his mouth, his ears. He groaned and moved away from her mouth.

'What's the matter?' Joe.

'Don't touch my ears, I'll come if you do.'

'Are you serious?' She smiled in delight at this news. 'Do you mean you get excited just by having your ears touched?'

'I'm afraid so.'

'Wow! What a time bomb you must be. Anyone could kiss your ears in the street and you would come!' She moved away from his over-sensitive ears and kissed his lovely shoulders and licked the length of his arms. She then concentrated on his hard, strong, calloused hands, licking between the fingers to the tips, sucking on each finger nail and finally on his fat thumbs, digging her teeth slightly into the rough skin. Laura was in an aroused state again with the novelty and beauty of the lovely firm youth beneath her. Her lips ran down the line of his chest and tugged at his nipples. 'Are they sensitive, too?' she asked.

'No, thank goodness,' he smiled.

She licked and bit gently at his taut stomach and belly and let her mouth find his pointed little penis just for a moment before teasingly leaving it to lick his thighs. Her hands rested either side of his cock, pressing down on his belly, and her head pushed and nuzzled his sex. Her mouth found his balls and her hands pressed his thighs apart so she could taste him and lick and tease the hot, almost hairless globes. Her fingernails pressed softly into the base of his penis and scratched the length of his shaft, pulling the loose skin over the tip and holding it there for a second before pushing it back down and scratching gently down to the root.

Joseph moaned and shook his head from side to side. Laura placed her hot little body on top of him, the buttocks next to his face, her sex pressed up against his chest, and she took the penis into her mouth, holding it firmly at the base and stroking his balls with her other hand. His mouth was on her sex, his strong arms holding her and moving her across his wet lips and sharp, nibbling teeth. They swayed together in a sweaty, oily orgy of desire, his tongue inside her, thrusting and darting, sucking at her sex lips. He held her buttocks apart with his strong hands, exposing her wet, swollen sex and anus to his ardent mouth.

Laura kept her fingers tight round the base of his short, fat penis and squeezed lightly to stop him from coming. She swallowed him to the hilt and suckled, her teeth digging in a little. She felt his thighs go tense as his breathing quickened. She allowed his penis freedom from her enclosed fingers and sucked strongly on the thick shaft. His cries were muffled by her sex as he came inside her mouth with little spurts that hit the back of her throat. She swallowed the hot sperm, coming almost immediately after him with an intensity that matched her first orgasm. They fell off each other and curled up like exhausted children, his head resting on her breast.

The next day, they woke to a perfect summer morning. Laura had a moment's concern that he would be embarrassed in the cold light of day and find her age off-putting. She needn't have worried: he was besotted with her. He made beautiful love to her that morning. She came with his hard little prick inside her and found it the perfect size and shape. Her sex seemed to close in and surround it, holding it firmly like her mouth had. It felt strangely pointed and aggressive – an exciting and persistent little weapon that he used with skill. She loved the way he flushed rosy red all over his face, neck and chest when he was about to come. They rolled round in the sweat of their combined bodies and their flesh slipped and slapped and aroused one another. His fingers were covered with her sex juices and he licked them and relished her salty taste.

'You must need some bacon and eggs for breakfast,' he joked.

'Not yet, I want more of you, first.' His lips traced her entire body, taking pleasure in her tiny perfect feet – feet which were as sensitive to touch as were his ears.

'Could you come with me only touching your feet?' he asked.

'I don't know. I shouldn't think so.'

He tried. He made love to her toes, kissing and licking and stroking each tiny, tanned digit with infinite care, as if she was a beautiful piece of sculpture he was preoccupied with. Her feet became all of her; all sensation was

13

concentrated on her two feet, her ten prehensile toes that spread and folded and stretched luxuriously under his tender ministrations. She felt wetter and wetter, and her sex pulsated with desire – jealous of the attention her toes were receiving.

'Stop! Please stop! I want you in me. Stick your cock into me. Fuck me!' she cried.

Her words acted like a long-awaited signal. He plunged into her ripe fruit like a knife, up to the hilt. She clung to his small white buttocks with clawing fingers and raised her knees, wrapping her legs and feet round his back, hugging him to her. They danced the crazy dance of sex together, moving rhythmically until they felt they would be joined forever by their sex organs. Her orgasms came in tiny flutters and deep spasms. She cried and yelled and moaned gently. Her face changed every time he made her come. First it was crazy with sex and desire, leering and lascivious, her lips dry, her eyes wild and unseeing. Then she was softened, gentle, her mouth open, relaxed, her lips soft and bruised-looking, her eyes closed, the flush gone from her cheeks, her damp hair flattened on her forehead, her breathing quiet.

It was then – when she was relaxed and made quiet by his efforts – that he felt that she was in his power. He had tamed her. His body was in control. He rammed into her, his short hard organ hitting her cervix and sliding nearly completely out of her to tease her clitoris for a moment before slamming back again to the hilt. He felt her wet pubic hair and her wide open sex lips rub on his balls and press them together. And it was the feeling that he was in total control – that in spite of her superior age and experience he was in the powerful position, on top of her, kneading into her, and she was finished, exhausted, spent, open wide and helpless under his superior strength – that made him burst into her, deep and long, emptying his seed with loud groans of satisfaction.

* * *

The summer passed in an erotic haze. Laura felt ten years younger, revitalised by the young man's strenuous demands. Her body glowed with health. She felt grateful for Joe's love and didn't want to hurt his young ego but her love for him was almost purely sensual. At weekends they escaped from London, driving through narrow lanes, looking for isolated meadows where they could make love. There was nothing better than sunbathing naked next to an ardent young lover – the sound of insects and seed heads bursting. Butterflies and bees were the only witnesses to their hot-skinned couplings, Hovering skylarks made music above.

On weekdays, he came home straight from work to her house, still covered in dirt and dust. She loved him like this. He was like a miner, covered in thick dirt, the whites of his eyes bleached in contrast. He always kissed her carefully, trying not to touch her clothes, just their lips meetings. One evening, though, she tempted him, pressing herself against his filthy overalls, licking the dirt from his face. Then she lifted her cotton dress, revealing her bare belly and sex, and offered it to him in sensuous writhings of her hips, like a belly dancer. She danced closer, her pelvis nudging his thigh. His penis strained through his overalls to meet her pushing, thrusting belly which was offered to him like a ripe fruit.

She pulled her dress over her head and rubbed her naked body against him. She undid his buttons and drew out the eager little cock. She knelt down on the kitchen floor, the bare boards hard on her knees, and sucked the pink, throbbing penis pointing at her. They had no contact except her mouth surrounding his sex. He was completely clothed except for the undone flies.

He found it difficult to stand with Laura kneeling at his feet, sucking hard on his swollen cock. He reeled, and held on to the pine table, regaining his balance. He knew he must stop her or he would climax immediately. He groaned.

She instinctively knew he wanted her to stop, and she

15

released his throbbing cock. Laura got on to the table, sitting with her legs off the floor, her hands braced on the wood behind her. His cock was almost, but not quite, at the right height for penetration. It just reached her sex, and he used his hands to grab her round the hips and pull her closer to him.

'I'm so dirty, I'll make a terrible mess of you,' he said.

'Yes, you will. Please do!' she replied.

He didn't need any more encouragement. He bent over her, her sex displayed on the edge of the table like an open flower, glistening with desire. His work-blackened hands smeared her clean, tanned skin. Her small breasts were tasted and sucked, the prominent nipples nibbled to erection. His work-dirt transferred from his face to her body. His sweat was strong and sweetly pungent, and she breathed it in deeply. She spread her legs and put her feet on the table top, lying back across the table. He stood, still fully-clothed, playing with this lovely naked toy. Her sex was spread open, the lips swollen and dark. Her clitoris was a pearly little peak.

His desire was too much and too young to hold back from immediate gratification. He fell on her, his penis finding her wetness and entering her completely, fiercely piercing the too tempting sex. Her head fell back, her throat swelled towards his mouth. Her mouth was open, her breath laboured. Her naked little body was smeared with dirt from his overalls and his hands and face.

He felt he was violating her, spoiling her clean fineness. He was in control. He was strong. He was enjoying his strength and potency. His penis had her impaled on the table. His hips undulated, girating his penis inside her, churning her swollen sex, which pulsated like a sea urchin, clutching at him and holding him tight.

He was a very lucky young man.

Gothic Blue

Portia Da Costa

Next follows an extract from *Gothic Blue* by one of the imprint's best-liked authors. Portia Da Costa specialises in stories with a dark and mysterious edge to the sex. In this excerpt, Belinda Seward – a contemporary young woman – has found shelter at a remote priory with her boyfriend after their car has broken down in a storm. The owner of the priory is the sensuous and melancholic André von Kastel who takes Belinda into the realm of the erotic paranormal. In this extract, Belinda is beginning to realise that André is not like other mortals – in fact, he may not be mortal at all.

Portia's other Black Lace titles are *Gemini Heat*, which features identical twin sisters who compete with each other for the attentions of an enigmatic art dealer; *The Tutor*, which is about a librarian employed to educate a young man who has led a sheltered life; *The Devil Inside*, a story of enhanced sexual perception; and *Continuum*, the story of a female office worker who is drawn into exploring games of punishment in a clandestine society. Her new Black Lace book, *The Stranger*, is due for publication in November and is a story of a young man who has lost his memory and calls one day at the house of a woman who is trying to rebuild her life. Together they find an unconventional love.

Gothic Blue

Count André von Kastel was waiting for her. Standing before one of the tall bookcases, he had an open leather-covered volume in his hand, and appeared deep in thought. He frowned suddenly, then flicked over several pages. Belinda cleared her throat to attract his attention.

When André looked up, the first thing she noticed was that his blue eyes were serious. The teasing quality she had seen earlier was conspicuous by its absence, and there was again an obscure aura of sorrow about him – something intense that came from deep in his psyche. He smiled to welcome her but still the sadness lingered.

'Good evening, Belinda,' he murmured, closing his book, setting it aside and coming towards her. 'How lovely you look. You truly are a sight to fire the spirits.'

When he reached her, he bowed over her hand again, clicking his heels. Belinda's heart pounded as his lips caressed her fingers.

André too had changed for dinner, and was now clothed from head to toe in black. Black silk shirt, black trousers and black shoes. Surprisingly, he was tie-less, but he was wearing the most elegant of antiquated dinner jackets, which suited him so beautifully that

Belinda caught her breath. His weird, striated hair was hanging loose around his shoulders, but despite its bleached look it appeared glossy and well kept. Belinda could have sworn it was even blonder than before.

'Thank you,' she said in answer to his compliment, feeling disturbed that he clung on to her hand.

'You are worried about your friend, are you not?' he said, giving her fingers a small squeeze before finally letting them go.

He's reading my mind again, thought Belinda, still feeling his firm, cool grip. 'Yes, I am rather. Johnny's usually so fit. It's not like him to come down with something.'

'Do not worry,' said André, his eyes hypnotic and soothing. 'I have examined him and basically he seems quite healthy. He is simply a little over-tired.' His mouth quirked very slightly, as if he was suggesting that *she* was the cause of Jonathan's tiredness. 'I gave him a herbal tonic. Something that will make him sleep deeply and renew his strength and vigour.'

'Thank you,' murmured Belinda again, her eyes sliding away from André's, unable to cope with the intensity of his look. She glanced around at the massed ranks of books. 'I didn't realise you were a doctor.'

He shrugged and somehow managed to capture her eyes again. 'I am not one.' He smiled, a little crookedly. 'I have a little medical knowledge but I am by no means a physician. Simply a dabbler in certain – ' he paused, his brilliant eyes dancing ' – therapies that have stood the test of time.'

'I'm very interested in alternative medicine – herbalism and aromatherapy and suchlike,' said Belinda quickly. It wasn't a lie. Standing here with André, she suddenly *was* interested. 'Do you have any good recipes and potions you can pass on?'

As she spoke, that strange shadow seemed to pass across his face again, but it disappeared just as swiftly when he replied.

'I would not exactly call them recipes,' he said, smiling, 'but there may be one or two things I can teach you. After dinner, that is.' He looked across to Oren, who seemed to be waiting for his orders. 'And now, I think, we shall have some champagne.'

This time, funnily enough, the wine was in an ice bucket. Belinda hadn't seen it when she had entered the library, but she noticed it now on the sideboard, coolly embracing a familiar, shapely bottle. With characteristic efficiency, Oren uncorked the frothing wine and filled two glasses without spilling the tiniest drop.

André took the two crystal flutes and handed one to Belinda, dismissing his servant with a slight nod as he did so. 'Not from my own country this time, alas,' he said, as he clinked his glass to hers, 'but delicious nevertheless. To your health, Belinda,' he murmured, 'and happiness.'

'What about long life?' she asked, as they sat down together. She felt intoxicated on just one sip of wine. 'Isn't that usually a part of the toast?'

André looked away then put his glass down by his feet. When he looked back at her, he seemed a mass of mixed emotions. His cultured face bore traces of irony, thoughtfulness and humour, as well as his slight but ever-present melancholy.

'Would you really want it?' he asked, his voice low and intent.

'What? You mean long life?' she countered, surprised by the sudden fire in the question. 'Well, yes, I suppose I do. Doesn't everybody?'

For a moment, André didn't answer, and Belinda got the impression that she had lost him somehow. Or somewhere. He was sitting right next to her – handsome, charismatic and desirable – but it felt as if she were seeing him across a huge gulf, a division of time and space it was impossible to quantify.

Belinda felt frightened. In spite of what had happened here on this very couch, she did not know this man at

21

all. She also had a feeling that if and when she came to know him fully, her present fears would seem as nothing by comparison.

'There are some to whom long life is a curse,' he said quietly. Then he reached down to retrieve his wine and downed it in one long swallow, his throat undulating sensuously as he drank. 'More champagne?' he enquired, on his feet again so fast it made her jump.

Belinda looked at her glass. She had hardly tasted the wine at all. She took a quick sip, then held it out. 'Yes, please,' she said, smiling as brightly as she could in an attempt to lift the suddenly sombre atmosphere.

'I'm sorry,' she said, when André returned with the wine, 'I think I've said something to upset you ... but I'm not quite sure what.'

'It is I who should be asking forgiveness,' he replied, his smile returned and his blue eyes unclouded and brilliant. 'I am being a poor host. I allow my worries to intrude at the most inopportune moments.'

'If you want to talk, it's OK, you know,' Belinda suddenly heard herself say. 'I know I'm a stranger ...' Colour flushed in her cheeks. She hadn't acted like a stranger earlier, when she had allowed him – and encouraged him – to touch her. 'But sometimes it's easier to tell your troubles to someone you don't know than it is to tell them to a friend or a loved one.'

For several seconds André stared at her unblinkingly. Belinda felt he was studying everything about her; her every thought, her every memory, her every hope and desire. 'You are a very kind and sensitive woman, Belinda,' he said softly. 'Perhaps I will confide in you. In a little while.' He smiled again, his eyes cheerful and full of promises. 'But first, we should enjoy our dinner, I think.' Draining his champagne, he put aside the glass, then rose to his feet, extending his hand to her like the courtier he most probably once had been.

He's like a prince in hiding, thought Belinda as she accompanied André to the dining room. A dissolute

prince, banished for some unspeakable crime of passion
and doomed to solitude for the rest of his days. It was a
desperately glamorous image, she knew, and made him
utterly fatal to women, especially imaginative ones like
her, who loved tales of high romance and gothic mystery.

She was laughing by the time they reached their
destination, and André gave her an amused look, as if
once again he knew her thoughts exactly.

'OK, I admit it,' she said, as André drew her chair out
and waited until she was comfortable before taking his
own seat. 'You ... and this place ... I hate to admit it,
but it really gets to me. I've got an ordinary life, an
ordinary job, and I meet ordinary people. All this is like
something from a book,' she said, gesturing around her.
'A foreign nobleman. A crumbling but fabulous house.
Antiques. Gorgeous pictures.' She paused, realising she
was gushing, and appalled by it. 'You've got me at a bit
of a disadvantage. Really.'

André laughed, a merry, husky sound that seemed to
dispel the last echoes of his sadness. 'It is *I* who is at a
disadvantage,' he said, laying his hand across his chest.
'I am at the mercy of your beauty, your compassion ...
and your open-mindedness.' He hesitated, as if debating
some thorny inner point. He seemed on the very edge of
revealing something, something which Belinda sensed
was crucial. 'You have much that I want, Belinda, and
much that I need,' he said at last. 'I am your servant,
believe me.' He bowed his head momentarily. 'And I
would do anything to keep you here in my company.
Anything.'

He spoke with such emphasis that Belinda felt chilled.
The words 'do anything' seemed to chime around the
room and envelop her, despite the fact that he had
spoken only quietly. It was a relief when Oren entered
the room, bearing their first course on a large chased
silver tray.

The meal was light and delicious but Belinda scarcely
noticed the fine cuisine. It was as if André had put a

spell on her; she could do nothing, really, but watch him and listen to his voice, and answer every question he asked about her. Revealing virtually nothing about himself, he seemed to effortlessly coax everything from her. Her past history; her present thoughts; her future hopes and dreams. Almost the whole of her life – even down to some of the most intimate details she had never told anyone about, ever – was described over the perfect food and heady wine. And when they were finished, she could hardly believe what she had disclosed.

Has he hypnotised me? she wondered as she studied the tiny coffee cup before her and smelt the divine aroma it exuded. It certainly seemed that way. She had just talked and talked and talked, while André had remained enigmatic, and listened.

He had also, she noticed, eaten very little of his excellent dinner. Just a few morsels here and there, and then only taken for her benefit, it seemed. As the strong but sublime coffee began to clear her fuddled head a little, Belinda had the most extraordinary idea ever.

He's not human, she thought, watching André push away his plate and fold his table napkin.

Suddenly, all the books she had read and the films and television shows she had seen seemed to conspire and produce an extraordinary conclusion – Count André von Kastel was a vampire, a ghost, or some other nether being who possessed strange powers and did not take ordinary nourishment.

Everything seemed to point to it. He slept during the day, he barely ate, and she was almost convinced that he had done some kind of magic trick with the wine that afternoon in the library. Plus the fact that he lived alone, in seclusion, with only three dumb servants to attend him, in a house that was crammed with peculiar artefacts. He even came from the appropriate part of Europe.

Belinda began to shake when André rose to his feet and walked around the table towards her. She felt foolish, letting her fancies control her, but when he stood over her, smiling slightly, she couldn't move a muscle and she couldn't seem to speak.

'What is it?' he asked softly, putting out his hand to her. 'Are you afraid of me?'

Belinda licked her lips. She was caught in the thrall of a being who had the combined sexual magnetism of a dozen cinematic Draculas, and even if he were just a man after all, she was sure that wouldn't lessen her growing fear of him.

'Belinda?' he prompted, making a tiny gesture of encouragement with his fingertips.

'I-I'm sorry, I think I've had too much wine,' she said, finally finding the strength to take his hand. 'I started imagining the silliest of things just then.' She stood up, half-expecting to swoon or something, but found herself quite steady on her feet.

'Tell me about them,' said André, tucking her hand beneath his arm and leading her to the door. 'Entertain me while we stroll on the terrace. I always enjoy a walk after dinner.' He patted her hand, his fingers cool but corporeal.

'It's too stupid. I couldn't tell you, really,' she insisted, as he led her along yet another corridor she hadn't been along before, that seemed to lead right through the centre of the priory.

'Try me,' he urged, as they reached an iron-studded door that surely only a man the size of Oren could master. 'I have heard many a tall tale in my time ... And told my fair share too.' He grinned and released her arm. Then he opened the huge door without effort.

The terrace that lay beyond was broad, stone flagged, and lit by a string of what appeared to be oil-burning lanterns. The sky was dark now, a rich shade of indigo, and the brightest of the stars were breaking through. A three-quarter moon rode above them like a sail. Belinda breathed in and smelt the perfume of many flowers, a rich fragrance that seemed to blend with André's cologne.

'This is so lovely,' she murmured, then hurried forward towards the elaborately-carved stone parapet so she could look out over the gardens beyond.

Why didn't I see this earlier today? she wondered, discovering that in the distance and to her left was the folly. She had approached the priory in broad daylight this morning and seen no evidence whatsoever of this long terrace. The whole house seemed to be remaking itself by the hour.

As she leaned over the parapet, she sensed rather than heard André join her. 'You were going to tell me what you had been thinking about,' he said, sliding his arm around her waist as if it were a perfectly natural thing to do with a near stranger, and as if they were about to take up where they had left off in the library. She felt his mouth brush the hot skin of her neck.

'I . . .' Feeling almost faint, she swayed against him. His lips were still against her throat, and filled with her insane notions of earlier, she expected him to attack at any second.

'Why do you fear me, Belinda?' he whispered, feathering a soft kiss against the line of her jaw. 'I am not what you think I am, believe me. I am just a man who is entranced by your beauty.'

He knows! thought Belinda as André turned her expertly and put his arms around her body to embrace her. He knows I thought he was a vampire. That I still think he might be one.

Cradling her head, André pressed his mouth to hers, probing for entrance with his tongue as she yielded. Belinda tried to keep her mouth closed and her brain sent the message to her lips, but with half a sigh and half a groan, she felt them open, admitting him to explore and taste her moistness.

The kiss went on for a long, long time, and as she enjoyed it, Belinda seemed to see a stream of inner pictures. Erotic images of herself and the man who held her.

First, she saw the way she must have appeared this afternoon: half-naked and sprawled across André's lap, moaning and crooning while he stroked her. Then, a second later, she seemed to be kneeling before him, on this very terrace, taking his strong, erect penis into her mouth. She could almost feel his fingers clasping her head as he thrust savagely, seeking the back of her throat, and she could almost taste the salt-sharp tang of come. The vision of fellatio melted then and changed to a picture of her leaning over a bed somewhere, possibly the red and gold one in her room, while André caressed her naked buttocks. He was teasing her, playing with her; dipping his fingers into her slit from behind, then drawing them up and back to fondle her pouting anus. To her horror the tiny portal seemed to welcome him, relaxing lewdly as a single digit entered.

The fantasy images were so real and so vivid that her body couldn't help but react to them. She groaned around André's intruding tongue and rubbed herself involuntarily against him. In response, his long, graceful hands sank immediately to her bottom, moulding her cheeks through the glistening dress, and pressing her to him.

Whatever his nature or strangeness, he was possessed of a living man's erection, and Belinda felt it bore into her belly. There were several layers of fabric between them, yet it was one of the most exciting sensations she had ever felt. He was like rock against her – like steel, like diamond – and despite the masking barriers, she seemed to feel his shape.

Massaging him with her body and feeling his fingers caress her buttocks in return, she began to see another set of pictures. But this time they were all of André only, in his tower room, fondling his penis until he came. She saw again, in every detail, the way he had arched with pleasure and squirmed like a wild man against the sheets. She almost seemed to hear his incoherent outcries, his mutterings and exclamations in his own

27

language. She saw him rising towards his climax, his body growing more and more tense as he strained to reach it, but at the instant he seemed to get there, the image faded. As she gasped in disappointment, he broke the kiss.

Panting for air, Belinda slumped against André's straight body, feeling grateful for his strength in her own weakness. She almost felt as if she had just had an orgasm herself, the rush had been so huge. She had certainly never been kissed like that before, and to her dismay, she felt a sudden urge to weep.

Confused, Belinda snuggled closer than ever, and as she buried her face in the hollow of André's shoulder, his hand came up and stroked her hair to soothe her. She heard him whisper something, his voice sounding vaguely Germanic but nevertheless flowing, and she realised he was speaking in his mother tongue to calm her.

'What are you doing to me?' she pleaded, drawing a little way away so she could look at him.

André looked at her steadily, his face appearing chiselled in the uneven radiance from the oil lamps and his eyes glowing with a fire both light and dark.

'I do not want to hurt you,' he said at length, using his thumb to brush away her tears. 'Only to arouse you, and enlighten you – ' he paused, a hint of a plea forming in the brilliance of his gaze ' – so you can help me.'

Belinda sniffed and he produced an immaculate white cotton handkerchief from his pocket and put it into her hand. Dabbing her eyes, she tried to think straight and ponder the significance of the words 'help me'.

It was the second time he had intimated that he needed her in some way, but Belinda couldn't begin to see why. She crumpled his snowy handkerchief, then frowned and tried to straighten it, knowing that there was no way she could put off asking the question.

'What are you, André? And why on earth would you need *me* for anything?'

He looked away towards the distant woods, as if seeking the right way to approach a difficult answer in their depths.

'I am just a man, Belinda,' he said eventually, still staring out across the gardens and the park, 'but I need you because – ' He paused, then turned fully away from her to face in the direction he was looking. His hands settled on the parapet, his fingers first splayed then gripping the stone tightly. 'You are beautiful. Desirable. Exquisite. I need your pleasure in order to be strong.'

It was Belinda's turn to seek an answer in the beautiful darkness. What did he mean by 'your pleasure in order to be strong'?

'I don't understand,' she said in a small voice, studying the shadows. 'You say you need my pleasure. Does that mean you are a – ' She couldn't say the word. It sounded ridiculous. Such things only existed in books and on celluloid.

'A vampire?' he asked, moving close behind her, his mouth brushing her neck just like the blackest Nosferatu's.

'Yes.' She was trembling again and gripping the parapet just as André had. She could feel his breath ruffling the fronds of hair at the nape of her neck, and the beating of his heart where his chest lay against her back. Both of these seemed to deny her mad suspicions.

'No, I am not a vampire,' he said, pressing a brief kiss to the lobe of her ear, 'although I can well imagine what it must be like to be one.'

Belinda could not speak. Her shudders doubled and re-doubled. He was skirting the issue. There *was* something wrong with him. Something different. She felt herself about to fall, to crumple face down over the parapet, but André's arms were around her again, holding her tightly against his body. His strangely cool body and his so very human erection.

He was still as hard as ever as he pressed himself against her, massaging his stiffness into the crease between her buttocks. 'Oh, Belle,' he whispered, 'I need you so much.' His hands moved away from her waist where he had held her, one sliding up to cup her breast, the other going downwards.

The fear Belinda felt seemed to have aphrodisiac qualities. She was still terrified but her body began to rouse. Her nipples stiffened, peaking beneath the fragile fabric of her dress and her chemise, and between her legs the silken moisture welled. When André pressed his palm against her pubis, she jerked and whimpered.

'I c-can't,' she sobbed, not knowing why she was trying to resist. What was the point in defending a barrier he had already breached? Hadn't he 'fed' this afternoon, when he had touched and stroked her; hadn't he been nourished by the orgasm she had then experienced?

'But you can,' he told her, his hands moving guilefully to squeeze and massage. 'It is so easy. I would never hurt you.'

Belinda went limp in his grasp, her body seeming to melt as the sensations quickly mounted. Her breasts were aching now, swelling inside the silk of her bodice, and her vulva was a pool of simmering heat.

'Oh André! André!' Moulded against him, she no longer cared who or what he was. He was simply caressing hands and a male body, superbly strong and fragrant.

Suddenly there were too many layers of clothing between them. Still held, she struggled in his grip, trying to reach the fastenings of the priceless period dress.

'Hush,' he murmured. 'Let me. It will be easier.' He took his hands from her body in an instant and set to work, deftly undoing the tiny buttons at the back of her dress.

Without André's hands on her, Belinda felt feverish, and she moaned for the return of his fabulous touch.

'Patience,' he said into her ear as the dress fluttered down on to the stone flags beneath them, forming a pale, fluid pool around her ankles. Too impatient even to step out of it, Belinda pressed her thinly-clad body back against him and circled her hips to work her buttocks against his penis.

'Touch me,' she begged, tugging at the cobweb-like chemise and knickers. 'I want you to touch me. Please. Like you did before ... I want to feel your fingers between my legs.'

Somewhere far back in her mind, Belinda was appalled. She was pleading and grovelling like some helpless nymphomaniac, calling out for a virtual stranger to lay his hands upon her sex. It wasn't like her, but it didn't seem to matter. She was another person here, transformed by André, her magician, into a thing of pleasure, pledged only to serve his whim. As his fingers slithered beneath the chemise, she grunted, 'Yes!'

Hunting among the layers of delicate silk, André soon had his hand inside her knickers, and with unerring efficiency, he worked it down to find her quim. One finger wiggled its way through the sodden curls of her pubic forest, and when it found her, Belinda crowed with lust and triumph.

'Oh God! Oh God!' Her cries rang out loudly in the mystical blue-black night, her bottom jerking as André flicked her clitoris. She was a breath away from orgasm, a heartbeat from coming gloriously and freely, but he kept her hovering, his touch wicked and as light as swan's down.

'Oh please,' she begged again, kicking her legs, heedless that she might tear the priceless gown around her feet. 'Oh please, André, please, I need to come. I can't wait. I'll go mad if I don't!'

One arm held her tight around her waist while the other slid loosely to her side. 'Don't worry, my beautiful Belinda,' he purred into her ear. 'You will have your release. But it will be all the sweeter for a little wait. A little craving.'

Belinda kicked again, sending the peach-orange dress

flying across the flags. 'You beast! You bastard! You really are a monster!' she howled, squirming and squirreling against him. Her sex was on fire and so engorged it seemed to hurt. She hissed 'I hate you' as he draped her forward against the parapet.

'Be still,' he ordered her, his voice soft yet seeming to resonate with command. She felt his hand lie flat against the small of her back, and though he held her lightly, she seemed to lose the will to move.

Belinda quivered finely as she lay prone across the parapet, toweringly furious yet more aroused than she could measure. She bit her lip as André stood behind her, and she sensed him studying her bottom. After a short pause, she felt him plucking gently at her knickers, then easing the fine, slippery fabric slowly downward.

When her drawers were around her ankles, he lifted the pretty embroidered chemise up to just beneath her shoulders and with a few deft tucks and twists, he secured it there. When that was done, she heard him step back to admire the view.

'Oh God,' Belinda moaned again, as she imagined the shocking vista before his eyes.

Her bottom and her thighs were completely on show, while her suspenders and her stockings enhanced their bareness. She could feel the fragrant night air flowing playfully across her vulva, its cool caress a blessed balm to her burning heat.

'What are you going to do to me?' she asked defiantly, fighting hard to keep the quaver from her voice. 'Beat me or something? Smack my bottom ... I'm sure that's just what you decadent aristocrats live for – a chance to humiliate the lower orders.'

'How wrong you are,' said André, his voice soft and far closer than she had realised. 'I only want to give you pleasure.' She could swear she felt his breath upon her back. 'Although if to be beaten *is* your pleasure, I would be far more than delighted to oblige you.'

'Don't be ridiculous!' she cried, yet at the same time

she imagined his hand crashing down upon her buttocks.
The idea should have been horrendous; revolting. But
suddenly, against her will, she seemed to want it. She
felt her sex-flesh pulse and flutter at the thought of
André smacking her bottom, and her hips began to
weave of their own accord. She pursed her lips to
prevent her voicing her wayward urges.

'I know ... I know ...' His voice was soothing and
she felt the brush of his dinner jacket against her thighs.
'Perhaps I should beat you?' He seemed to reflect for a
moment. 'But not just yet. Tonight we will enjoy a
simpler pleasure.'

He *does* know, she thought, feeling herself sink to a
delicious nadir of shame. He understands what I want
before I do. He anticipates the way I think and what I
feel. How will I ever keep a secret while he's near?
Belinda tensed a little, feeling suddenly vulnerable.

'Relax ... relax ...' murmured André, his long hair
tickling her back as he sank to his knees at her side.
'There is no need to keep secrets from me. I have no
wish to harm you.'

Belinda stiffened involuntarily. The more André con-
firmed his strangeness, the more her fear of him
increased. And as the fear grew, so did her arousal.

He must be able to see how much I want him, she
thought, unable to prevent her thighs from shaking. She
could feel his breath on her now, his cool breath, like a
breeze that teased her naked bottom. His face was just
inches from her vulva. She imagined him flaring his
nostrils and drawing her scent; her strong female odour.
She could smell it herself, so André must be drowning
in it. She pictured him studying the engorged folds of
her sex then putting out his tongue, pointed and mobile,
to taste and lick her. The idea made her cringe with
shame, and yet, with all her might, she craved it. And in
acknowledging that need, she knew that he too knew
what she wanted.

But still he kept his distance. Inches seemed like feet or yards. His breath and his masculine aura seemed to tantalise and caress her, but his fingers and his tongue remained aloof.

'Well, do something if you're going to!' she cried, unable to bear the waiting any longer. She felt like an exhibit in a gallery or some infernal experiment in responsiveness. Was he waiting to see how wet she would get without the benefit of contact? Was he waiting for her to crack and reach to touch herself? Or perhaps to have an orgasm, just from need?

'Patience,' he whispered, laying his fingers on her flank. 'You are so beautiful. Let me admire you a moment, before I pleasure you.'

Belinda let out a low, frustrated cry. Her swollen sex was calling to him, begging for him. She kicked her legs and felt her knickers at first constrain her then slide off over her shiny satin ballet pumps, one foot after the other. Kicking them away, she edged closer to the parapet, trying to press her pubis against the stone and get relief.

The hand on her thigh moved inward, fingers splaying, thumb beginning a rhythmic stroke. It moved back and forth, less than an inch from her anus, sliding over the sensitive skin with ineffable lightness. As she groaned, his left hand mirrored his right, and then both his thumbs were working in concert, stroking the area around her rosy entrance with the greatest care.

Belinda pushed back towards him, feeling both her sex and her rear portal pout rudely. Her body seemed to speak of its own accord. Choose! it demanded of him. Take me! Take whatever you want . . . it's yours . . . take everything!

The thumbs edged closer together, right into the channel, their soft pads brushing the forbidden opening. Liquid gathered in her vulva, pooling as it never had before, then became too much to be contained and overflowed. She could feel her sexual juice trickling down her inner thigh and landing in a sticky puddle on the stone. Shame made her whole body flush, but it made no difference. The fluid only ran faster than ever, oozing out of her like honey from a jar.

'Oh please! Oh please!' she begged again, unable to bear being touched yet not touched, being viewed but not allowed to come, being so wet and needy she was running like a river. 'Oh please,' she grunted, shoving her whole body towards him and tilting up her hips.

His answer was to dig into the flesh of her bottom with his thumbs, exert a measured, devilish pressure, then slide them outwards again, parting her lobes like a ripe peach. Her sense of being exposed increased exponentially as the entrances to her body were stretched wide, but she urged him on by pressing backwards and stretching them wider –

When his tongue touched her sex, she almost fainted.

It was just the very lightest contact at first. His tongue-tip was furled, extended, probing like a dart into her sacred inner sanctum. Moving like a hovering, nectar drinking bird, it circled the snug mouth of her vagina, then seemed to flatten and lap at her welling fluids. The feeling was so sublime and so longed for, she began to come.

As the pulsations lashed her vulva, she felt André grip her tightly and his tongue point again and dive inside her. Squirming, she reached beneath herself and rubbed her clitoris.

'Yes!' encouraged André, his cultured voice muffled against her bottom.

Belinda rubbed harder, her whole body in manic, jerking motion as the sensations spiralled up to a new intensity. She could hear herself sobbing, shouting, grunting; her sex seemed to be a mile wide, a vast landscape of pure, lewd pleasure; every inch of it beating like a misplaced heart.

The next moment, she felt André withdraw his tongue

from her vagina then slither it backwards until it rested against her anus.

Oh no! screamed a scared little voice inside her; then suddenly the same voice was howling out anew in perfect ecstasy. Furled again, and as stiff and determined as before, his tongue breached the puckered aperture between her buttocks.

'Oh no! Oh no! Oh no!' she crooned, appalled by the power of what she was experiencing. This was an unthinkable taboo. It couldn't be happening. She couldn't be feeling such pleasure because he was doing *that* to her. She couldn't be coming even harder than she had before . . .

After a while, Belinda seemed to wake up from a dream of sobbing and disorientation. She was aware of what had just happened, but her mind was trying to stop her from believing it. No man had ever done such a thing to her before, and the strength of her own responses confused and confounded her. Shame and horror vied with delicious wonder. She didn't know what to think, but she couldn't deny what she had felt. The pinnacle of pleasure from the basest kiss of all.

As her shoulders heaved and her teardrops fell down into the garden below, she sensed André rise behind her. What he had just done should by rights have abased him, and yet it dawned on Belinda that precisely the opposite had happened. If anything, her awe of him had increased. He was remarkable. Uninhibited beyond belief. A sexual prize she was unworthy of and had not earned.

'Do not weep,' he whispered, leaning over her. 'There is no shame in enjoying the *feuille de rose*.' His arms slid around her and lifted her from the stone, and when she was standing, he gently turned her to face him, using the very tips of his fingers to erase her tears. 'And it pleased me to kiss you there. Your *cul* is enchanting. I cannot imagine a man who could resist its tender beauty and its tightness.'

Belinda buried her face in the lapel of his dinner jacket,

very aware of her own vulnerability. Her pretty chemise had slid down over her back but her buttocks were still naked. She could feel herself blushing again, thinking of André's cool aristocratic face pressed tight between the cheeks of her bottom.

'Hush ... hush...' A long, graceful hand settled on the back of her head, ruffling and smoothing her short hair. Belinda felt a great calm flow over her, a feeling of being exactly in the right place in the world. What André had done had been wonderful. How could she possibly have perceived it as wrong?

'That's a pretty name for it,' she said at last, looking up into his lambent blue eyes.

'*Feuille de rose*?'

'Yes. Trust the French.' She suddenly found herself laughing.

André chuckled too. 'Yes, as a nation they have an aptitude for the *bon mot*,' he observed, smiling at her. 'But the description is valid. Have you never taken a glass and studied yourself?' His eyes twinkled. 'The entrance is soft and a dark, dark pink, and it is ruffled like the petals of a rosebud.'

'I-I've never looked,' she said nervously. Would he think her less of a woman if she wasn't fully familiar with her own sexual anatomy? She had taken her body for granted until now; perhaps not revelled in it as much as she should have.

'Never?'

'Never.'

'Then why not begin tonight?' He eyed her intently, his expression indicating an order rather than a question.

'I – ' Belinda began, then she fell silent as André slid his fingers beneath the hem of her thin chemise and whisked it up over her head.

'But how can I look at myself here?' she protested when it too fluttered down on to the flags of the terrace. She fought the urge to cover herself, especially her nipples, which were as hard and dark as plum stones.

37

'You cannot,' he replied, reaching gently for her breasts and cupping them, 'but I can.' He bent down, kissed each delicately pointed crest, then met her eyes again. 'And I have been promising myself this privilege all night.' He reached out and enfolded her in his arms, crushing her near-naked form to his fully-clothed body.

If Belinda had felt vulnerable before, she felt doubly so now. She was standing on an open terrace, at night, virtually nude. Her flimsy suspender belt, her stockings and her ballet shoes were no protection, especially from the mysterious, audacious man who held her. Any second now, he might bend her over the parapet and perform whatever outrage he so desired on her unprotected body. It might be more than his tongue that entered her this time – and yet, snuggling closer, she longed for the deepest of debasement.

For a while he just kissed her and held her, his mouth quite circumspect as it roved across her face, exploring briefly but always returning to her lips. Occasionally, he would mutter a scrap of a sentence against her skin, something unintelligible in his own language that nevertheless made her quiver.

Presently, his mouth settled firmly on hers again, his tongue pressing for entrance then possessing her completely the instant her lips yielded. At the same time, his hands began to range across her body, visiting her breasts, her thighs and her buttocks. In sliding circles, he rubbed and aroused her and his fingers delved repeatedly into the grove between her legs, touching her sex and the sensitive 'rosebud' of her bottom. Aflame anew, she couldn't stop herself from moaning, uttering her muffled entreaties around his tongue.

'You want me,' he said, releasing her mouth and looking down at her. It was a statement of fact, not a question.

Belinda tried to look away, but he cupped her jaw in his fingers and prevented her.

'You want me ... I know that,' he said again, with a

strange expression on his face that puzzled her. She watched him bite his lip in perplexity, then heard him sigh.

Sensing the sudden return of his melancholy, Belinda moved her body against his invitingly. She found it difficult to say the words, but actions were easy enough. She shimmied sinuously, rocking her belly against the bulge of his erection.

'Would that things were different . . .' he said quietly, his eyes on her face, their brilliant blue suddenly darkened to indigo. He was aroused, she could tell. There was no denying the truth of his hard, swollen cock against her. But the very fact of it seemed to cause him sorrow instead of joy.

'What's wrong?' asked Belinda, thoroughly puzzled by the contradictions. She suddenly realised that she had perhaps never wanted a man this much ever in her life, and she couldn't bear the idea of being thwarted now. A second ago, she had been sure he desired her.

'I *will* tell you,' he said, placing a cool hand on either side of her face and making her look at him. 'But first we will share pleasure as best we can.' Releasing her, he stepped back a pace, then reached for her hand. 'Come. We will go to your bedroom. We can be more comfortable there.' He gave her a small, almost nervous smile, and began to lead her across the terrace towards the house.

'But my clothes – ' She looked back towards the pools of pale silk that were the dress and the lingerie. 'And I left my bag and my flower in the dining room.' Why was she protesting? The things were André's so what did it matter?

'You do not need clothes,' he said, urging her forward, his playfulness returned. 'Come, I want you to walk naked through my house. I want to see your breasts and your bottom sway as you move. Indulge an old man, Belinda. Please be kind.'

More confused than ever, she obeyed him, very conscious of the bounce of her breasts with each step and the way her bottom rolled voluptuously from side to side. And what on earth had he meant by 'indulge an old man'? He had been flirting with her as he had said it, yet the words themselves had seemed to carry an odd significance.

He wasn't old, not by any means. Not really. Yet as she thought about it, Belinda wondered exactly how old her intriguing host was. It was hard to put a precise age on him. His features were peculiarly ageless; neither old nor young. He could have been anywhere between his early twenties to his late thirties, and his streaky hair made him even more of an enigma.

'Why are you frowning?' André asked suddenly as he stepped aside to let her pass into the main hall. 'Please do not spoil a masterpiece with such a worried look.'

Wondering what he was referring to, Belinda spun around and saw herself and André reflected in a long mirror which she hadn't noticed before.

The contrast between them was stunning: André was a dramatic and ominous figure in his sombre black clothing, while she was a pale, gleaming vision of delicate curves. The minimal scrap of lace around her hips and her gossamer fine stockings only appeared to increase her nakedness rather than cover it, and the glossy amber of her pubic curls was a brilliant splash. Once again, she felt an overpowering urge to try and cover herself, but before thought could become deed, André grasped her arms.

'Do not hide, Belinda,' he whispered, drawing her arms back and making her straighten her shoulders. Her breasts lifted proudly as if displayed. 'Your bare body is sublime. A treasure. You should exhibit it as often as you are able.' Starting to blush again, Belinda looked away, but André released her and made her turn her head. 'Look ... Look into the glass,' he murmured. 'See your own beauty.' His hand passed across her breasts, then down over her belly to rest briefly against her pubis, the dark sleeve of his coat making her skin look white and pearly. There seemed no trace left of her holiday tan. 'Would you like to watch while I caress you?' His voice was low, like velvet in her ear, and the expression on his face was almost predatory. 'Would you like to see your own face when you are in the throes of ecstasy? See it grow savage as you reach the peak of pleasure?' His mouth was against her neck; she could feel his teeth. 'Would you, Belinda, would you?'

'No! I can't! I don't want to!' She jerked away from him, aware that she was lying but also frightened. Her body was moistening at the thought – the image of her naked hips bucking, her face twisting. Her thighs spread wide while a strong hand worked ruthlessly between them. 'Please, no,' she whispered, turning in towards him then almost collapsing against the dark-clad column of his body.

He held her again, soothingly. 'Do not worry,' he said into her hair, 'there is no compulsion. You need only do what you want to do, Belinda. I would never force you to do anything against your will.'

Belinda snuggled against him, breathing in great lung-fuls of his heady rose cologne. Within her, she could already feel her fears transforming into desires. It was on the tip of her tongue to tell him she had changed her mind and that she would be glad to fulfil his wishes, when he patted her back and then released her from his arms.

'Come along, to your room. We can relax there and feel comfortable.'

Belinda nodded and gave him a small shy smile, wondering how it was that she could suddenly change from a self-possessed and rather bossy young woman into a creature so pliant and submissive. It was less than a day since she had first set eyes on André von Kastel, and already she was obeying his every word.

The Ninety Days of Genevieve

Lucinda Carrington

Lucinda Carrington's *The Ninety Days of Genevieve* was one of the most popular Black Lace titles of 1996. When Genevieve Loften begins business negotiations with the aloof and attractive James Sinclair, she doesn't realise that a 90-day sex contract is part of the deal. As a career move, playing along with him may provide a huge pay-off. However, she is not used to behaving the way Sinclair likes her to behave, or wearing the kind of clothes Sinclair seems to prefer. The following extract introduces Genevieve to some of Sinclair's little games. From here on in, Genevieve learns to balance her high-pressure career with the fascinating world of fetishism and debauchery.

Lucinda Carrington's other Black Lace book is *The Master of Shilden*, which tells the story of a young interior designer – Elise St John – who takes a job redecorating a remote castle and finds herself torn between the affections of two very different men. The only thing they seem to have in common is a hatred of each other and the ability to satisfy Elise.

The Ninety Days of Genevieve

*T*he house looked very ordinary. A neat front garden, flower-patterned net curtains. Genevieve knocked on the dark-red front door. An elderly lady opened it.

'I'm Miss Jones,' said Genevieve, following instructions, 'I've come to collect some – er – things.'

'Go straight in, dear,' the old lady nodded. 'Georgie's in her workroom now.'

Wondering if Georgie would turn out to be another old lady, Genevieve went through the door and found herself in a room that indicated whatever clothes you bought here they would certainly not include anything either lacy or frilled.

There was leather everywhere. The tangy scent of it perfumed the air. Hides were stacked on the floor. Boots with impossible heels stood against the wall. Whips and harnesses hung on hooks. Faceless tailor's dummies were masked and gagged with demonstration items. There were long gloves, heavy belts and bras so studded with metal they looked like armour. A workbench was piled high with work in progress. Genevieve stared round in amazement.

Georgie was a bubbly blonde who looked hardly out of her teens. She wore a Save the Seals T-shirt and jeans.

45

'It's a terrible mess, I'm afraid,' she apologised cheerfully. 'My girlfriend says she can never understand how I find anything. I've got your stuff all boxed up.'

Genevieve inspected the nearest dummy. It was dressed in a close-fitting female bodysuit made of lustrous black leather. The head was completely covered by a tight cap with holes only for the nose and mouth. Chrome zips, all obviously very carefully positioned, circled the thighs, the breasts, the midriff, the arms, and curved up between the buttocks. The legs ended in high-heeled, front-laced boots.

'Nice, isn't it?' Georgie said proudly. 'One of my specials. Imagine standing there in some kind of restraint harness, not knowing which zip's going to be undone, which bit of you is going to be used or played with next? But what's really good is that it's a dozen outfits in one. If you fancy a different game you can take the whole suit apart and use bits of it. The leggings can be thigh boots, the sleeves are gloves. There's a bra and a corset, whatever. I always thought anyone would look good in just the hood and long boots and maybe a wide belt. Actually I saw a painting a bit like that once in a proper art gallery, this woman standing there in this shiny leather gear, and there were all these serious people looking at it and saying how symbolic it was.' She giggled. 'I just thought it was a turn-on, and I bet that's why the artist painted it, really.'

Genevieve stared at the bodysuit. A turn-on? Yes, she had to admit that it was. The leather made it seem faintly aggressive but the obvious sexual positioning of the zips implied submission. She imagined the chrome teeth opening slowly. She imagined the cool touch of air on the exposed skin. And then the tips of fingers, or the tip of a tongue, exploring.

Yes, definitely a turn-on for a certain type of person. Her type? What would it feel like to be sheathed in that body-hugging leather? She turned round. A dummy behind her was wearing a complex corset, laced down the back and covered with straps, buckles and studs. She thought it looked incredibly uncomfortable. 'Do a lot of people buy these things?' she asked.

'Gosh, yes.' Georgie nodded. 'And a lot more probably would if they could afford them. I don't come cheap, but I use the best leather and none of my straps pull off at the wrong moment, unlike some of the stuff you can buy. When you're laced up in one of my restraints you stay laced up until your master or mistress releases you.'

Genevieve stared at the corset, trying to visualise where various straps would go, how they would feel when they were pulled tight. The more she stared, the easier it was to imagine this blatantly sexual garment on a real body, or to be more precise, on her body.

She had never really understood the erotic appeal of leather clothing before, or perhaps it would be more honest to say that she had never thought about it. But she began to think about it now, surrounded by this cornucopia of fetishist designs. She imagined the leather corset encasing her, the straps digging and constraining, and realised that she found the idea exciting. She reached out and touched the leather. It was smooth and sensual.

Georgie watched her. 'Nice, isn't it? Almost as nice as stroking a cat. Yours is the same quality. The best.'

'Mine?' Genevieve was startled back to the present.

'Your corset,' Georgie said. 'The one your fella ordered.'

'You've made me a corset?' Genevieve felt her face flush. Her eyes returned to the model on the dummy. She felt as if James Sinclair had read her mind.

'You bet.' Georgie nodded. 'Rush job and guess the measurements time, but it'll fit. Your fella gave me a rough guide to your size and I made it adjustable. You'll feel great in it. Promise.'

Genevieve felt her cheeks growing hot with embarrassment at the thought of it. It was one thing imagining yourself in one of these unambiguously provocative outfits, or maybe even wearing one for a long-time partner you knew and trusted. But Sinclair was virtually a stranger. 'But my – friend expects me to wear it when I go out with him,' she said.

'Well, why not?' Georgie shrugged. 'Where are you going? To a club?'

'To a restaurant.'

'But I bet he'll take you to a club afterwards,' Georgie said. 'He'll probably want to show you off. I would if I'd paid all that for your gear.'

'Show me off?' Genevieve repeated. Good God, was that what he was planning? She was horrified. And yet deep down in her mind a little tremor of excitement began.

Georgie looked at her in amusement. 'You're really new to all this, aren't you?'

'New to what?'

'Bondage. S and M. Master and slave.'

'Well, yes,' Genevieve admitted.

'You'll love it,' Georgie enthused. 'My girlfriend takes me to The Cupboard. I have to wear a collar and chain and this really short skirt, and boots of course. The Cupboard's for lesbians so it probably wouldn't be your scene, but I've had more spankings there than I've had hot dinners. There's this marvellous dyke, really strong, she bends me over and really goes to town. My girlfriend loves to watch.'

'And you don't mind?' Genevieve asked in amazement.

'Of course I don't mind.' Georgie looked surprised. 'It turns me on. If I minded my girlfriend wouldn't let anyone do it.'

'I wouldn't let anyone do that to me,' Genevieve said, with conviction. 'In public or anywhere else.'

Georgie looked at her and then laughed. 'You'd be surprised what you'd do,' she said, 'with the right partner.'

* * *

Knowing what to expect didn't make the sight of the corset any less startling when she unpacked it. Black leather, dull-sheened, with so many straps and buckles she wondered if she would be able to do them all up correctly. The box also contained a pair of seamed black stockings and some ridiculously high-heeled shoes. She searched for panties and could not find any. Obviously an oversight, she thought, and put on a pair of her favourite black silk bikini briefs.

It did not take her as long to lace herself into the corset as she expected. It was beautifully made and the straps seemed to find their correct position automatically. She soon discovered that they were intended to display and emphasise various parts of her anatomy. They plunged between her legs, scooped under her buttocks, and circled her thighs like narrow garters. They drew black lines round her breasts and she realised that if she tightened them they would pull her into a provocative jutting shape. She deliberately did not tighten them too much. It looked sexy but it was also uncomfortable.

One of the straps seemed to be designed to go straight across her breasts and was fitted with two little expanding rings that she could not see any use for. She could not detach them so she left them alone. The stockings polished her legs with a glossy lustre and the shoes fitted perfectly. How had he known her size?

She looked at herself in the mirror and saw a woman with her face and a stranger's body. A leather queen in fetishist gear. She thought about the bondage clubs. There were women who would let others see them dressed like this? She guessed there were, but she was not one of them. Or was she?

She posed, at first self-consciously and then with increasing lack of inhibition. Her figure, she decided, was fine: good breasts, long legs, neat waist. She had nothing to be ashamed of and plenty to display. Would she really do it? The idea was suddenly exciting.

She covered the corset with a dark blouse and a loosely

tailored suit made of silk, not wanting anything too tight or the buckles and studs would show through. She twisted her straight blonde hair into a loose knot and applied the minimum of make-up. Outwardly she looked almost prim. Only the shoes and stockings had a sexy look.

But when she walked she was constantly aware of Georgie's leather tailoring. The straps pulled and the studs pressed, reminding her all the time of exactly what she would look like if anyone removed her clothes. And James Sinclair was going to remove them at some point in the evening. That was one thing she could be absolutely certain of.

A taxi called for her promptly and took her to the Garnet. He was waiting, elegant in black. He smiled and surprised her by putting his hand behind her back and drawing her close for a chaste kiss on the cheek. She smelled the faint and expensive tang of his aftershave. His hand moved down her spine and she realised that his apparently friendly gesture had an ulterior motive. He was feeling for proof that she had obeyed his orders. 'Good,' he said, his fingers lightly tracing a line of hidden studs. 'You're obedient. But I always thought you would be.'

The muted sounds of the restaurant murmured round them. A middle-aged couple sat discussing the wine list. A waiter hovered discreetly. The subdued lighting gave the interior a sense of peaceful intimacy.

He took her arm and led her to a table. She had a horrible feeling the leather was creaking, that everyone knew exactly what she was wearing under her primly tailored suit. He held her chair for her, the perfect gentleman.

'No problems dressing?' he wondered mildly.

'I overcame them,' she said.

'A good fit?'

'Tight,' she said.

'It's supposed to be tight,' he said pleasantly, smiling.

He leaned across and took her hand, pressing her fingers. 'Like this.' He squeezed briefly and let her go. 'It's a restraint corset. A mild one, but you're supposed to know you're wearing it. There are better versions. Much better. Think about that.' He beckoned to the waiter. 'Did you fit the rings?' he asked her.

'Rings?' she repeated blankly. The waiter hesitated near their table.

'The nipple rings,' he said.

She felt her face growing pink. Surely the waiter could hear their conversation? 'I don't understand you,' she faltered.

He ordered for both of them and the waiter moved silently away. He leaned forward. She reflected that they must have looked like a couple of lovers. 'There should have been a strap with rings on them to cross your breasts,' he said. 'The rings were to fit round your nipples, nice and tight.'

'Oh,' she said, blushing. 'I didn't realise that was what they were for.'

He surprised her by laughing. 'You are an innocent, aren't you? I'm going to enjoy teaching you!'

This simple comment made her skin prickle with sudden excitement. She was already beginning to realise that her erotic education had been sadly lacking in variety. She would enjoy learning with him as her tutor but she did not intend to give him the satisfaction of knowing that he had already virtually won her over.

'I haven't agreed to anything yet,' she said sharply.

He gave her a wry look. 'Haven't you?' he asked softly. 'I'm not going to argue. Enjoy the meal.'

She did enjoy it. He discussed plays, films and music, entertaining her with anecdotes, intriguing her with his ideas. She sat stiffly because of the corset and wriggled occasionally as the metal studs on the leather garter bands dug into her thighs. He said nothing but she knew he noticed her movements and she was sure they amused him.

'Now,' he said pleasantly, when they finished their coffee and liqueurs, 'go to the ladies.' He indicated the door on the other side of the room with a tilt of his head.

'But I don't want to,' she said in surprise.

'What you want doesn't matter.' He smiled and reached across the table to hold her hand. 'Get this straight. If we make a deal you do as you're told. Walk over there. Go in. Stay a few minutes and walk back.' His strong fingers held hers. 'Don't hurry. Just walk.'

'I couldn't hurry if I wanted to in these damned shoes,' she said tightly.

He laughed. 'I like them. They make you walk like a tart. And that's what you are, aren't you? You're with me because you expect me to pay you. With a signature and not money, but the principle's the same. I've bought you, and tonight I'm going to get my money's worth. Starting now. So walk.'

She swayed over to the door past the small tables and the respectable dining couples. There was a large gilt-framed mirror in the ladies. She looked at herself. A fashionable woman in a silk suit, her hair neat, her face discreetly made-up. And wearing a leather bondage corset under her conventional outer clothes, the restraining straps digging into her flesh, reminding her of the other image of herself she had watched earlier on, posing. A tart, was she? In a way she had to admit that he was right. They were negotiating a contract, but he was controlling the terms. She walked back to the table aware that his eyes were on her all the time. He stood up.

'Right,' he said. 'I think it's time for me to inspect the goods I paid so much money for.'

Sinclair lived in a tall Georgian house in one of the more exclusive London squares. She found it difficult to manage the high steps to the front door. He did not offer to help her, but watched as she tottered uncomfortably.

Inside her heels clicked on the marble-tiled floor in the hall.

He opened a door and she found herself in a room that was both masculine and elegant. There were oil portraits on the walls, large leather-covered chairs, a polished wooden floor and discreet lighting from red-shaded lamps. He walked over to one of the chairs, turned it so that it faced her and sat down.

'Get your clothes off,' he said.

'I thought we were going to discuss your terms,' she began.

'We are,' he agreed. 'But not with a desk between us. You're not at work now. Just do as you're told. I want to see if Georgie's work is still up to her usual standard.'

Genevieve stripped slowly and was pleased to see him shift position as she peeled off her blouse. Maybe he was getting an erection already? She hoped so. The sooner he was hard the sooner he would take her to bed and she could remove the now increasingly uncomfortable corset.

She left her skirt until last. When she finally let it fall to the floor she saw his expression change from the relaxed look of a man enjoying a performance to obvious annoyance. He stood up, came towards her and hooked a finger in the front of her silk panties. 'Did I tell you to wear these?' he asked coldly.

'You didn't include any,' she began. 'So I thought . . .'

'Let's get one thing clear right now,' he interrupted. 'If we come to an agreement we do things my way. If I don't give you panties it means you don't wear panties. Understand?'

She nodded, speechless. He went to a drawer and took out a pair of scissors. He pulled the panties away from her body and cut them. Her favourite underwear ended up in pieces on the floor.

'That's better,' he approved, inspecting her. 'You're a natural blonde. I thought you would be. Turn round.' She did so. 'Spread your legs. Bend over slowly, then straighten up.' She heard the leather creak as she moved. 'You've got a nice, sexy arse,' he told her pleasantly. 'But I guessed that too.'

'I don't see how,' she said, still with her back to him.

'I always let you walk in front of me,' he said. 'The perfect gentleman. Didn't you notice? Then I used my imagination to decide how your bottom would look if I stripped you. And how big your nipples were. And how fast it would take to get them erect. Little daydreams like that help keep me awake at boring shareholders' meetings. Don't feel too flattered. I do it quite often with women that I meet.' She prepared to face him again. He said sharply: 'Stay as you are.' She stood still. 'Now,' he said, 'walk over to that door, and take your time.'

When she reached the door she realised that it was drilled with inch-wide holes.

'Turn round,' he said. 'Back up.'

He went to a cupboard and took out some wooden pegs and narrow leather straps. He positioned her exactly how he wanted her, flat against the door, legs apart, arms stretched above her head, her body forming an X. He pushed the pegs into the holes nearest her hands and feet and bound her wrists and ankles with the straps.

'That's fine,' he said. 'Every house should have a door like this. You know, Miss Loften, it was worth buying you dinner just to see your legs nicely apart like a high-class whore waiting for action.' He stood in front of her. 'Although a real whore would have known how to prepare herself.' His hands took her breasts and his thumbs stroked her nipples lightly. She knew he was watching her face for signs of enjoyment. It was difficult not to oblige him, especially as her body was betraying her anyway and she felt her flesh peaking into two hard buds. He took the strap with the rings on it and clipped one ring over her aroused nipple, tightening it until she gave a yelp of protest.

'Next time perhaps you'll do it yourself,' he said.

Her other nipple was treated the same way. He pulled on the strap that connected the rings forcing her breasts together and giving her a deep cleavage. The pressure and the tugging made her realise how arousing it was to be manhandled in this way. The sensations became even more intense when he began to tighten the other straps so that both breasts were pulled upwards, and then he adjusted the front lacing of the corset, nipping her waist in by at least two inches, so that she gasped.

He backed away from her and gave her a slow once-over. Even the passage of his eyes aroused her. He turned, went over to a chair and pushed it until it came to rest a few feet away from her. Sitting down, he put one leg over the arm and lounged back. A quick glance proved to her that he had enjoyed restraining her with the pegs, the straps and the rings as much as she had enjoyed being his victim.

'I don't think we've got much to discuss,' he said. 'I always knew that under that cool and efficient exterior there was a highly sexed woman just waiting to be liberated, and your behaviour so far has proved that I'm right.'

She wasn't going to give in that easily. 'Don't jump to conclusions,' she objected. 'I want that business contract. That's why I'm cooperating. And I'd hardly describe this,' she tugged at her bound wrists, 'as liberating.'

'Wouldn't you?' he said softly. 'Lots of women would. Right now you haven't got to think. You haven't got to make decisions. You're free just to be yourself.'

'*This* isn't being myself,' she protested quickly.

'Isn't it?' He smiled. 'Are you sure? Do you know yourself that well?' He paused. 'Here's the deal: for ninety days you'll obey my orders. When I want you I'll call you, and you'll play the games I choose, no arguments. When you're with me I'll let you know who you're going to be. A lady, a whore, a slave, the choice is mine. I will promise that whatever I arrange for you, I'll protect you from being recognised by anyone who might know you. If you really object to anything I suggest you can back out, you've got that option, but if you do the deal's off. Agreed?'

'Yes,' she said.

'Don't you mean "yes please"?' he asked her softly.

Ninety days? Three months? Did the idea of being his sexual slave whenever he decided to exercise his power over her excite her or appal her? She was not sure. 'I'll do whatever you want,' she said quickly. 'But just remember this is strictly a business deal.'

He stood up and walked towards her. She would never have believed that she could find being forced into this kind of erotically humiliating position exciting. Normally she hated being uncomfortable. Now her swelling clitoris was already peeping through the bush of her pubic hair. He put one finger on her and stroked gently. The sensation was so intense that she writhed against her restraints and groaned.

'You'll do whatever I want, will you?' His mouth moved over her neck and his tongue found her ear, lazily tracing patterns, probing. 'Let's see if you mean that. I want you to make me come, but not too quickly. Think you can manage that?'

He took the strap that joined her nipples and tugged. The rings that circled her sensitive flesh caused her tremors of erotic pain. Her body quivered and shook. All she wanted now was relief, either manual or from penetration. She moaned and thrust her hips forward.

'Answer me,' he said.

'Yes,' she groaned. 'Yes.'

She almost said please, her need for relief was so great. Swiftly he moved back, unzipped his trousers and lifted out his cock and balls. His erection was impressive but she did not have much time to admire it before he entered her smoothly, his hands behind her now, cupping her bottom, lifting her towards him. Her wrists and ankles pulled against their restraints. Her nipples, aroused from the embrace of the rings, rubbed against his coat, causing her extra delight.

'I've been looking forward to this,' he murmured.

He thrust into her, slowly at first and she matched his rhythm, clenching her internal muscles, squeezing, relaxing, pulling him deeper, letting him withdraw. She wanted to make it last too, not only to please him but for her own pleasure. But as his hips moved faster a glance at his face showed her that he was no longer in control. And neither was she. All that mattered now was release from the mounting sexual tension that gripped her. He climaxed just before she did, a hoarse groan of pleasure deep in his throat matching her own intense cry of relief.

She relaxed limply against the door and watched as he tidied himself up. Even returning to its unexcited size, his penis was impressive and she noticed that he was circumcised. He removed the pegs and straps that secured her. For a moment she remained standing against the door, then she took an unsteady step forward. She felt his hand on her arm.

'Sit down,' he said.

She collapsed into one of the armchairs. The leather felt warm and sensual against her skin. He poured her a glass of wine and one for himself, clinked his glass against hers, smiled, and said, 'Here's to the next three months.'

The following day a small parcel arrived by special courier. It contained three pairs of silk bikini briefs, lace-trimmed, beautifully handmade. A simple message card read: BUT NEXT TIME, OBEY ORDERS.

There was certainly something exciting about being given sexy orders by someone you really fancied, she thought later. She began to slip into a daydream, remembering the authoritative tone of Sinclair's voice, re-living the restaurant meal and her later experiences at his house. A bang on her door startled her back to reality.

The postman handed her a large, well-wrapped box and asked her to sign for it. After removing the heavy-duty tape and outer paper, she found an envelope. The message inside was simple and direct: GET USED TO THESE. ESPECIALLY THE SHOES. WEAR THEM ON SUNDAY AFTERNOON. LEAVE YOUR HAIR LOOSE. WAIT FOR ME AT FOUR.

Inside the box she found a zipped purse containing make-up: eye liner, eye shadow, and bright-red lipstick – a colour she would never normally wear. There was also a pair of black shoes with absurdly high heels and thin ankle straps, a very short black skirt with long zips instead of side seams and a white blouse with three buttons and a plunging neckline trimmed with a flouncey frill. There were similar frills on the elbow-length sleeves.

She stared at the outfit in amazement. Get used to these? She held the skirt against her waist and realised that it would barely cover her bottom. And there were no panties in the box. This time she knew better than to consider wearing a pair of her own. She knew that *Get used to these* meant exactly that. But did he really expect her to go outside in a skirt that looked like an extended belt, and no knickers? She knew that he did. But surely only just to his car? If she ran, she told herself, no one would notice her lack of underwear.

She picked up the shoes. Could she run in these? Could she even walk in them? No wonder he suggested that she get used to them. On impulse she slipped them on. Although they were uncomfortable they also felt extremely sexy. She sat down and stretched out her legs. She had small ankles and the thin straps emphasised this asset. She pushed aside the silky skirt of her loose kimono and looked critically at her legs. Not bad, she thought.

On Sunday afternoon Genevieve laid the clothes Sinclair had sent her out on the bed. What was important was to decide whether she really could walk outside dressed in this micro-skirt and plunge-neck blouse.

It was only a short journey from her apartment door to the street, and then she assumed that she would just have to walk to Sinclair's car. It was also true that most of her neighbours had gone to their country cottages for the weekend, but how would she feel if someone did appear unexpectedly and recognised her?

Her apprehension disappeared after she had applied the make-up. She stared at herself in the mirror. With her eyes darkly outlined and heavy with mascara, and wearing the bright-red lipstick, she had completely altered her appearance. When she loosened her hair and put on the clothes the transformation was complete.

She had not tried them on before because she had not had time. Apart from her first attempt at balancing she had not tried the shoes on either. Now she realised that the skirt was even shorter than she had first believed. It barely skimmed her crotch. And the blouse was too small. It tugged across her breasts with the buttons pulling and her nipples showing clearly through the thin material. She looked like a hooker. No one would ever recognise her. She could not believe that a change of make-up and these tarty clothes would make such an instant difference.

She put on the shoes and stood up. Despite the fact that the shoes were obviously meant to restrict her to tiny steps, and curtail her freedom, there was something about their overtly sexy design that made her feel strangely powerful. It was as if by trying to control her they actually captured and controlled the men who enjoyed looking at them.

She practised walking and realised that if you altered the way you moved it was not too difficult to strut about in the raunchy but uncomfortable heels. Her main problem was not balancing or walking but preventing the skirt from riding up with each step she took until both the curving underside of her bottom and the golden triangle of her pubic hair were clearly visible.

She hoped she would not have to walk far. Just to the car would do fine. She had no doubt that Sinclair would be picking her up by car and that wherever he was taking her, whatever he had planned for her, it would be indoors. He surely could not expect her to go out on the street dressed like this?

She heard the powerful sound of an engine and went over to the window. A massive black and chrome motorcycle pulled up to the kerb. The rider was clothed from head to foot in tight, black leathers, a space-style helmet with a dark visor covering his head. He carried a similar helmet under his arm. She tried to persuade herself that this was a stranger waiting for someone else. In a minute he would mount his machine and ride away.

But even in leathers there was something familiar about the tall, slim figure. When he blasted impatiently on the horn she knew she was right. A motorcycle? How could she ride on a motorcycle in this skirt? It was hardly long enough to cover her bottom. If she sat astride the pillion it would probably go up round her waist.

Did he really expect her to show herself in public wearing the kind of clothes that made her look like a total exhibitionist? The kind of woman men instantly thought of as a good lay? Her first reaction was anger, but she had to admit that the idea excited her too.

And, she reminded herself, she had not chosen this situation. It had been forced on her. Well, more or less. She knew she could invoke the back-out clause but that would be the end of any chance of a deal with James Sinclair. It would also probably be the end of her chances of early promotion. She went downstairs and into the street.

He stood by the powerful, chrome-tanked machine. His leathers fitted him as if they had been tailored, accentuating his broad shoulders and slim hips. She found her eyes drawn to the bulging trouser zip and quickly looked away. She wasn't going to give him the satisfaction of knowing that she found his sexual equipment exciting.

He hardly moved his head but she knew she was being checked.

'Very nice,' he said. His voice was unexpectedly clear and she realised there was a small speaker in the helmet. 'Lift your skirt.'

There was no one else on the street but she still flattened her hands protectively against her thighs. 'I'm not wearing anything under this,' she said.

'You'd better not be,' he said. He handed her the helmet. 'Put this on.'

She took it and held it. 'I can't ride pillion dressed like this.'

'Why not?' He sounded surprised. 'It's a nice warm day.'

'It's obvious why not.' She tried to tug down the ultra-short skirt. 'You've only got to look at this outfit to know why not.'

'You look fine,' he said, and she guessed he was grinning. 'Put the helmet on.' She lowered the helmet over her head. There was a click and his voice sounded in her ear. 'You look like a typical biker's tart. I'm going to take you for a ride, and I guarantee you'll remember it for the rest of your life.' He swung one long leg over the saddle, kick-started the bike and his dark-visored helmet turned towards her. 'Get up behind me.' She hesitated. 'Get astride.' His voice was hard. 'Or I'll pick you up and dump you on and if any passers-by get a good look between your legs that won't bother me at all.'

The street was empty but she wasn't sure if anyone was watching from the windows. She approached the bike cautiously. Suddenly she felt as if she was acting in a play. She was a different person in these clothes and with the added disguise of the helmet no one would ever recognise her. Let him take her for a spin round the block. If anyone saw her they wouldn't have time to realise that she was more undressed than dressed.

She climbed astride the pillion. The saddle felt warm against her naked skin. She managed to tuck the lower edge of her skirt under her bottom. If she sat down hard she thought she could keep it there. Well, she decided, this isn't so bad after all. She slipped her arms round his waist, feeling the smooth, sexy texture of the leather. The bike roared away from the kerb.

It soon became obvious that he did not intend to take her for a short ride, but he did stay on the side roads and before long they were passing boarded shop fronts and decaying rows of terraced houses, a mute and depressing memorial to what had once been a thriving East End community. The few pedestrians out walking turned to stare, although whether it was at the powerful, macho lines of the motorbike or at her she wasn't too sure. But she was sure that it was going to be impossible to keep the skirt secure.

He slanted round a corner and she slithered towards his back. The skirt slipped from under her bottom and she was acutely aware that anyone in a car behind them would have a perfect view of the cleft between her buttocks and her white, rounded cheeks spread by her weight against the black padding of the pillion seat.

And there was a car behind them. She glanced over her shoulder. She could see the driver grinning. She tried unsuccessfully to tug the skirt down.

'Stop,' she requested through her helmet speaker.

'What for?'

'There's a car following us. The driver's looking at me.'

He laughed. 'Looking at your arse, you mean? And you're enjoying it, aren't you?'

'Certainly not.' It was her best boardroom voice.

He laughed again and reached behind her, clasping one of her buttocks with his leather-gloved hands, pushing her skirt up even more. His strong fingers massaged her flesh, squeezing and pinching, forcing her to wriggle and shift her position, lifting her bottom off the pillion seat. The car driver tooted enthusiastically on his horn.

'Stand up.' His voice was hard now. 'Unzip your skirt. Make his day.'

'No,' she protested.

'Do it!' he said.

He turned the bike into a narrow side street and slowed down. They were between high padlocked wooden gates and disused buildings now. There were no pedestrians. The car stayed behind them. Suddenly she felt a great sense of freedom. She was anonymous in these clothes, with only her overly made-up eyes showing behind the helmet visor. Her best friend wouldn't recognise her. To hell with modesty and convention.

She stood up on the footrests, her legs bent, knees pointing outwards. He kept the bike upright and slow. The car braked gently behind them. She found the zip tabs and pulled, opening the skirt at both sides. The zips made a tearing noise. The skirt was reduced to two flaps.

Sinclair reached behind again and lifted the back flap, exposing her fully. She knew that the unknown voyeur now had a perfect view of her naked bottom.

'Loving this, aren't you?' The car crawled behind them, showing no inclination to overtake. Sinclair's voice sounded mockingly in her ears. 'I bet our Peeping Tom thinks he's in heaven. It can't be everyday you get to see an arse like yours for free.' He slowed down and beckoned to the car. 'Well, he's seen you. Now we'll have a look at him.'

The bike glided to the kerb and she lowered herself back on the saddle. The car slowed until the driver was level with them. His window was open. Genevieve thought he looked like the kind of man who would have two teenaged children and a nearly paid-for house. She found herself wondering what his wife was like. Middle-aged, she guessed. Not the kind of woman who would wear a frilly blouse with the buttons coming undone.

'You've seen her arse.' Sinclair's voice startled her, coming clearly from the helmet speaker. 'Want to have a look at her tits?' She was surprised to find that the unexpected schoolboy crudity of his language excited her. His voice in her helmet ordered, hard-edged: 'Show him.'

She tugged the flouncey frills aside without a second thought and displayed herself. Behaving like this was so out of character that she felt as if she was acting in a film. The driver's smile turned into a gape of surprise. She put her hands under her breasts and lifted them slightly. The man pursed his lips in a silent whistle.

'Delightful, isn't she?' Sinclair observed. 'And she likes being handled.' His voice switched inside her helmet too. 'Lean forward, baby. Let him touch.'

Again she felt a strange sense of unreality. She turned towards the car window. The man swivelled in his seat and reached for her. He squeezed and cupped her, bouncing her breast appreciatively. His thumb found her semi-erect nipple and rubbed it into full and sensitive hardness. She felt her breath quicken.

'That's enough.'

The motorbike rolled forwards, taking her out of the driver's reach. He grasped the steering wheel again.

'Put her on the back seat,' he suggested. 'I can think of some other bits of her I'd like to rub.'

The visored helmet turned. Sinclair's voice sounded faintly amused. 'Save it for your wife. Go home and give her a treat.'

'I couldn't . . .' the man faltered in surprise. 'I mean, she wouldn't . . .'

'How do you know what she'd do? Have you ever suggested anything unusual? Whatever you're thinking, go home and do it to your wife. Surprise her for once. I bet she'll love you for it.'

He accelerated and roared off down the road. Genevieve had to circle him with her arms to keep her balance. Her exposed breasts pressed against the sensual smoothness of his leather-covered back. Her skirt flapped behind her. For all the protection her clothes were giving her now she might as well have been naked.

'Stop,' she cried.

'Why?'

'I want to make myself decent.'

'I'd rather you didn't bother,' he said. 'Anyway we're nearly there.'

They pulled up outside an anonymous, high gate. He dismounted and pushed it open. The bike cruised into what had probably once been a builder's yard, a small paved area surrounded by ramshackle sheds and garage doors.

He dismounted and watched her slide off the pillion. Then he stood the bike on its stand and closed the gates. She fumbled with the buttons of her blouse and he came over to watch her, standing with his booted, black-clad legs apart, his face hidden behind the dark visor.

'Did it turn you on?' he asked. He sounded interested.

She glanced up. 'Having to behave like a whore on a motorbike? Certainly not!'

He laughed. 'Lady, you're a liar.'

He was right, although she would never have admitted it to him. It was a little difficult to admit it to herself. It had turned her on. The freedom of it, knowing that she was unrecognisable. She would never have believed that the hard insistent fingers of a stranger fondling her could have given her a sexual thrill.

She reached for the helmet strap wondering what he was planning now. Did he intend to take her into one of the disused sheds? Stretch her out on the paving stones? Not very imaginative, she thought, but what else could you do in a place like this?

'Leave the helmet on,' he said. 'Get back on the bike.'

Surprised, she went to straddle the pillion.

'Not that way.' He walked towards her. 'Turn round.'

She obeyed, lying with her back against the petrol tank, her legs apart. He took two narrow silk scarves from one of his pockets. Lifting her arms above her head he positioned her exactly how he wanted her and bound her wrists to the handlebars.

After looking at her for a moment he pushed up her skirt and fondled her clitoris gently. The touch of his leather-covered finger made her gasp. She waited for him to unzip his trousers, straddle the bike, start to give her some lasting relief from her mounting sexual tension, although she hoped he would arouse her for a little longer first.

Instead he stepped back. 'You're about ready,' he said. He turned. 'Gentlemen, she's all yours.'

Four young men came out of one of the sheds. They wore T-shirts and jeans and looked fit and muscular. She could imagine them working out with weights. They stood round the motorbike, two on each side, and she saw their eyes admiring her.

The man in black leathers said: 'Get on with it.'

They each took up a position where they could reach her body easily and began to play with her. Unhurriedly. Expertly. One of them kissed her arms, his lips tracing lines to the crook of her elbow, licking and teasing the delicate inner skin. Another caressed her ankle, undid her shoe, removed it and lifted her foot to his mouth. He sucked her toes one by one, taking his time. The third man kissed her neck under the padded rim of the helmet. One finger stroked the underside of her breasts. He avoided her nipples although they were hard with obvious desire.

Her fourth tormentor ran his tongue round her navel. She willed him to move his mouth down to her throbbing clitoris, but he did not. He flicked and tickled her skin. His fingers tantalised the top of her thighs but stopped short of her pubic hair. It was an incredible sensation, to have so many men working on her at once, teasing her, finding erogenous zones she did not know existed.

Someone was drawing light patterns on the palm of

her hand. Someone else was massaging her shoulders. A gentle slapping made her breasts jiggle. The man stimulating her toes now moved to her kneecap, making it tingle with the same lightly sucking kisses he had used on her foot. The hands working on her breasts teased insistently but avoided the two hard buds that she most wanted them to handle.

She suppressed a groan of sheer frustration. She was wet and throbbing, aching for a male touch between her legs and on her nipples. The tall figure in black leather stood watching her from behind the blank black visor, legs braced apart. She could see his erection bulging against his zip and hoped he felt as sexily uncomfortable as she did.

The fingers and tongues moved over her skin. She strained at the scarves that held her captive. Hands slid under her buttocks and lifted her slightly. Hands pushed her thighs wider apart. She imagined a tongue on her clitoris giving her relief but instead a mouth merely kissed her inner thighs. She moaned with delicious frustration.

'You want them to fuck you, don't you?' The voice in her helmet startled her. 'Well, they're not going to do it, lady. Their job is to warm you up. When you want it badly enough you can try asking for it, and I might oblige.'

A mouth nuzzled the underside of her breast, a tongue tickled her belly, another licked the sole of her foot.

'You want it good and hard?' He was actually voicing her exact thoughts. 'Then beg for it. I want to hear you beg.'

But a perverse obstinacy gripped her. If she didn't obey what else would he make them do to her? 'I won't beg,' she said defiantly. 'Never!'

He laughed. 'Enjoying yourself too much, are you? Let's see how you like it when it gets a bit rougher.' She heard the outside speaker click on. 'Gentlemen, turn her ladyship over. And then get to work. Warm up her arse for me.'

The scarves were loosened. They lifted her bodily, forced her to straddle the bike face down and retied her wrists to the handlebars. She stood with her legs braced apart. But not for long. They caught her ankles lifting her feet from the ground, stretching her out. She felt the cool chrome of the petrol tank against her breasts, the smoothness of the saddle between her thighs.

'Let's see how you like this,' James Sinclair's voice said politely in her ears.

The hand that landed on her bottom made her yelp as much in surprise as pain. The slaps that followed were hard and stinging. Watched by the blank-visored man in leathers they took it in turns to give her a thorough spanking. And they made no secret of the fact that they were enjoying every minute of it, enjoying the way she struggled, the way her body reacted, the way her hips jerked when she tried unsuccessfully to evade the undignified punishment. But whichever way she wriggled and twisted the descending hands always found their target and left their glowing pink imprint on her flesh.

She guessed they were probably turned on by the noises she was making too, and she knew her gasps, squeals and protests were quite clear to Sinclair although he did not seem in the least bit inclined to heed them.

And did she really want him to? Not just yet, she startled herself by thinking. She had never been spanked before but it was arousing her as intensely as all the previous sexual tricks she had been subjected to. She was wet and her swollen clitoris ached for relief.

She remembered Georgie. Was this how Georgie had felt when her dyke friend up-ended her? No wonder she went back for more. As each hand landed her vagina clenched and unclenched. Her moans took on a new urgency. Finally she gasped: 'Make them stop.'

'I thought you were enjoying it?' He sounded faintly mocking, pretending surprise.

'Just stop,' she groaned. She knew she could not bear this mounting sexual tension for much longer.

'You want fucking, lady?' He might have been asking her if she wanted a drink. His voice was suddenly hard. 'You want it, you ask for it. Properly.'

The young men changed over. New hands gripped her ankles. A new palm left its stinging imprint on her bottom. Her body jerked and quivered.

'I've asked,' she said. 'I've asked already.'

'Wrong words,' he said. 'I want it plain and simple. I want it basic. I want to hear that snooty boardroom voice of yours begging for it.'

'Please,' she said.

'Try again.'

'Fuck me,' she moaned. 'Please.'

'And again,' he ordered. She repeated the request, more urgently this time. 'Not bad,' he said. 'You sound as if you mean it.' He touched the external speaker. 'Playtime's over, gentlemen.' They stopped at once, standing back. 'Now it's my turn.' He straddled the bike behind her. His leather-gloved hand smacked her behind. 'Straighten up.'

She jumped with surprise and did as she was told. Was he going to untie her? She heard the zip of his trousers opening and the next moment he had leaned over her, his hands slid under her armpits and captured her breasts. His erect cock pressed against her bottom as he fondled her. As she wriggled she felt it growing even harder from the friction she was providing.

She found it intensely stimulating to be bent forward, hands tied, and used like this. The fact that he was fully dressed in his black leathers added to her pleasure. His gloves were tight fitting. The leather gave his fingers a sensual smoothness. Her nipples were already aroused by the spanking. When he rolled them between his finger and thumb the sensations shuddered down to her clitoris.

He entered her easily. She was so wet she felt she

69

could have taken a cock twice as big and twice as long. Not, she remembered, that there was anything small about his.

Rhythmically he began to thrust. She let her head fall forward and saw the reflection of his hands massaging her in the chrome petrol tank. The image excited her. It made her wonder what she looked like, half-naked, being taken from behind by an anonymous man in leathers.

It was then, as the sensations mounted, that she realised the four men were still watching. Instead of embarrassing her it added spice to her predicament. And they could not see her face. They had never seen her face. The helmets guarded them both from recognition. She could be as wanton as she liked. The thought encouraged her to try and control her partner's orgasmic thrusting. When she felt him speeding up, felt his body trembling with imminent release, she moved away from him and nearly broke contact.

Angrily he grasped her thighs and pulled her close, pushing into her again, filling her. She teased him with quick vaginal contractions and was delighted to hear him groan with pleasure. Her apparent compliance fooled him into thinking that she was going to let him have his own way. He relaxed his grip and she immediately pushed forward again.

But this time he grabbed her more roughly. She heard his breath rasping in the confines of his helmet, coming clearly through to hers. His superior weight pinned her down on the bike. Her knees bent and her high heels slipped on the ground. His hands held her close. He thrust deeply, pulled back, and thrust again until she began to match him with her internal muscles and the smooth pumping of her own hips.

'That's better,' he said softly in her ear.

His fingers slid round to her clitoris. He rubbed it lightly and thrust faster. The clitoral stimulation was so intense that she felt herself coming and could not control it. She cried out: 'Yes, now! Please!' Her legs kicked and her feet slipped and it was only his hands round her waist that kept her in position as they both climaxed together in a violent spasm of delight.

Lord Wraxall's Fancy

Anna Lieff Saxby

The year is 1720 and the beautiful and spirited Celine Fortescue has been coerced into marrying the dastardly Lord Odo Wraxall. Celine's father is the governor of St Cecilia – the turbulent Caribbean island where Wraxall owns a vast estate – and he believes the marriage will be a profitable one. Once betrothed to Wraxall, Celine soon realises that his sexual proclivities are a little unusual and his appetite for the pleasures of the flesh seems unquenchable. He is, in fact, an immoral libertine – but a highly imaginative one. This scene shows Celine partaking in one of Wraxall's theatrical parties and, despite her reluctance to play the part of Persephone, becoming overwhelmed with desire and succumbing to the opulent surroundings – and her husband's sexual magnetism. Her former lover, Liam O'Brien, is in the island's jail. Odo Wraxall has plans for him; but Liam seems to be one jump ahead on everyone.

Lord Wraxall's Fancy is Anna Lieff Saxby's first Black Lace novel. We hope there will be a sequel sometime in 1998. Wraxall makes an excellent rogue to Celine's feisty character and the historical detail in the book is meticulous.

Lord Wraxall's Fancy

Celine dreamt she was lost among black trees, and woke with a start. It was night. Shadows stood tall in the corners; the mirrors reflected a darkness only slightly less profound. The room smelt of sex and Wraxall's perfume.

She rose and padded across the floor, the silk bedcover draped around her. To her surprise, the French windows opened easily. Somehow she had expected them to be locked. Lord Wraxall was very sure of her. Celine pulled the coverlet tight around her shoulders and passed out on to the veranda.

The night was sultry. Carriage-lamps moved on the distant road, and from the Rotunda chinks of light showed between heavy curtains. Celine gazed out over the shadowed plantation, trying to make sense of her feelings.

Her body felt silky and relaxed, languid with eroticism. Her feelings for Lord Wraxall were unchanged. No, she thought, say rather that something had been added: desire? Yes, and something darker. Dangerous yet alluring, it tempted her onwards.

She remembered he had known her mother. Where, and when? Had they been lovers? Was this fever in the blood, this need to submit, another legacy?

The door to her chamber opened, and light spilt across the floor.

'Madame?' said a woman, softly.

Celine cleared her throat. 'Here.'

'*Bon*,' said the newcomer. She pushed the bedroom door wide, murmuring orders to the servants accompanying her. Candles were lit: chambermaids brought in a clutter of cosmetics, silks, and ewers of perfumed water. The woman made a noise of disapproval.

'Come in at once, madame!' she snapped. 'Do you want to catch an ague?'

Celine could not help laughing a little as the woman closed the window and, scolding in island French, pulled the curtains to. Her abigail, sure enough. Being ordered around so brusquely was almost like having Bess back. She examined her new maid while the bath was brought in and filled. This was no English country rose, but an exotic – a hibiscus or an orchid.

The woman stared back with bold, bright eyes. She was honey-gold and rounded: there was a haunting familiarity about her. Her tawny hair was crowned with a garland of wheat and poppies. Her thin robe, the colour of ripe corn, skimmed the ample contours of her body. She clapped her hands, and the lesser servants rustled away.

The abigail beckoned. 'Quickly, madame. There is little time. The company is gathering.'

'Company?' asked Celine. She knew she had seen this woman before. Not among the servants waiting on the steps, though: somewhere else.

'But of course. You think I dress like this to make beds? Milor' has ordered an entertainment for your wedding. Did he not tell you?'

'It was mentioned,' said Celine. She breathed a deep sigh of relief as her stays were unloosed. 'What's your name?'

'Does it matter?' said her new maid, with a shrug. 'I

am a slave. I have no name. He calls me Ceres: my last master, something else.'

The woman lifted the hem of Celine's chemise. Her fingers trailed across bare flesh as she slowly raised the wisp of silk.

Celine shivered at her touch. She knew Lord Wraxall had taken this creature: perhaps in this very room, on the black bed, he had granted her the satisfaction he had refused his bride.

'You should not have slept in the corset, madame. It has left marks on the skin, you see? Milor' will be angry. We must see what the bath can do.'

Celine thrust her hands away. 'Don't touch me!'

'*Oh la la*, are you jealous?' asked Ceres, with a low chuckle. 'Does it pique you that he has had me – that he will have me again? Then you must resent the whole house, madame, down to the boy who cleans the knives.'

She stepped closer. Her hands slipped down over Celine's hips.

'Come, *doudou*, let me wash you.'

Revolted, Celine pushed her off and stepped into the tub. Her nudity made her feel very vulnerable. She lowered herself into the warm water. It lapped around her, seeking out the tender folds of her body, supporting her breasts as she lay back so that they formed two swelling, snowy islands crowned with pink. She tried to ignore the maid, but remained very conscious of her gaze.

Celine soaped her arms, her torso. She rinsed the crawling suds from her stomach and long legs. She squeezed the sponge between her thighs, massaging the sensitive flesh. Ceres licked rouged lips.

'Let me help you, *chérie*,' she said huskily.

Celine glanced at her. The other woman's eyes were heavy with lust. Her nipples were huge and hard, peaking the fabric of her robe. Ceres knelt down and leant close, dabbling her fingertips in the tub. Celine could smell the musk of her arousal, even through the lily-perfume of the soap.

'Give the sponge here, to me,' purred Ceres, sliding her fingers up the inside of Celine's leg. 'I can show you things even milor' has not thought of.'

With an angry exclamation, Celine slashed her hand across the surface of the water, sending a great cascade of it into the kneeling maid's face. Ceres started to her feet with a scream of fury. The front of her gown was soaked to transparency, and foam dripped from the wilting corn-ears of her crown.

Celine stepped out of the bath and reached for a towel.

'You are a servant, Ceres: act like one,' she said, coldly. 'Address me as "milady" at all times. Take no further liberties. I have never flogged a servant yet, but by heaven, I will do it if you provoke me further!'

'You think you are so high above me,' sneered Ceres, her eyes glowing with scorn. 'You are too good even for me to touch, yes? Well, let me tell you, he will tire of you. If I could not hold him for more than a week, what will you manage, *milady*? Two days? Three? Not much longer, I think. And then you will be ours to play with. After the footmen have finished with you, you will be begging me for a woman's gentleness.'

'That's five lashes, slut,' said Celine. She finished drying herself, and tossed the towel aside. 'You may dress me now.'

Ceres clenched her fists. 'I spit on you,' she hissed.

'Ten,' said Celine. 'Well? Am I to wait all night?'

Muttering under her breath, but not so loudly that Celine was forced to take notice and punish it, Ceres picked up a drift of white silk. She shook out its folds and held the garment up at arm's length, displaying it.

It was a *chlamys*, a long Grecian tunic. No more than two rectangles of spider-fine gauze, shot through with metallic threads, it was caught together at shoulder and hip with clasps of gold. The silk was so delicate that the flames of the candles could be seen though it, haloed as if by cloud.

'I won't wear that,' said Celine, flatly. 'It's indecent!'

'Milor's choice. Shall I tell him you do not care for it?'

Celine buried her face in her hands. It was outrageous, but, like every other of Lord Wraxall's demands, it had to be met.

'Very well,' she said. 'I swore obedience. How does it go on?'

It took nearly an hour before Ceres was satisfied. She gave a final twitch to the filmy draperies and stood back, frowning critically.

'Not my best effort, but it will do.'

Celine looked with awe at her reflection. A slender goddess, crowned with flowers, gazed back at her with soft, wild eyes. She had never dreamt that she could look so immodest – or so beautiful.

The *chlamys*, its glittering weave so fine as to be almost invisible, flowed in sculptured folds down to her naked feet, hiding nothing. Golden ribbons bound her waist and crossed between her high breasts. Her nipples were tinted to the same shade as her mouth, and Ceres had clipped short her pubic hair. The lips of her sex, delicately rouged by the same expert hand, glowed through the transparent fabric.

Celine swayed. The light of the candles shimmered on the spider-gauze. It was as if she had dressed in water, or mist, gilded by the first sun of spring.

'It's wonderful,' said Celine, flushing. 'But I can't be seen like this. Haven't you heard the carriages? There must be dozens of guests assembled.'

'Milady will follow orders, as do we all,' snapped Ceres, and led her out.

The darkened house was silent. Celine's breath came fast as she followed her maid downstairs, through shadowed galleries, and out into the colonnade.

Looming overhead, the dark bulk of the Rotunda blotted out the stars. Ceres knocked twice. Tall double doors swung open at her signal, and sighed shut again behind them.

Inside was a small lobby, painted scarlet from ceiling to floor. The only light came from the eyes of a Balinese devil-mask set above a curtained doorway. From within came the sound of drums: loud, savage and insistent.

Ceres drew the hangings aside. The drums stopped short.

Her heart racing like a runner's, Celine stepped into the room beyond.

It was hung with sooty velvet and blazed with candles, black and myrrh-scented. The circular space was crowded with people, but she saw only one.

Her husband sprawled in an ebony throne opposite the entrance, all the light and darkness of the room concentrated in his eyes.

He was robed in brocade the colour of midnight, and crowned with black lilies. He smiled, and sipped red wine from a cup made of a skull.

'Welcome to the Underworld,' said Lord Odo Wraxall.

Celine stood at the head of a shallow stairway. On either hand, the interior of the Rotunda descended in tiers to a central space, and each broad circle was packed with watchers, sprawled among the cushions.

Every head was turned towards her. A hundred candles burned in the wall-sconces, as many more in the clawed, iron chandelier that hung from the centre of the gilded dome. Her thin tunic concealed nothing, merely accentuating her nudity. There was no place to hide from the stares.

Lord Wraxall set down the cup and rose, gathering his dark brocades around him. In silence, he stepped down from the dais and crossed the Rotunda to stoop above her.

His robe parted with a hiss of silks and he snatched her into its shadowy folds. He was naked beneath it. His body crushed against hers, breast to breast and thigh to thigh: she felt the quick response of his phallus, stirring into hardness against her groin.

Someone cheered hoarsely, and the watchers burst into applause. Celine cried out with shame and confusion, pushing against Lord Wraxall's chest.

Odo's grip tightened. 'Are you afraid?' he asked.

She buried her face in the hollow of his shoulder, and nodded.

'There is no need,' he whispered. 'Tonight, you are the Queen of Hades. Nothing shall be done without your consent. Come.'

He cloaked her in the parted wings of his mantle and guided her down the stairs. All eyes followed them as they went.

Celine clung to him, grateful for the concealment of his robe. She peeped curiously between her eyelashes at the room, as Odo led her across it.

Murals ringed the Rotunda's walls. Fallen angels, gold on red, copulated with beasts between the black-curtained windows. Behind the throne, a private room had been walled off. Three steps led up to its arched doorway. The hangings that screened it were caught back, and a low bed stood within.

From the inner chamber to the lobby, the Rotunda's topmost tier swept round in two half-moons, massed with servants. Women, shaved bare as babies, posed there among the ranks of drums: apart from their high-heeled shoes, they wore only scarlet stockings and half-masks.

The invited gentry, all male, lolled in full evening finery of silks and gems on the levels below. There were too many familiar faces among them: men Celine had danced with, friends of her father's, guests at his table.

Lowering her eyes, she drew closer to her husband. Together, they ascended the dais. He drew her down beside him on the black throne. There was room for two, if they sat close. His naked flank pressed against her.

Lord Wraxall raised his hand. The drums began a low muttering.

'Gentlemen, you know the rules. Let us commence.'

With a squeal of its chain, the central chandelier was lowered. Slaves doused its candles, and those burning round the walls, plunging the Rotunda each moment into deeper gloom.

Ceres danced in the growing darkness, her face an exaggerated mask of woe. She sang to the beat of the drums. The language was unknown to Celine, but every word spoke of tragedy, of a loss almost too great to be borne. Pain twisted inside her: she, too, had felt such a parting.

'What does she say?' she murmured. 'It sounds so sad.'

Lord Wraxall's hands drifted over Celine, just touching her.

'Forgive me, but I am disinclined for translation at this moment. It's Doric. A lament of Demeter.'

He moved the folds of his robe, so that he could see her body. Celine shrank away, embarrassed by his too-public caresses.

The Rotunda was in semi-darkness. A few flames still burned here and there among the guests, sparkling from buckles and jewelled sword-hilts.

Only the circular space in the middle of the room was fully lit, drawing the eye. Iron candle-holders, each as tall as a man, stood around its circumference, illuminating the heap of crimson cushions in its centre.

Odo's lips brushed her neck. Slowly he slipped the *chlamys* down from Celine's shoulder. His mouth left a track of kisses on her skin, following his hand over the swell of her breast to toy lightly with her rouged nipple. He found Celine's hand, lying loosely on her lap, and carried it to his loins.

His manhood was fully erect. For a moment Celine felt its virile heat pulsing within her palm. Then she recoiled, and snatched her hand away: she could not touch him so openly, before this crowd of lecherous onlookers.

On the lowest tier of the Rotunda, Ceres swayed and wailed. A man crouched at her feet, pawing her bare legs. He clutched at her and pulled her down beside him. Her song broke off with a most untragic squawk and giggle.

'I wonder why I invited that oaf,' Odo murmured pensively. 'No style. No finesse. The efforts of a Heliogabalus would be wasted on such dullards.'

He beckoned. A black slave, in stockings embroidered with pearls, stepped into the centre of the room, and spread herself on the cushions heaped there.

She stretched out her limbs, making herself comfortable. More pearls were sewn into the tight cap of her hair and the triangle of her pubis. They trembled in the candle-light, gleaming against her sombre skin.

A bell chimed. The audience shifted in their places. After an introductory roll, the drums fell into a slow rhythm, like the beating of wings.

'First conundrum,' announced Lord Wraxall.

The curtains of the lobby parted with a sudden rush. As if blown there by a gale, a man stood poised on tiptoe at the head of the stairway. He was white, chalk-white, from head to foot: an albino. His hair was a snow-cloud, and his eyes were red. For an instant he waited there, arms outspread, and then with a slow, gliding pace, he began to descend the steps.

Lord Wraxall reached for the skull-cup, and passed it to Celine.

'You will drink,' he said. It was not a question.

Celine turned it in her hands, putting off the inevitable. The cup was wide and shallow, its polished bone bowl set on a stem of fluted gold.

The albino circled the supine slave-girl, his eyes fixed on her, his arms moving as if in flight. In the shadows, one of the guests reached orgasm with a grunt.

'Drink,' repeated Odo. 'Do you fear I mean to poison you?'

The wine was red: it burned in her mouth, heavy and sweet, with a faint aftertaste of bitterness. She closed her eyes and swallowed. Maybe it would be best if she was a little drunk. A last drop trickled from the corner of her mouth, and Odo bent to kiss it away.

'Now watch,' he said. 'See if you can guess my riddle.'

The black girl writhed on the cushions, caressing her breasts. She moaned softly and toyed with her sex, opening herself for all to see.

With a last flutter of his hands, the albino descended to settle between her legs. His pallid skin was a startling contrast to the darkness of the woman moving beneath him. His arms stilled, and folded behind his back. He stretched out his neck over her. His white hair feathered across her breasts.

The wine coursed with a strange heat through Celine's veins. She could feel the skin of her nipples creasing as they tightened. Odo's hands, travelling across her body, seemed to imprint a pattern of fire that remained, and glowed, even after they had moved on.

On the stage below, the albino's phallus thrust at the gateway of pleasure. The woman held herself wide, guiding the blind guest within.

'Solomon and Sheba,' called a man. He stood up. His coat was red. Candle-light glinted on gold braid. Celine knew him.

'It's Solomon and Sheba, I say,' insisted Captain Cathcart. 'You know, "I am black but comely, oh ye daughters of Jerusalem."'

'Wrong,' said Lord Wraxall. He smiled. 'Pay your forfeit.'

Two of the masked women descended from among the servants. Captain Cathcart blustered insincerely as they began to unfasten his clothes. One of them slipped her hand into his breeches, and the officer's laughing protests changed to a groan of lust. The women twined their arms around him. They bore him back into the shadows.

Lord Wraxall held out his goblet to be refilled. 'Continue.'

The albino's manhood entered the woman's body by slow fractions. Their groins met and kissed, white hair tangling with black. He held himself there, pressed hard against her, while the drums beat ten times. Then, as gradually, he began to withdraw.

Fingers trailed across Celine's flesh.

'Shall I take you thus?' whispered Odo. 'Inch by inch until you whimper? Or would you like me to be rough, to handle you masterfully? Do you have a preference, madam? Answer me!'

He tweaked her nipple, and Celine cried out softly at the harsh caress. Excitement boiled inside her. Her sex throbbed, swollen and heavy. All the heat of the wine seemed to be concentrated there, radiating out from its centre to her every nerve-ending.

It could not just be wine that had brought her to such warmth and eagerness. She felt not far short of wanting any man. Celine moaned with despair and need. Something had been put in the cup.

She pressed against her husband, arching her back to bring her breasts forward to his mouth. In the lit circle at the centre of the Rotunda, the albino thrust again and again. He raised his head and called out once, wordlessly, then fell to lie upon the slave-girl, still as death.

'*Dieu*, I have it! Leda and the swan!'

'M. de Goudet wins,' said Odo. 'Will you choose your prize, sir?'

'Christ,' complained one of the watchers, bitterly. 'These aren't going to be *Greek* games, are they? Have a heart, Wraxall. We don't all know Homer.'

De Goudet, small and round, scrambled into the lit circle. He took the woman's arm and pulled her upright. He ran his hands across her dark skin.

'This one,' he said huskily, and retreated, taking his trophy with him.

The bell rang a second time.

'Next riddle,' proclaimed Lord Wraxall.

From opposite sides of the room, two naked men stepped down the tiers and into the light. Charles and Rupert, the footmen.

They were perfectly matched, of identical height and build. Their skins were the same shade of polished bronze: they might have been twins. Charles raised his right hand in an imploring gesture. Rupert mirrored it with his left. They moved closer. Palm met palm. Eyes reflected eyes.

Celine fidgeted on the throne. The aphrodisiac burned in her flesh: one thing alone could quench that fire. She slid her hand under Lord Wraxall's brocades, and ran her fingers down the springing length of his cock, from the tip to the warm weight of his scrotum.

Odo shifted position, and his robe fell away, leaving him uncovered. His look was inscrutable, but his shuddering breath told its own tale. He, too, had drunk of the wine. He brushed away the transparent silk covering Celine's loins, and sank his hand between her thighs. His fingers moved in the wetness between her labia: she thrust to meet them.

She was desperate for his body. Why didn't he take her into the inner room? He must know she wanted to feel him on her, wanted more than his fingers inside her. She moved the ring in his glans. His phallus jerked.

'By hell, you learn fast,' said Odo huskily. 'Leave me be, now.'

'I desire you,' she whispered. 'I need to have you. Why do we wait?'

'I said no more, woman! I'll not have those pretty fingers of yours make me spend before time. Watch the players.'

The footmen were very close now, face to face, their postures symmetrical. Charles took Rupert's cock in his right hand: his twin mirrored the gesture with his left. On the same beat of the drum they began to pump each other's engorged flesh. Celine made a little grimace and looked away.

'I know nothing of the classics,' she murmured.

'A pity. I like my wit to be appreciated. You should at least be familiar with the tale of Hades and Persephone. Shall I instruct you?'

'I had rather learn other things. Touch me.'

'Madam, you are importunate,' whispered Odo. 'Come, then, for once you shall be the teacher. Show me what you want.'

He allowed Celine to guide his hand once more between her thighs. The juices of her readiness slicked the skin. Lord Wraxall found the hood of her clitoris and drew it back, teasing her softly.

'In the ancient world,' he said, moving his thumb in tiny circles, 'the goddess of crops and gardens was called Demeter – Ceres, if you prefer the Latin. She had a daughter, Persephone, fair as the spring. Are you listening?'

'Yes,' lied Celine.

The hot wetness of her sex throbbed around his fingers. She could feel the head of his erection against her leg. His lips were warm, and his long hair brushed over her breasts.

'One day, as the daughter of Demeter gathered flowers, the dark god Hades, Lord of the Underworld, passed by in his chariot.'

In the audience, someone cleared their throat.

'Hades saw Persephone, and wanted her in that instant. He – '

'Hm hmm!' came the sound again, louder.

'The devil!' Odo muttered, with uncharacteristic energy. 'How inopportune.'

A man stepped forward into the light. He was elderly, and stooped, and should have known better than to choose puce satin.

'Yes?' said Odo.

Celine panted with frustration. This interruption was agony to her. She pressed close to Lord Wraxall, tracing a line from his collar-bone to his nipple with her tongue. She bit the taut brown nubbin gently.

'Narcissus, who loved his own reflection in the pool?'

'Correct, sir. And your prize?'

The man considered, looking from Charles to Rupert, to Charles again. 'One hardly knows,' he said. 'They are both so . . .'

'Take the pair,' said Lord Wraxall, with a hint of impatience. As one, the footmen stood. They linked arms across the man's back. Walking in step, they ushered him into the darkness, eyes fixed on each other over his bent head.

'Now where were we, madam?' murmured Odo. 'Ah, yes, the legend.'

'No more delays,' said Celine passionately. 'You know that I want you, that I need your body. Please, my lord . . .'

'You are sure?' he whispered. 'Shall I take you? Shall it be now?'

'Yes,' she answered, her voice shaking. He gathered her to him, picking her up in his arms. With a drive of his powerful thighs he rose smoothly to his feet. He looked down at her and smiled. His lean strength supported her weight without effort. Celine nuzzled against his chest, kissing the smooth tanned skin.

'Very well,' he said, and laughed. 'Remember, it was your choice.'

Holding her close, he looked out proudly across the silent room. The bell chimed. 'Gentlemen, the third riddle!' cried Lord Odo Wraxall.

At first she did not understand. It was only when he began to descend the stairs leading to the Rotunda's centre, that she realised what he had planned for their wedding night.

'My lord, not here!' she hissed, in horror. 'Not before them all!'

'Too late,' said Odo mockingly. 'Did you not, just now, consent?'

He sank to his knees, lowering her on to the heap of cushions. They were still warm from the previous occupants. Celine could smell sweat on the plush, sharp and masculine. From the audience, she heard a growing murmur.

Odo's hands trailed across her, teasing her back to arousal with his sensualist's skill. Celine was unable to still her body's response to his touch. He had tricked her: she would never have knowingly agreed to this. But her hunger for him was too deep. Even now, even here, she wanted him.

'Mother of God,' said someone, in heavily accented English. 'What then is the prize for this conundrum, Wraxall? You, or her?'

'I'll make you a gift of the answer, Don Alvaro,' he said, 'since I cannot give you my person, or that of my bride: the Rape of Persephone.'

He bent and kissed her. He parted her thighs.

'Look at me,' he breathed.

The robe had slipped from his shoulders: apart from the black flower-crown, he was naked. His body was that of an athlete, superbly conditioned: his face was the face of a jaded roué.

'You are mine: look only at me.'

He leant over her, his hands playing on her breasts. His hair fell down about her in dark curtains. He moved, and she felt the ring in his penis stir against the curls of her mound. Slowly, he unfastened the four clasps holding her last covering and let it fall. The watchers sighed.

'I am in hell!' cried Celine.

'Indeed you are. How quickly you have learnt to play the game.' His lips met hers, and his mouth held the taste of darkness. 'The Underworld, too, has its delights: I know them all. Let me show you, my Persephone.'

His fingers slipped briefly within her. His cock-tip rubbed against her clitoris. Torn between desire and anguish, she allowed him to bring her legs up, and around his waist. His phallus moved between her sex-lips.

He found the entrance to her vagina, and lingered there for a moment, supported on his outstretched arms. Candle-flames burned in the shadows of his eyes. Then, with a sigh, he thrust slowly forward, sheathing himself to the hilt in the scabbard of her loins.

His prick was warm, immense, filling her to capacity, almost to straining point. Celine moaned with shock and delight. She felt the ring in his glans nudge delicately at the neck of her womb. She felt it rolling as he drew back, felt it pressing against the pleasure-spot on her inner wall.

He thrust again, a little faster. Without conscious thought, she moved to meet the stroke, gripping the shaft of his cock, as he had taught her.

'Gently,' he said. 'Give me time to please you.'

Celine tightened her legs about his waist. She heard the rustle of silks as the watchers stirred on the tiers above. She tried to blot out her sense of them. Let them witness her passion. Only the moving hardness of her husband's phallus was of moment now: the feel of his pubic bone thrusting against her clitoris, and the heaviness of his balls brushing her inner thighs.

With leisurely skill, Lord Wraxall penetrated her again and again. She heaved beneath him, urging him on to push deeper, harder. Her hands slipped up and down his arms, across the muscles of his back and shoulders.

Her hips pumped. The muscles of her vagina fluttered, tensing and relaxing on his shaft in an increasing tempo. Celine had never known such ecstasy; the feel of him within her so sensual and erotic, that it was close to agony. She could not bear it. He could not continue; he must not stop.

Celine murmured little words of endearment, hardly

coherent, as she felt the first sweet stirrings of her climax. Her need overmastered her. She clasped her hands behind Odo's neck and pulled herself up to him, sobbing against his mouth as her orgasm peaked, burst, and scattered, sending its piercing shards through every fibre of her body.

She sank away, gasping, but Lord Wraxall barely paused to let her get her breath. All slowness was abandoned now, all subtlety. He lay full-length upon her, crushing her beneath him. His kiss was savage. He grasped cruelly at her breast, and thrust into her with a raw animal lust for satisfaction.

Lord Wraxall's rough dominance excited Celine even more than his earlier delay. Incredibly, she felt desire spark into life again. His ardour enflamed her. She raised her knees, clawing at his back and buttocks. Their loins drove together. She felt the heat run through her, and the tension building once more to the exploding point. Crying out wildly, she came.

And this time, Odo came with her, finding his release with a deep growl of fulfilment.

There was a minute's awed silence, then a tumult of applause.

Odo raised himself on one elbow. 'Well, Lady Wraxall,' he said, a little breathlessly. 'I was right about you, was I not? You have an inborn talent for the sport.'

Celine tightened her sex-muscles on his phallus: it was hardly less firm now than when he had first taken her. The feel of it thrilled her. Maybe it was the effect of the aphrodisiac, or – as he said – a natural hunger. Maybe it was his superlative skill at the act of love. It did not even matter that her heart was forever closed to him. She had tasted the pleasure of a man's body for the first time, and she wanted more.

There was no need for her to speak. Without once withdrawing, Lord Wraxall pulled her close, and got to his feet. Celine twined her limbs around him, and clasped her vagina around his hardening cock. He took her back to the throne and held her there, impaled on his manhood, while he kissed her, long and succulently.

Then he reached out for the skull-goblet, and placed it in her hand.

'Drink, Persephone,' he said. 'The night is long, and lies before us.'

It was dawn. Where early light penetrated the Rotunda's drapes the guttering candle-flames were wan and sick-looking. The drums were silent, overturned. The room was a chaos of torn garments and entangled bodies.

A bar of sun fell across Celine's eyes. She lay, with her head in Odo's lap, on the cushions of the lowest tier. Making a soft noise of protest, she turned away from the sudden brilliance.

Every muscle ached after the night's unceasing exercise in Lord Wraxall's arms. He had been a stranger to fatigue, taking her publicly and repeatedly in positions that made Celine flush with shame as she recalled them.

She had knelt for him, stood, crouched. She remembered straddling his hips while two of the masked women held her, supporting her weight as they raised and lowered her on the upright shaft of his penis.

The aphrodisiac's effects were fading, but still potent. Beneath her bitter remorse, Celine sensed a submerged excitement. Odo's hand lay on her neck, his fingers twining in her hair. She knew that he would only have to caress her breasts, her thighs, to bring that hunger boiling to the surface.

She sat up, and his hand slipped from her neck to her shoulder. He stroked it, fingers moving softly.

He lay, half-reclining, banked up by cushions. One knee was raised, supporting his outstretched right arm. He turned the goblet in his fingers. It still contained some dregs of wine.

Lord Wraxall's left hand moved from Celine's shoulder and down her arm, brushing the swell of her breast. A drowsy need awakened, and she sighed.

'What, still eager?' murmured Odo. 'Madam, you surprise me. I expected you to be exhausted by now.'

He pulled her close.

'Can't we go away from here?' she whispered, against his skin. 'Be alone?'

'Why this sudden need for seclusion? I thought you found my poor efforts at entertainment stimulating.'

Celine wanted to deny it, but the memory of some of the lewd games she had witnessed returned to refute her. The groom, who had ogled Celine's breasts so fiercely on the steps of Acheron, had urinated into his girl's mouth before satisfying his lust between her thighs. Captain Cathcart had guessed correctly for once: Danae and the Shower of Gold.

Odo's steward, in a false beard, played Zeus and Ganymede with one of the stable lads. The sight of the two men coupling had excited Celine dangerously. When Mr Jeffries had parted the young man's buttocks and thrust within, she had felt a desperate urge for Odo to spoil her of that second, secret virginity. But she had not voiced her thought, and now she was glad of it. She had been wanton enough: at least that shame had been spared her.

Lord Wraxall's hand cupped her breasts one after the other, squeezing the pale half-globes. Her nipples felt tender, and very sensitive from the greed with which he had suckled on them. It only needed a touch to send arousal darting swiftly down to the centre of her sex.

Only a very little more of this, and she would forget her reservations and be begging him to mount her again. It was too late for modesty. If anyone wanted to watch, they would see nothing which had not been done before them time and again.

She let her hand move down Lord Wraxall's body, and ringed his rapidly hardening cock with her fingers. Odo shifted an inch or two, making it easier for her to pleasure him.

'Will you drink?' he asked, offering her the goblet.

Celine shook her head.

'As you will, madam. It's true you don't appear to be in need of it.' He took a sip himself, and grimaced. 'Nor, for that matter, am I.'

The groom who had acted in 'Danae' snored noisily on the cushions a few feet away. With a flick of his wrist, Lord Wraxall sent the dregs of wine spattering into the man's face.

The groom started awake with an oath and dodged, adroitly, as Odo threw the cup at his head. It fell, and rolled clattering across the floor, leaving droplets that burned like rubies where they crossed the track of the sun.

'You, whatever your name is.'

The groom scowled into the shadows, slitting his tilted hazel eyes against the light. Then he realised who had spoken. He snapped to his feet.

'Martin Piggott, my lord. Undergroom, my lord.'

'Aptly named,' remarked Odo. 'You were grunting swinishly enough. Get me some coffee, Piggott, and quick about it.'

The man bowed himself obsequiously out. Lord Wraxall moved to the edge of the tier and sat there, raking through his hair with long fingers.

'Come round here in front of me,' he said.

Celine complied. Head a little to one side, he examined her naked body. His look was like his touch: intimate and exciting. She took a step closer. Odo slipped his hands up her flanks.

'Do you know, Lady Wraxall, you please me greatly,' he said, with idle courtesy. 'It's a pity I have to attend the assizes tomorrow. Even a half-day's absence from your charms will seem too long. I swear a man might use you for a month and not be wearied. A month? Say three!'

Celine had not forgotten her maid's warning that Odo would soon tire of her, nor the threat that she would

94

then be made over to his servants. The idea was frightening, and she thrust it aside.

Better to think of the assize-court. Her former lover Liam was to be tried tomorrow, and he would go free. She had purchased Lord Wraxall's testimony, and Liam's life, with this carnal marriage. That was worth any shame or remorse.

Odo's fingers closed on her waist; he pulled her towards him. He caressed the rounded flesh of her buttocks. His mouth, warm and wet, travelled across her stomach.

'Yes,' he whispered. 'I'd say at least three. We have a precedent, after all: that was the time Persephone stayed in the Underworld. But I never finished that tale, did I?'

He drew Celine down until she knelt before him, and bent to kiss her. She went to him easily, opening her lips under his. This new life need not be so bad: though she could not love Odo, he had taught her to desire him. And three months seemed to her endless – a lifetime

'Listen, now,' he continued softly, between kisses. 'Demeter went into mourning for the loss of her daughter, snatched away by Hades. The crops failed, the fields were sterile. It was the world's first winter.'

He guided her hands to the junction of his parted thighs. Celine stroked his balls, feeling their skin crawl and tighten.

'And then?' she murmured. 'Ah, God, I want you inside me.'

'Oh, the girl was found. But Hades refused to release her. She had eaten, while in his dark kingdom: only three pomegranate seeds, but it was enough. She was forced to be his, for as many months. As you will be mine. Though it is not pomegranate seed that you will swallow.'

Tangling his fingers in Celine's hair, he pulled her down until her lips brushed the head of his fully erect manhood.

'Suck me, Persephone,' he said.

Obediently, she dipped her head, and ran her tongue down from the tip of his phallus to his scrotum. His prick throbbed with readiness for her, a drop of moisture exuding from its eye. His groin smelt musky with the juices of the night. She could taste herself on him.

Celine closed her hand around the thick shaft of his penis, masturbating him, while she kissed his testicles. She rubbed the hard length from head to root, very slowly. She could feel his need. He was sweating and trembling for her, eager as a rutting stallion.

'It's not your hands I want, madam. Suck my prick.'

He held his phallus at the base, and pressed it fiercely between her lips. As she had in the black bedchamber, Celine teased his glans with her tongue. But Odo's lust was keyed too high to be satisfied by half-measures. He made her take all of it, driving the full length of his shaft into her, deep within her throat. Celine fought for air. Her eyes watered.

Odo pulled back sharply. His penis still crammed her mouth, but at least she could breathe.

'This is a skill I expect you to acquire,' he said, hoarsely. 'And fast, madam. Hold your breath and swallow as I thrust: inhale on the withdrawal.'

He pushed in to her throat once more. Celine's hands tightened on him: her nails dug into his thighs.

'Yes!' he hissed. 'Once more.'

It was none too simple at first to follow the instructions he gasped out. Even when she had learned the knack of it, she sometimes lost the rhythm and had to come up for air, choking and sobbing.

'Don't stop, damn you!'

'But you go too fast!'

Cursing, Odo scrambled back on to the cushioned ledge, dragging her with him. He lay on his back and positioned her so that she crouched over him. With hard hands he pushed her down on his rigid phallus.

'Take me at your own pace then,' he panted. 'But do

it. Do it, madam. Take my whole prick. Take all of me. I want to come in your mouth.'

His head was between her parted thighs. He kissed and sucked her sex, while he thrust his penis once more between her lips. It was better for her this way, easier, more exciting. Celine gave a muffled cry of pleasure as she felt his tongue on her clitoris. She palpated his testicles, and swallowed the great shaft of his cock, in slow, repeated mouthfuls.

Lord Wraxall heaved beneath her. His hands clenched on her arse. His lips and teeth aroused her wildly. He thrust his tongue inside her, lapping the juices trickling from her vagina.

She felt herself approaching climax and sucked him harder, faster. Odo's hands moved across her back and buttocks in soft, scattering motions. All his control was gone now, lost in lust. He moaned and nuzzled her clitoris: his hips rocked more rapidly. His prick pulsed with orgasm and he clutched her to him. His seed filled Celine's mouth in hot spurts.

The pungent semen burned on her tongue as her own pleasure reached its apogee. She came, with a sob of ecstasy, to the convulsive movements of his mouth, and sank down across his body. She lay there, shuddering, for a while.

Odo moved one of her legs so that he could lie pillowed against her thighs. Celine roused herself, and kissed his penis.

'The devil's in that mouth of yours, Lady Wraxall,' he said. 'A little more practice and you could seduce Satan himself, I believe.'

'I thought I already had,' murmured Celine.

Lord Wraxall laughed. 'I don't aspire so high. Though I have my moments.'

There was something in his tone that penetrated her trance of satisfaction. Celine rose on her elbow to look at him.

'Shall you come to town with me on Saturday?' he said.

'Why?' asked Celine, with some suspicion.

Odo shrugged. 'Any number of reasons. To visit your father; to show off your trousseau. To keep me company. Perhaps to say goodbye to that lover of yours: I won't deny you a last farewell, after the enjoyment I've had from you.'

Celine's heart leapt. 'Do you really mean it?' she exclaimed.

'Assuredly,' he said. His eyelids lifted: he gave her a hard stare. 'But in the market square, madam, before the whole town. You will not touch, nor will you say one word I do not hear. And you will never see him again.'

'I promise,' said Celine in a shaken voice. 'If you grant me this, my lord, I won't ever, ever forget it. I'll – '

'I dislike sentimentality,' he said. 'No more of this mawkishness, I beg.'

He shook her off, and padded across the room to retrieve his brocade robe. Celine propped her chin on her hands, and watched him go. Her dark eyes shone. It was unbelievable that he would be so generous.

The Rotunda's door banged in the wind, then slammed shut. The groom pushed through the curtains from the lobby and stood at the top of the steps.

'Have you not forgotten something, Piggott? I sent you for coffee.'

The man vacillated. His face was white in the shadows. Odo beckoned: Piggott came slowly down the stairs, and stopped just out of arm's reach. He was shaking: a nervous tic made the corner of his mouth twitch.

'My orders are not to be disobeyed: I thought all my people knew that.'

Piggott cringed, and began to babble.

'There's a messenger come from town, my lord. They've sent for Cathcart and the other officers. The gaol was broke last night: gaolers drugged, sentries sand-bagged, prisoners away!'

Lord Wraxall snatched a handful of Piggott's neck-cloth and twisted it.

'All the prisoners? All? Liam O'Brien too?'

'Every one,' wheezed the groom. 'There'll be an empty gallows Saturday.'

At first Celine did not understand the implication of his words. Then the full horror of their meaning burst upon her. She started to her feet with a wail of anguish.

Lord Wraxall whirled to face her. 'You,' he said, 'will be silent!'

'I won't!' she cried, in a throbbing voice. 'That's what you meant, isn't it? "A last farewell in the market square, before all the town"! You were going to take me to see him hang, you whoreson bastard! You've never had any intention of letting Liam go. And you swore – and I believed you. God's death, I thought you were being kind! How could I have been so stupid!'

Lord Wraxall curled his lip.

'I told you, madam,' he said, coolly. 'I tolerate no rivals. And watch your language.'

She flung herself on him, nails raking at his eyes. Odo thrust the choking groom aside and caught Celine's wrists in an iron grip, twisting them until she shrieked. He forced her down, to lie sobbing on the floor at his feet. He smiled.

'I have remarked before how well tears suit you, madam. Don't dry them all before I return with O'Brien's head. Or would you prefer another part – for old times' sake?'

'I hate you!' screamed Celine.

'I know,' he said. 'I find it most enlivening.'

He turned his back on her, and shrugged into the robe. He glanced once at Piggott. The groom flinched and scrabbled away.

'As for your wagging tongue,' said Lord Wraxall, in tones of ice, 'I'll deal with that later. You've cost me a rare pleasure, my man. Her face, as she watched him die, would have been a picture. 'For now, get a saddle on Brown Molly. And find my valet. I want riding clothes, my cloak, and my sword.'

And with that order, he left the room.

Celine stared after him, her mind in turmoil.

The Black Orchid Hotel

Roxanne Carr

When asked what their ideal male fantasy character would be, many Black Lace readers have mentioned a preference for firemen. Always fit and ready for action, to many women they are the nicest men in uniform. In the following extract Maggie, the proprietor of the Black Orchid Hotel, begins to explore a more down-to-earth kind of sex than that which she is used to having in the luxurious surroundings of her hotel. Brett Tunnock is a fire safety inspector with an impressive physique. He's been called in to investigate a small fire at Maggie's premises. One visit is not enough, as far as she is concerned, and it isn't long before Maggie and Brett are taking things more than a step further.

The Black Orchid Hotel closes the series which began with *Black Orchid* and continued with *A Bouquet of Black Orchids*. Roxanne Carr's other Black Lace titles are: *Western Star*, set in the wild west of America; *Jewel of Xanadu*, set in the time of Marco Polo at the palace of the Kublai Khan, and *Avenging Angels*, a contemporary story of female sexual revenge set in a Spanish holiday resort.

The Black Orchid Hotel

———— ❦ ————

Maggie was on duty when Brett Tunnock, the fire officer, turned up for the promised inspection of her premises. Maggie followed him around the building, paying more attention to his nicely muscled buttocks than to his occasional attempts at small talk. Making love to other women was all very well, but she would never want to give up the singular pleasure of a hard male body entering hers.

Brett Tunnock was a fine specimen, she saw now. Probably in his mid to late-forties his thick, dark hair was greying at the temples and he had the kind of face which reflected his personality. The network of lines around his eyes and at the corners of his mouth were arranged in such a way that suggested he was a man who liked to laugh. There was a lively intelligence in his deep-blue eyes and a fullness to his lower lip which held a wealth of sensual promise.

Underneath the bulky uniform he had worn the night before was a well-toned body, shown to pleasant advantage in his pristine white shirt and tailored trousers. Obviously, his job kept him in trim, but a man of his age would have to work hard to maintain such a physique and Maggie was impressed by the evidence of such self-discipline.

'Well?' she asked him when they had completed their tour, finishing up, at her suggestion, in Maggie's office. 'Do we pass muster?'

Brett sat in the chair she had indicated, looking completely at ease. 'I'll send you a copy of my report,' he replied. 'Meanwhile, the police will want to interview everyone who was at the hotel last night.'

'Really? Is that absolutely necessary?' Maggie said, her heart sinking at the thought of her clients' reaction to being told they were under investigation. After all, the activities on offer at the Black Orchid Hotel were nothing if not secret. And if the press should get hold of the story ... Maggie suppressed a shudder.

'I'm afraid so,' Brett said coolly. 'Procedure.'

Maggie smiled politely at him and offered him coffee. She could not help but notice that his eyes followed the movement of her legs as she sat down opposite him, and she crossed one over the other slowly, displaying them to advantage in her short skirt.

'Have you been in the fire service long ... Brett?' she asked, allowing her voice to drop huskily on his name.

'Fifteen years. And you, Maggie – how long have you been in the hotel trade?'

Maggie suppressed a smile at his assessment of her job. 'Not long at all. I like to keep a little variety in my life. I'm easily bored.'

Brett narrowed his eyes and Maggie knew that he had not missed her *double entendre*. Though all her instincts urged her to take things a step further, she waited, judging that he was the kind of man who would want to feel as if he had made all the moves. He did not disappoint her. Leaning forward, he fixed her with a frank gaze, his lips curving slightly into a smile.

'What bores you, Maggie?' he asked, his eyes twinkling with amusement.

'Oh, you know,' she replied airily, 'the usual things. Routine. Commitment. Lack of imagination ...' she paused to enjoy the expression in his eyes.

At that moment the coffee arrived and Maggie smiled at Susie, the new 'waitress', who brought it in. The girl kept glancing at Brett as she walked across the room. Laying the silver tray on the coffee table between them, she leant towards him giving a view of her pert breasts, but Brett didn't notice her, his eyes were firmly clamped on Maggie.

Susie retreated with a small shrug of her narrow shoulders and Maggie made a mental note to advise the girl that the idea was not so much to offer herself at every available opportunity, but to try to second guess the needs of the clients. The fact that the handsome fire officer wasn't even a guest at the hotel was another point against her.

Maggie smiled slightly as Susie left them, knowing that the girl was more than capable of engineering such an indiscretion just so that Maggie would punish her. Perhaps she would, Maggie mused, filing the incident away for future reference. There was bound to be an opportunity to educate the girl whilst at the same time fulfilling a guest's fantasy. There usually was.

'You seem very distracted suddenly.'

Maggie pulled her attention back to the man in front of her and lifted the coffee cup to her lips before replying. The hot liquid was strong and bitter, just as she liked it. Putting the cup carefully back on its saucer, she looked Brett Tunnock straight in the eye.

'I was wondering if you might like to join me for lunch?'

For a moment Maggie thought she had gone too far too fast; Brett sat back in his seat and regarded her through narrowed eyes. Then he smiled, flashing white, even teeth at her.

'That's very hospitable of you,' he said, rising slowly to his feet.

Maggie stood up and moved round the coffee table until she was standing toe to toe with him. They weren't touching, yet she could feel the healthy, animal warmth of his body reaching out to her. The perfume of his aftershave was light and understated, allowing the scent of man to predominate. Maggie flared her nostrils, enjoying this first contact of their senses.

Brett's eyes ran unhurriedly across her face and down the front of her body. Maggie had the feeling that he too was enjoying the subtle sensuality of his first sensory contact with her. Instinct told her that he would be the kind of lover who liked to take his time, to relish each and every experience to the utmost without feeling the need to rush. Anticipation made her skin tingle and her secret flesh swell and moisten.

Slowly, very slowly, Brett reached for her. His strong, square-tipped fingers cupped her cheek and slid behind her head to the nape of her neck. Maggie stood absolutely still, enjoying the exquisite tension of waiting for his lips to touch hers.

His hand was warm at the base of her skull, the skin slightly rough against the softness of hers. Maggie felt her stomach tighten, her breasts hardening as they strained towards him. His eyes were on her lips now, caressing them, as if imagining how they would feel and taste. Just as Maggie thought he would never kiss her, he lowered his head and brushed the sensitive surface of her lower lip with his before pressing a small, closed-mouth kiss at the corner of her mouth.

Maggie sighed, her lips parting slightly as his warm breath tickled over the surface. Again he brushed her lower lip, this time with his top one, before pressing gently at the centre with his thumb, exposing the sensitive inner surface. His tongue probed lightly at the tender skin as his free arm came around Maggie's waist, pressing her to him.

Reaching her arms up, around his neck, Maggie gave in to the overwhelming urge to sway towards him. As she had expected, his body was hard and unyielding, forcing her softer curves to mould themselves against him. She felt weak at the knees, more so as he began to kiss her properly, his tongue seeking access to her mouth, his lips closing over hers.

It was the most erotic kiss Maggie had enjoyed for a long, long time and she found herself clinging to him, not wanting it to end. When, at last, they broke apart, she saw her own excitement reflected in his eyes and knew that Brett was as overwhelmed by this first contact between them as she was.

To her relief, he resumed kissing her at once, his fingers working on the tense muscle at the top of her neck, kneading and squeezing until she felt she would dissolve with the pleasure of it. At first she had planned to invite him back for dinner another night, assuming that he would be the kind of man who would appreciate the chase, but now she wanted him with such urgency she knew she lacked the self-discipline to stick to her original strategy. As soon as he came up for air again, she would suggest that they lock the office door and . . .

Maggie started as a discordant electronic bleeper sounded from somewhere in the region of his trouser pocket. A cold waft of air came between them as he pulled away, shooting her a rueful grimace as he took out the bleeper and switched it off.

'Do you have a phone I could use?'

'Be my guest.'

Maggie stood back as he went to the telephone on her desk. Without the heat of his body she felt unnaturally cold and she shivered, folding her arms around herself. Watching Brett's face as he spoke, she knew he was going to have to leave.

'I'm sorry,' he said, reaching for his jacket and making for the door. 'Another time?'

Maggie shrugged, disappointment making her stomach churn. Brett crossed the room and pulled her into his arms for one last, hard kiss.

'When I'm off duty – when we can take things slowly.' He ran the tip of his forefinger from her lips, down her throat to her cleavage. 'All right?'

Maggie nodded, unable to speak for her mouth and throat had dried and it had become inexplicably hard to breathe. Brett smiled, a wholly masculine, knowing smile which made her feel weak, then he turned on his heel and was gone, leaving Maggie staring after him.

Later that week, a phone call came through for Maggie. When her assistant told her who was on the line, she hurried from the room to take the call.

'Brett?' she said, picking up the receiver in her office.

'Hello Maggie. I hope I'm not interrupting anything?'

Maggie had forgotten how his voice sounded; deep and mellifluous, it set her nerve endings tingling.

'No,' she replied, 'nothing at all. I was beginning to think you were never going to ring me.'

His chuckle was low and rich. 'I'm sorry. It's just that when we make love I want to be able to give you the time you deserve. I've been working odd shifts. In fact, I'm on duty now.'

Already aroused, Maggie found the thought of Brett's lovemaking intensely pleasurable. 'I could come down to the fire station now,' she suggested.

Brett laughed. 'Shameless hussy. No, Maggie, I don't want a quickie up against a fire tender, I – .'

'Sounds like fun to me,' Maggie interrupted with a laugh.

'Another time maybe. Like I said before, I want the first time we come together to be long and slow. I want us both to savour every minute.'

His seductive voice was having a profound effect on Maggie. 'When do you go off duty?' she asked him, her voice husky with need.

'Six o'clock.'

Glancing at her watch, Maggie saw that it was already 2 a.m. She didn't feel in the least bit tired after her rest that afternoon. She knew she wouldn't be able to sleep anyway until she had eased the very specific ache which started in her womb and radiated through her, in ever increasing circles of lust.

'If I come down to the station, could I hang around until your watch ends? I wouldn't get in the way, and then I could go home with you at six.'

Brett was silent for a minute. When he spoke, his voice was thick with suppressed excitement. 'All right,' he told her. 'I'll leave the side door open – the men are mostly in the mess room. Try not to let them see you. My office is on the first floor, straight up the stairs. You can't miss it.'

'I'll see you in about an hour,' Maggie told him. She was so aroused she didn't know if she was going to be able to wait that long.

'I'll be waiting,' he promised.

Smiling to herself, Maggie replaced the receiver.

The fire station was eerily quiet as Maggie let herself in by the side door and crept up the metal stairs. The tap of her high-heeled sandals sounded overloud and she tried to walk on the balls of her feet. As she passed a door on the landing she heard the low murmur of voices and guessed this must be the mess. Moving quickly past for fear that someone might come through the door, she made her way right to the top of the stairs where Brett had his office.

He was sitting at his desk, in his shirt sleeves, writing a report. Maggie had a few brief seconds to study him before he saw her. She saw that he looked fit and tanned, but tired, as he had when he had attended the second fire at the hotel. Without his bulky, protective clothing, she could see the definition of his body and she felt a small mule's kick of desire deep in her stomach.

Part of the thrill of this escapade was, she knew, the idea of finding her pleasure outside the hotel and the club. What Brett was offering her was a respite from her usual sexual routine and she was looking forward to the experience. She liked Brett and she knew from the way he kissed her in his office that he would be an accomplished lover. For once, Maggie decided, she would lie back and let a man make love to her, without any effort on her part. Her skin tingled at the thought.

Brett looked up as she entered and smiled at her. 'I wasn't sure that you'd come,' he said, striding across the room and taking her into his arms.

Maggie tipped her face up for his kiss, clinging to him as he bent her back slightly over his arm. The kiss left her feeling breathless, aching for more.

'I said I'd come,' she pointed out when she had recovered. 'I always do what I say I'm going to do.'

Brett smiled and went back round his desk. 'You said you'd hang around here until I finish, then come home with me,' he reminded her.

'Yes. And I will,' she said.

'I have to finish this report. There are magazines in the rack under the coffee table – help yourself.'

His eyes mocked her gently and Maggie realised that he fully expected her to grow bored within half an hour and go home again. Flashing him a challenging smile, she went over to the couch which sat against one wall of his office and rummaged under the coffee table for something to read.

She could feel Brett's eyes on her bottom, moulded by the flimsy jersey fabric of the dress she had changed into and she took her time, hoping the sight was disconcerting him. She'd worn the dress deliberately, because she guessed it would be the kind of thing he would find attractive. Though it was a 'look-at-me' red, it skimmed rather than clung to her figure, its skirt falling in soft swirls to her mid-calf. It was a modest dress, almost demure apart from the colour, and the way it moved around her figure as she walked.

He would be able to tell that she wasn't wearing any underwear by the way the fabric clung. Sitting down on the couch, Maggie slowly crossed one leg over the other, deliberately giving Brett a flash of tanned thigh as her skirt rode up her legs before she smoothed it back down again.

The magazine she had picked up soon bored her and she leant forward to put it back and look through the stack for another one. Near the bottom there were several copies of a soft-core girlie magazine. It had been years since Maggie had looked at one of these and she picked it up out of idle curiosity.

Glancing at Brett, she saw that he was pretending to be absorbed in the report he was writing. From the tension apparent in every line of his body, she guessed that he had noticed what she had picked up and was finding it difficult to look as if he hadn't. She smiled to herself as she opened the pages.

Acre upon acre of naked flesh sprung from the page, the colours vivid, drawing the eye. Maggie recoiled from the 'in your face' photography – gynae shots of pouting, wet-lipped women invariably sucking a forefinger as they stared into the camera with dewy, lambent eyes. She closed the magazine with a small sound of disappointment.

'I didn't know that was there,' Brett said, looking up from his report as she put the magazine away.

Maggie regarded him sceptically. 'Really?'

'Honestly. You look shocked – I'm surprised at you, Maggie. I thought you'd be more open-minded.'

Maggie laughed aloud. 'I am about what I do. But to me what's in that magazine is a distortion of what sex should be about.'

'How so?'

She had all his attention now, she noticed. He swivelled in his chair so that he was facing her, the report he was so keen to finish lying forgotten on his desk. Maggie picked the magazine up again and flicked thoughtfully through the pages, aware of Brett's eyes trained on her face, as if gauging her reaction.

'I know men's sexual psyche is more attuned to the

visual than most women's, but in my experience there's room for a wider range of stimuli than this.'

Turning the magazine around, she showed Brett a photograph of a woman sitting, knees bent and apart, spreading the lips of her sex with her fingers. Brett's expression was unreadable as he looked from it to Maggie. She glanced at the photograph again before closing the magazine and putting it aside with a grimace of distaste.

'That looked like an anatomy lesson,' she said.

A ghost of a smile flitted across Brett's features.

'They never had anatomy lessons like that when I was at school.'

'Thank God they didn't – what a warped view of womankind to present to an adolescent of either sex.'

'So – what do you suggest would improve it?'

Maggie smiled slowly. Her eyes never leaving Brett's, she said, 'I would treat my male readers with a little more respect. Acknowledge that they're capable of more than just a knee-jerk reaction...' keeping her voice deliberately smoky, Maggie allowed the fingers of one hand to drift across her breast, circling the areola with the very tip so that the skin puckered and hardened.

'I'd have a long, slow build-up, to entice the reader to linger over each and every photograph.' She transferred her attention to her other breast, cupping its fullness in her palm and squeezing, almost absently, her thumb brushing the hardening tip. 'Maybe a striptease, revealing the model's body inch by beautiful inch.'

'But you'd still end up with what's in there in the end,' Brett pointed out reasonably.

'Yes – but it would make more sense. Have more impact.'

The Adam's apple in Brett's throat moved as he swallowed and she knew that she had thoroughly unsettled him. *That'll teach him to expect to be able to ignore me in favour of a report*, she thought triumphantly, knowing that she was being childish, but not able to give a damn.

'Anyway,' she continued, taking her hand away from her breast and picking up a copy of an angling magazine, 'you carry on with what you were doing. I don't want to be a distraction to you.'

From beneath her lashes, she watched as Brett tried to do as she had suggested. He couldn't concentrate, and after a few minutes Maggie saw that he laid down his pen with a grimace of disgust.

'How long is it until you go off duty?' she asked him, her voice low and husky, infinitely seductive.

Brett glanced at his watch. 'Just over an hour,' he said.

'Is there a lock on your door?'

Catching her drift, he raised his eyebrows, but did not get up from the desk. 'Long and slow. That's what we agreed, and that's what I'm hanging out for.'

Maggie pouted, her eyes dancing with amusement. 'Are you *sure* you can wait that long?' she teased him, uncrossing and re-crossing her legs.

Brett groaned. 'Yes – I can. I have to attend a debriefing. Will you be all right on your own?'

'Of course,' Maggie replied, watching him as he stood up and took his jacket off the back of his chair. The fabric of his regulation trousers was stretched tight over his crotch. She hoped that fatigue and the necessity for routine would not diminish it entirely before she got him home.

'Would it be all right if I had a look round?'

Brett looked doubtful as he put on his jacket.

'I won't touch anything,' she promised.

'All right. I'll meet you back up here in half an hour, OK?'

Striding over to her he bent and kissed her, full on the lips, taking her by surprise. His mouth was firm and warm on hers and, by the time he broke away, Maggie was trembling.

'*Touché*,' he murmured, his eyes roving her face and

113

the hectic flush which had crept into her cheeks. 'Now we both have something to think about.'

Maggie watched as he strode away, aware that her heart had quickened in her chest. She hadn't been one hundred per cent certain why she had come tonight, whether because she had strong feelings towards Brett, or simply because she knew he would be able to occupy her thoughts, thus directing them away from Jake. It didn't really matter. He wanted her; she wanted him. It was all refreshingly simple.

After a few minutes, Maggie got up and went to look around the fire station. Although the whole place was flooded with light, there was a quality to the silence which she knew she would only find at this hour, just past dawn. From the walkway she could see that there were two fire engines below, both equipped ready for action. At the end of the walkway there was a round hole cut into the metal, wide enough for a large man to slide down the fireman's pole.

As a child, Maggie had always wanted to try this method of descending quickly downstairs. Glancing around her, she reassured herself that she was alone before kicking off her shoes and wrapping herself round the metal pole. Clinging on for dear life, she slipped slowly down the pole, conscious of the smooth metal rubbing against the front of her body, setting up a wonderful friction between her legs. She hadn't realised quite how much she had turned herself on whilst in the process of teasing Brett until she felt the easing of tension caused by the slow, sensuous slide.

At the bottom, she stood for a few moments, still pressed against the pole. It would not take long to bring herself to a climax by rubbing herself against it, but she decided that she would save that first orgasm for Brett. The anticipation was excruciating, but she knew that a little self-control now would pay dividends in the very near future.

Wandering around the tenders, both looking very

large now that she was on the ground floor with them, Maggie eyed the reels of hose and imagined them being pulled slowly between her legs. She winced at the lewdness of the thought, running her fingers along the shiny paint of the fire engine as she made for the stairs.

Retrieving her shoes, Maggie resisted the temptation to take a second trip down the pole. Instead she sat down and waited impatiently for Brett to come back up to the office.

'Ready?' he asked her as he returned to the room at last.

'Oh yes,' Maggie smiled. 'I'm more than ready.' Smiling, she walked over to Brett and put her hand in his.

Brett lived in a stark, sixties-style flat overlooking the sea. Its furnishings were of the type that is found in rented accommodation, though Maggie barely noticed her surroundings at all as they were hardly through the door when Brett started kissing her again.

Knowing that now there were no restrictions, no outside constraints to stop them, added an urgency to their love-making that thrilled them both. Until now they had only been able to snatch the odd kiss in Maggie's office or Brett's – now there was no chance that anyone was about to walk in on them, all the barriers had been removed.

His fingers were warm against her bare skin as he slipped them under her long hair to caress the nape of her neck.

'Maggie, Maggie,' he murmured against her throat as he steered her through the living room and into the bedroom.

Sinking down on to the bed, Maggie was aware of the pink streaks across the early morning sky outside and she was glad that Brett made no attempt to close the curtains. They were high, about six storeys up, and there was nothing opposite but the sea and sky.

She stretched, like a cat in the sun, watching Brett

through narrowed eyes as he undressed. Removing his jacket, tie and then his shirt, he was silent as he watched Maggie watching him. His chest was broad and muscular, only lightly furred with hair which, as he moved and the light shone through it, Maggie saw was beginning to take on a tinge of grey. The long, hot summer had perfected his tan and his skin glowed bronze, smooth and healthy. Maggie imagined how it would feel and sat up on the bed, trembling with anticipation.

Brett dispensed with his trousers with an economy of movement which Maggie admired, removing his socks at the same time. Underneath he was wearing plain black cotton boxer shorts which barely contained his erection. He left them on as he sat on the bed next to her and ran his fingers through her hair.

'I've been waiting for this,' he told her, his eyes on her lips as she replied,

'So have I.'

Reaching for him, she ran her hands over his shoulders and down his arms. His skin felt like warm silk. Placing one hand over his heart, she felt it pound against her palm and her own pulse quickened. She could smell the sharp tang of fresh male sweat as he folded her in his arms and her head swam dizzily. He was so big, so solid. There was something very primitive about being clasped against his chest and Maggie's body responded at once.

'Let me take off my dress,' she murmured against his hair, 'I want to feel your body against mine.'

Brett helped her to pull her dress over her head, his eyes widening in delight as he saw that she wore nothing at all underneath it.

'God, you're beautiful,' he breathed, his lips moving against the tender place behind her ear. 'But you're moving too fast.' He pulled back, holding her face in his hands and staring deep into her eyes. 'Nice and slow – remember. I want it to last.'

'It doesn't have to be only once,' Maggie protested

half-heartedly. Her heart was hammering in her chest, the adrenalin pumping through her veins making her feel jumpy. There was so much tension in her she felt she might snap.

Brett did not smile, though his eyes shone. 'I want to touch every inch of you with my fingers, with my lips. By the time you leave I want to know your body so well I could draw a map for the Ordnance Survey series.'

Maggie laughed and his eyebrows rose.

'You think I'm joking? Turn over.'

Eyeing him quizzically, Maggie rolled on to her stomach, watching him over her shoulder as he reached into a drawer in the bedside table and took out a bottle of oil. She gasped as he unscrewed the top and, holding the bottle high, he dribbled it across her back.

'Lie down,' he said. Gentle fingers smoothed her long hair to one side and Maggie closed her eyes. Arousal churned through her, hot and impatient, and she tried to calm it, to match Brett's slow, steady pace.

The bed dipped as Brett straddled her, one knee on either side of her hips as he began to work the sweet-smelling oil into her skin. Maggie groaned involuntarily as his fingers dug deep into her muscles, dissolving the tension in her back until she felt boneless, incapable of independent movement.

The silence in the room grew thick with tension as Maggie's body grew more and more fluid. Brett's fingers were firm and sure, but Maggie could swear that there was electricity in their tips as he gradually shifted his attention to her bottom. It was bliss to lie with her cheek against the cool pillow while Brett oiled her buttocks and the back of her legs, right down to the soles of her feet.

'Roll over,' he said from the end of the bed, a gruffness in his voice which betrayed the effort such self-control was costing him.

Maggie moved very slowly, rolling on to her back and easing herself up the bed so that her head was propped on the pillows. Her eyes followed his hands as they massaged the oil into her feet and between her toes, almost tickling her, his touch just firm enough to make it pleasant. She sighed as he circled her ankles and began to work up her thighs.

Raising her arms above her head, Maggie settled back on the pillows as Brett's oily fingers neared the junction of her thighs. The folds of flesh still hidden by her closed legs were swollen and moist and Maggie could already feel a dull pulse beating at the apex of her labia. If he touched her there, now, she knew she would come.

Brett didn't touch her there. Instead, when he reached her groin he turned his attention to her arms. Maggie gasped as his hands, slippery with oil, smoothed the skin in the dip of her armpit before sliding easily up her arm to her elbow. Once he reached her wrist, he lifted it and brought her arm down gently.

'Mmmm – where did you learn to do that?' Maggie moaned as he began to manipulate each finger in turn.

'I had a girlfriend once who was a beauty therapist,' he told her.

'And she taught you how to massage?' she asked as he turned his attention to her other hand.

'Caroline liked to receive as well as to give,' he explained.

'Fair enough. I can see why too – you must have been a quick learner.'

'I practised a lot.'

He pressed his lips against the corner of her mouth, teasing it into a smile with the very tip of his tongue.

'Really?' she whispered, her heart pounding as she contemplated where he would spill the oil next. So far he had paid minute attention to every part of her except those areas that would drive her wild: her breasts, belly and the soft, melting folds of flesh between her thighs.

Sitting up, Brett smiled down at her. Maggie caught the wicked gleam in his eye and shivered.

'Oh!' she gasped as he spilled oil over her breasts. It

ran in little viscous rivulets from the tip of her nipples down over the mounds of her breasts and pooling in the valley between them. It was into this cleft that Brett passed the palms of his hands, pressing gently so that Maggie felt she would melt into the mattress.

For a few moments he ignored the aching peaks of her breasts, so that when, at last, he began to stroke and knead them, they quivered with suppressed delight. Maggie felt her nipples harden still more and was compelled to allow her thighs to roll apart slightly to ease the pressure on her sensitive vulval flesh.

Brett saw the movement and smiled at her. Bending his head he caught the very tip of one nipple between his lips and nibbled on it, sending little shock waves of pleasure down from her breasts to her mons.

'Uh-oh, that's so-o good,' she moaned, writhing against the sheets as his hands moulded her waist and hips, his thumbs brushing across the taut plane of her stomach. 'Please, lower . . .'

Brett chuckled softly and dipped his head to place a wet, open-mouthed kiss at the top of the naked crease between her labia. Maggie gasped. She had expected him to oil her shaven mons too, maybe even to work the oil into her already dew-soaked skin before sliding himself into her. She hadn't expected him to begin this slow, leisurely exploration with his lips and tongue.

Under pressure from his tongue, she felt her labia open to him, the intricate folds of flesh peeling apart, eager for the touch of his lips inside each secret channel. Brett licked and sucked at her swollen flesh as if he was tasting the juiciest, most exotic fruit. Carefully avoiding the little promontory of her clitoris, Brett teased and tantalised every inch, drawing a series of involuntary sighs and moans from Maggie's lips.

She felt his tongue wiggle into the elastic-walled channel of her vagina and she shifted her hips, wanting to feel him deeper, firmer. Her fingers ran restlessly through his thick crop of hair, her knee moving caressingly against the thick shaft of his penis, pressing against his boxer shorts. She wanted that inside her instead of his tongue and she moaned incoherently, trying to communicate her need.

Brett lifted his head and gazed down at her, his eyes lambent with desire. His fingers fumbled with the fastening to his boxer shorts and he drew them down, flinging them carelessly aside as he straddled her.

His penis was not particularly long, but it was thick, solid looking, its foreskin already drawn back, the glans smooth and shiny. Maggie felt an atavistic fluttering in the pit of her belly as she imagined it entering her. The long massage and tantalising oral stimulation had left her with every nerve tingling, aching for satisfaction.

Reaching for him, she enclosed him in her hand and stroked the silky skin which moved over the steel-hard core.

'I want you,' she said, her eyes boring into his, 'now.'

Brett sat back on his heels and pulled her into a sitting position. Lifting her at the waist, he reversed their positions so that he was lying on his back, his head towards the end of the bed, and she was straddling him, her sex poised above the strong, straight staff of his cock.

As she sank slowly down on to him, Brett pulled himself up, holding her in his arms so that her breasts were crushed against the hard wall of his chest and her pubic bone ground against his.

They sat like that, very still, for a few seconds. Maggie could feel the breadth of his cock stretching her internal walls, giving her a feeling of fullness that sent ripples of pleasure through to her womb. Slowly, he began to rock her, so that he was moving inside her.

Maggie could see her own face reflected in his eyes as he moved forward to kiss her. The pace was slow and gentle, and yet somehow they managed to maintain the tension. It gained momentum as they moved as one, in silence, rolling so that Brett was on his back, then over again so that he was on top of Maggie.

A fine film of sweat made their skin stick then slip. Maggie felt as though a slow-spreading fire had started at the point where their two bodies joined and was sweeping gradually through her, consuming her with heat. Breathing seemed difficult and her heartbeat became faster as Brett began to move more deeply in her, thrusting now with increasing urgency.

'Ahhh,' Maggie let out her breath sharply as an orgasm took her by surprise. Without any kind of direct stimulation, the bundle of nerve endings in her clitoris could take no more. The silky, cleated walls of her sex convulsed around Brett's moving penis, setting up a chain reaction along its length so that, in no time, he joined her, tipping over the edge with an impassioned cry of release.

They clung together for a few moments, Brett's lips roving across Maggie's heated face and neck as he muttered endearments. Afterwards, they lay side by side, the duvet pulled up around their necks. The daylight streamed in through the uncurtained window, but neither were in any state to notice. In his sleep, Brett turned towards Maggie and drew her in close to him.

She lay, warm in his embrace, for several minutes. She felt as if her arms and legs had suddenly become impregnated with lead, they were so heavy. So were her eyelids and, within minutes, Maggie was also sound asleep.

The Bridal Gift

Jan Smith

In the Middle Ages, a maid's wedding night was a time of fearful anticipation. In this second of four original short stories in this anthology, Jan Smith tells a tale of the old practice of *droit de seigneur*. Young Isobel is unprepared for married life with her new husband, Jamie. Her family are enjoying the music and drinking but she is experiencing some wedding-night nerves. In steps Christian de Vallibus, recently returned from the French court, to assist in Isobel's education.

Jan Smith has written two Black Lace books. They are: *To Take a Queen*, set in the time of Scottish Highland clans fighting in the fourteenth century, and *Palazzo*, a contemporary story of two women's sexual adventures in the mysterious city of Venice.

The Bridal Gift

'*A* toast! A toast to the newly-weds!'
The cry was taken up with enthusiasm along the table. The old man beamed at the couple, his face already betraying the effects of the best part of a cask of ale.

'To my lad, Jamie, and his bride Isobel – the comeliest wench this side of Edinburgh. May their union be a long and fruitful one. Here's to a teeming belly, lass!'

Laughter followed his words. Isobel blushed to the roots of her hair at her father-in-law's indelicacy, but still summoned a smile for her own father. He was steward of the Lord of Dirleton, and a respected man. And she was a dutiful daughter.

She picked up a honey cake to nibble on and let her gaze slide to the youth lounging beside her. Jamie had been her father's choice for her husband, but she had no complaints; he was a favourite with the ladies, with his ebony curls and eyes the colour of cornflowers. He had been whispering with his brother, Ramsey, and now turned to her.

'Would you care to hear Ramsey's jest, Isobel? 'Tis a rare one.'

His brother put a warning hand on his arm. 'But not for a maid's ear, in faith.'

Jamie looked at Isobel, noting her reddened cheeks and lowered lashes. 'You have the right of it.' He dropped his hand to grip her thigh through the cloth of her gown. 'I'll tell it to you in the morning, sweetheart. When you are a maid no longer.'

She almost choked on her cake. Her bridegroom's hand remained where it was, clutching her thigh. She grew warm under her kirtle, as if his fingers were communicating with something in the core of her body, sending the blood singing through her veins. She closed her eyes. The sensation provoked by Jamie's hand took her back to another place, another time:

She was standing at the edge of the tarn.

'Come on, Bella! The water will cool you off.' The boy shook his hair out of his eyes and waved for her to join him in the deepest part of the pool. She hesitated, and then plunged in, gasping.

'It's too cold.' She could barely force the words between her chattering teeth.

'You'll soon get used to it.' The boy's eyes were warm as a summer mist. 'Especially if I tickle you.'

'Nay!' She shrieked and struck out towards the other side of the pool. Their laughter rang across the moorland, disturbing a pheasant that flapped up and away over the heather.

She couldn't remember exactly when their ducking and splashing had taken on a more sexual note, or how the boy's hand had found its way beneath her shift. All she could recall was his touch on her budding breasts under the water, and the sensation of his lips on her numbed ones. A few days later, he had gone from Dirleton to the glamour of the French court. She hadn't seen him since.

'Dreaming of tonight, sweeting?' Jamie's whispered words brought her back to the present and caught her off guard. She shook her head and blushed again. He glowered at her, before taking his hand from her thigh and turning back to his brother. She sighed. Jamie had a reputation for whoring, and had even fathered a bastard on one of the village lasses. He could not fail to be disappointed in her – she had so little experience of men.

The celebration was becoming more unruly. The two minstrels her father had employed were trying to outdo each other, to the delight of the ladies, who were clapping their hands and urging them on to bawdier and bawdier verses. Heads turned as a figure appeared in the doorway. He strode towards the gathering, two deerhounds panting at his heels, his clothes steaming and his features obscured with grime under the broad-brimmed hat. The laughter and music died away as he shook the snow from his cloak.

Isobel's father was the first to move. He bowed deeply. 'My lord! We did not expect you so soon.'

'I received your news about my father's death in Avignon. I have made better time than I thought, in spite of the weather. What is happening here?'

'Saving your presence, we are celebrating the marriage of my daughter, Isobel. You remember her?'

The eyes under the brim of the hat locked with the girl's. Christian de Vallibus smiled. 'Of course.' He swept off his hat and bowed in her direction. Then he turned to the steward again. 'Some wine. My throat is parched.'

Isobel's father rushed to fill a tankard, which his new master emptied without pausing for breath. Still, no one spoke.

De Vallibus wiped his sleeve across his mouth. 'Is it not customary to ask the permission of your lord before undertaking such a union?'

'Your father had already given his blessing,' stammered the older man.

Grey eyes swept the table, resting only momentarily on Isobel's flaming face. 'In that case, I will add my blessing to his.' He removed his gauntlets and began to unfasten his cloak. 'Can you spare someone from the celebration to settle my horse, and help me bathe?'

The boldest of the minstrels took up his lute again and conversation resumed, ripened this time with speculation.

'As you wish, my lord. I will have the water heated straight away.'

'There is one final matter.' De Vallibus straightened as he slung his cloak over his shoulder. 'I claim *droit de seigneur* of your daughter this night. Her bridegroom may have her back tomorrow.'

The lute player broke off his tune with a twang. Everyone stared, open-mouthed.

'But my lord . . .' Isobel's father's face was grey, as if it had been hewn from stone. 'I pray you. That is an old custom, long since out of favour.'

De Vallibus smiled. 'But still my right, by law. Is that not so, Strachan?'

The steward nodded. 'It is. But surely, my Lord, you cannot . . .'

'Bring her to me when I have bathed.' Then he turned on his heel and strode towards the staircase, closely followed by his hounds.

Isobel shivered as her aunt stroked a brush through her curls and braided them again before securing them with a filet. She was still wearing her wedding clothes: the heavy surcoat, embroidered with seed pearls, and the tightly fitting green kirtle beneath.

'Courage, lassie.' Her aunt's eyes met hers and slid away again. ''Tis but one night.'

The girl realised she had no choice. If she refused de Vallibus's command her father's goods would be forfeit, and, if he chose, he might cast out the whole family to fend for themselves. She followed her aunt in a daze as the woman knocked at the door to the chamber and entered.

Their lord was seated in a chair near the fire, his two hounds sleeping at his feet. He had changed out of his travel-stained garments and now wore a robe trimmed with marten-fur which was belted loosely at the waist.

The door behind her closed softly, and she realised she was alone with him.

He was watching her. She returned his gaze, searching his face for the boy she had known. As a child it had been easy to forget he was some years older than her, but now his features had lost the softness of youth and the eyes that were once so light were as dark as pewter. His face had a sensual, almost cruel look. Until he smiled. Then she thought it was the sweetest thing she had ever seen.

'Aren't you going to come closer, Bella? I don't bite.'

She remained where she was, standing stiffly by the door.

He stood up and approached her. 'Are you really so afraid of me?' he asked, searching her face. 'We were friends once.'

'You *dare* to remind me of that?' Tears stung her eyes. 'You have shamed me in front of the whole village. Jamie will never forgive it.'

'Bella!' He grasped her shoulders to prevent her from turning away from him. 'How can you think I would hurt you? I would sooner hurt myself.'

Isobel opened her mouth to protest at his hypocrisy, but found it swiftly covered with his own. His lips teased hers, playful, intimate, robbing her of her breath and her will. His tongue pressed against her teeth demanding entrance and she opened herself to it, allowing him to plunder the softest parts of her mouth. When he drew back she leant against him, too shaken to trust her legs.

'Christian! For pity's sake . . .'

He silenced her with a finger on her lips. 'No more words.' He stood back. 'You can leave now. Walk away if you wish. I will exact no retribution from your family. But if you stay, and give me this one night, I will give you something in return that you will value greatly. I give you my oath.'

She looked at him, her eyes huge in her face.

'If you stay, I will expect you to obey me without question.'

Still she made no move.

'What is it to be?'

Slowly she took a step towards him, and then another. Before she knew it, he had captured her face in his hands and was kissing her eyelids, her nose, her chin. She reached up to clasp his neck and heard him groan.

'Bella,' he whispered. Then he pushed her away. 'Go to the bed and take off your gown.'

She stared at him.

'It was your choice to stay, and therefore to obey me.' His voice was teasing. 'Come, sweetheart.' He took her hand and pulled her over to the bed with its striped canopy and tester.

'I will need some help. The laces . . .'

'Willingly.'

He watched as she loosened the girdle that clasped her waist, and then raised her hands to the laces of her surcoat. She fumbled with them and pulled her surcoat over her head, leaving her standing in only her kirtle. The garment had laces not only down the back, but along each of the tightly fitting sleeves. Christian frowned when he saw them, then reached for something on his coffer. She flinched when she saw what it was.

'Softly, sweetheart. Patience is not always a virtue.' He sliced through the laces with his dirk, until the only thing keeping the kirtle up was Isobel herself. She clutched her arms over her breasts, guessing that he must also have cut through her chemise and probably her small clothes too. Christian took her hands and pulled them down. Then he tugged at her sleeves until she was standing naked before him, save for her stockings and shoes. He looked down at her.

A blush mottled the milky skin of her throat and breasts, almost matching the tips of her nipples in colour. A riot of emotions swept through her as Christian's eyes devoured her shoulders, breasts, belly, and the coppery curls between her legs. It was the first time a man had ever seen her naked. She was filled with shame, and something else too: something hotter, more urgent.

'Unbind your hair.'

She battled with the compulsion to cover herself, raising her arms instead to remove her filet and unpin the coils that were wound around her head. Her hair fell in auburn waves over her shoulders.

Christian's face had grown dark. 'Now undress me.'

She looked at him. She had expected to submit to him, not to take an active part in the proceedings. As if reading her mind, he laughed.

'A wench can bed a man too, love. 'Tis not necessarily something to be inflicted upon her.'

Emboldened by his words, she reached out to tug at the belt that held his gown. It loosened, and the gown parted to reveal his body. His arousal was shockingly obvious. Unembarrassed, he watched as the girl's gaze travelled up from his lean, muscled legs, over his groin to his chest, and then inevitably back to his groin again. He gave a throaty laugh.

'God's nails, but I could grow accustomed to the way you look at me. Touch me, sweetheart.' He took her hand and guided it to his manhood. Once the urge to snatch her hand away had passed, Isobel found the hot, silky skin with its core of iron strangely pleasing. Her fingers curled instinctively around the shaft, and she watched enthralled as a single drop of liquid pearled at the tip.

'Enough.' Christian's voice was hoarse. 'Or I'll spill my seed untimely.' He caught her face and drew her mouth to his. 'Kiss me back, Bella!'

He thrust his tongue into her mouth for her to taste it, spicy with wine, and then bit her lips, her chin, her throat. She was soon swept along by the force of his desire, and started to return his caresses greedily. They devoured each other for many minutes before her hand reached out, almost of its own accord, to brush his manhood. It was the signal he had been waiting for. He guided her backwards under a fresh onslaught of kisses, until they fell together on to the bed. His hands moved lower to cup her breasts for the first time. She stiffened and then arched against him as he tugged at the delicate tips with his fingers. He dropped his head to suckle them, and Isobel gasped. She had never felt anything like it in her life. An invisible, glittering cord spun out from her breasts and tightened between her legs. He teased her another few moments with his lips and teeth, and then moved lower, to her belly, where he snaked his tongue into her bellybutton. Then he moved lower still. Realising his intention, modesty overcame her passon, and she cried out, 'Nay!'

'Nay?' He looked up at her, his chin resting on her belly.

'I . . . I cannot . . . 'Tis not seemly.'

'Indeed it isn't. But didn't you swear to obey me?'

'In truth, I did,' she gasped, 'but . . .'

'Then honour your word; I wouldn't do anything to hurt you.' He resumed his journey down her body, pressing hard, biting little kisses into her flesh, until he reached the curls between her legs. She flung her arm over her eyes, scarlet with shame, but did not think to interrupt him again. She felt him pause, then smooth the ruffled hair. His touch sent tingles through her body which turned to flames as his fingers spread the lips of her sex. It did not feel as it usually did, but swollen and strangely fluid. She bit back a moan. He dipped his fingers into her and she melted inside. Moisture trickled from her sex, down her buttocks and on to the coverlet. Quivers shook her as he found her most sensitive, secret core. She moved her hips instinctively to meet his fingers, driven by a need as old as time itself, until she lost all consciousness of where she was, and even who she was. Her belly began to contract and shivers ran through her buttocks and loins. What was happening to her? she wondered wildly. Was she dying? She climbed the crest of her pleasure and tumbled to the very edge of it.

Then, suddenly, her lover pulled away. She cried out at the shock of it. Christian pulled her arm away from her face and forced her to look at him through her lashes; they were jewelled with tears. Her lip trembled, and he gathered her in his arms.

'Hush. There is time a-plenty for that.' He wiped her face, and pushed something soft into her hand. She looked down to see that it was silk, torn into strips. Christian stretched out his long limbs on the bed beside her. 'I want you to bind me.'

Once again, he had shocked her. She stared at him.

'No jest, sweetheart. Bind my ankles and wrists to the posts of the bed.'

She frowned, confused.

He sighed. 'Do I have to remind you of your oath again? That would be the third time.'

So she did as he asked, binding his ankles and wrists securely to each corner of the bed, although she couldn't imagine the purpose of such an exercise. When she had finished she stood back to look at him. He was spread-eagled on the coverlet, his well-muscled limbs akimbo, his manhood swollen. Her cheeks flamed as she suddenly realised how defenceless he was.

He smiled. 'Climb up on me, love.'

Shyly, she climbed on to the bed beside him.

'Not like that. Sit astride me, as a man would a horse.'

Her eyes widened but she obeyed, being careful not to touch his manhood. He looked at her as she sat astride his thighs, taking in the tight tips of her breasts and the curves of her body, still flushed with her thwarted orgasm.

She returned his scrutiny, curiosity warring with her natural modesty. Her gaze crept down to his manhood. It was long, rising from the curls between his legs like the sturdy shaft of a fighting stave but, with Christian so securely tied, it had lost some of its menace. She longed to touch it again.

Reading her expression, Christian grinned. 'I pray you, take as many liberties as you wish.'

She ran a finger along its length. The man froze beneath her and bit back a groan. Encouraged by his response, she mischievously wrapped both hands around it. It twisted and she giggled. He let out his breath with a sigh.

'Do you recall the feeling you had when my fingers were inside you? You can do the same thing for yourself, with that.' He nodded at what she held. ''Twas fashioned to fit where my fingers were.'

Her eyes widened at such a possibility. She examined his manhood again, with renewed curiosity. Surely it would never fit inside her? She shuffled forward, and then raised herself on her knees to slide the tip of it between the still swollen lips of her sex. She rubbed it up and down the moist flesh and gasped as pleasure sang through her. She discovered her enjoyment was particularly intense when she applied it to a particular spot. She rubbed it there again, faster and faster.

'Have mercy,' gasped Christian.

Chastened, she stopped and looked down at his cock. Its head was glistening now with her juice. If his manhood could give her such pleasure merely by rubbing against her, how might it feel when taken inside completely, as Christian had said? She raised herself higher on her knees and slipped it between the lips of her sex again, pushing it deeper this time. At first it found resistance, but when she slid it further back it seemed to find a spot that accepted it.

'That's it, sweetheart.'

Heat tumbled over her. Closing her eyes, she took a firmer grasp on the base of his manhood and pushed it further in. Once more, it met resistance. Her eyes flew to Christian's.

"Tis natural. Push down on it. There might be a little pain, but 'twill pass, I swear.'

She bit her lip, hesitated, and then did as her lover suggested. Something gave inside her with a tiny sear of pain. She sobbed, and rammed herself down completely. Christian bucked and gasped as he was swallowed to the hilt by the tight channel.

Isobel threw her head back, overwhelmed by the sensation of being so crammed with flesh. It seemed to nudge against the very core of her. She pressed herself against the man's pelvis, and found that the pleasure she thought had fled came flooding back once more. She ground herself against him and her hands crept lower, until she slid one finger instinctively between the lips of sex. It found a nub of flesh she had never discovered before, pushed forward by the shaft of Christian's cock. She ran her fingertip experimentally over it and gasped as her pleasure doubled. By raising herself on her knees, she found she could draw Christian's cock in and out of her, stoking her pleasure even more. Her whole body was beginning to shudder, and she clenched the rod of flesh inside her convulsively, grinding herself harder and harder against Christian's groin.

Then, just before the most beautiful, shimmering forgetfulness sluiced through her, she opened her eyes to look down at the man beneath her. His eyes were clenched tightly shut, his face twisted as if in pain as he arched up to meet her thrusts. She hesitated a moment, worried that she was hurting him, but her own pleasure would not be denied. She gave one final thrust of her buttocks on to the stiffened rod of flesh inside her, and was sucked suddenly into a black whirling eddy. She heard a woman cry out, as if from a great distance away, her cry accompanied by the shout of a man.

She lay slumped across Christian's chest, as the sweat cooled on their skin. When she looked up at last she saw he was smiling down at her.

'I never dreamt . . .' she began.

'Hush. There is more yet.'

'There is?' Her expression was eager and incredulous.

He nodded. 'Untie me.'

She did as she was told. He settled her on his knee, then handed her a goblet of wine, which she drank. She met his glance shyly.

'What would you say if I told you someone had witnessed our coupling?' he said.

She sat up and looked wildly around. Seeing no one else in the chamber, she relaxed again. 'Surely . . .' she began.

He interrupted her. 'You may reveal yourself now, Jamie.'

To Isobel's horror, a tapestry in the corner of the room stirred and her bridegroom emerged, still dressed in his wedding finery. She put up her hands to cover herself.

'For shame.' Christian swatted her hands away. 'He is your husband.'

She stared in consternation at Jamie, ready for the rebuke she knew must come. His handsome face was as flushed as her own, and he was breathing heavily. As he drew closer to the bed, she saw the bulge in his breeches.

She turned mutely to Christian, dumbfounded.

'I wished not only to bestow a gift on you, but your bridegroom too. I must confess that at first he was not too eager to watch us, love. But he soon changed his mind when he saw how lovely you were. Kiss her, lad, did she not do well?'

Jamie bent to press his lips to her mouth. His sapphire eyes locked with hers. They were not filled with condemnation, as she had feared, but with admiration and lust.

'You call yourself a man? That's not a proper kiss.'

Jamie kissed her again, more deeply this time, parting her lips with his tongue. He groaned as he felt her respond, and reached for her breast, grasping the nipple. Heat thumped between her legs.

'I want you to tie Jamie to the bed, as you did me,' said Christian. 'When he has undressed.'

Taking the hint, the youth quickly stripped off his jerkin and breeches, until he was standing straight and proud in front of them. His cock was thinner than his master's, but just as eager. Christian's cock give an answering leap under Isobel's buttocks.

Jamie lay on the bed as Christian had done, and allowed Isobel to bind his feet and ankles. She moved to straddle him, but Christian stopped her. He pulled her to him, and pushed his hand between her legs, delving it into her moisture, teasing her until she was twisting in his arms with frustrated desire. Jamie watched them avidly from the bed. Christian bent and whispered in her ear. 'The only way I will permit you to achieve satisfaction this time is with your bridegroom's tongue.' She frowned, sure she had misheard, but he merely smiled and guided her back to the bed. She looked longingly at Jamie's cock, but Christian pushed her away from it.

Jamie lay frowning, uncertain, as Isobel climbed on his chest and pushed her knees into his armpits.

Christian gave a shout of laughter. 'You will have to get closer than that. You would fare better if you turned around.'

Blushing, she did as he suggested. Christian helped to position her knees on either side of Jamie's head. When she looked down she could see her husband's blue eyes scowling at her past the curls between her legs. She suffered a throb of shame, but there was a deeper throb in her sex that demanded satisfaction. The knowledge that he was at her mercy sent a thrill of power surging through her. Jamie twisted in his bonds, and gave a cry of protest as she lowered herself on to his face. At first he remained impassive beneath her, but then he groaned and began to lap at her. She cried out and arched her back. As she did so, she saw that Christian had taken Jamie's cock in his hand, and was sliding his fingers casually up and down the shaft. Her shock was overcome, however, by the urgent guzzling between her legs.

The feeling was exquisite torture to her, and she smeared herself more and more deliriously on to Jamie's face. Then she realised with a dark thrill that her juice must be mingled with the seed that Christian had pulsed into her earlier. The thought brought a moan from deep inside her, which was echoed by Jamie's muffled groans. Christian took his hand from Jamie's cock, with the result that the youth became frenzied, darting his tongue in and out of Isobel's sex, sobbing into it. Then suddenly, like a cord snapping, Isobel experienced release. It swept up from her toes, over her buttocks, her sex and breasts, until she cried out into the room.

Jamie continued to suck at her, driven by his own desperation. She squirmed and felt a pair of strong arms lift her to the floor. Together she and Christian looked down at the youth tied on the bed. His black hair was tousled, his handsome features polished with sweat and musk. He arched his bursting groin into the air.

'I pray you,' he begged.

Christian bent and kissed him full on the lips. Jamie turned his head away, but Isobel saw his cock jerk violently.

'Release him, Bella.'

She did so. As soon as the last tie was unfastened, however, Jamie grabbed her and rolled her beneath him. 'Can I, love?' Surprised by the fact he had thought to ask, she merely nodded. With a groan, he pushed her thighs apart and slid his cock into the well-oiled channel between them. She gasped and dug her fingers into his back, then opened her eyes again in surprise as she felt someone kissing her hands. Christian had climbed on the bed behind Jamie and was running his palms over the other man's smooth skin, even as he took Isobel's fingers into his mouth. Jamie shuddered at his touch, and Isobel felt his cock spasm inside her as Christian ran his finger down the cleft of his buttocks. Isobel shuddered in turn. Jamie kissed her furiously, groaning against her lips as the other man cupped his balls.

Christian's fingers drifted up to where the shaft of Jamie's cock was swallowed by Isobel's sex and grasped it hard, while his other hand spread the cheeks of his arse. Jamie clasped her tighter to him and froze. Slowly, Christian pushed his cock into that virgin cleft until all three of them were bound together. They were motionless at first, stunned by the sensations that were flooding through their bodies. But then, tentatively, they began to move. Minutes later, all three reached orgasm together, frantically, in a tangle of limbs and searching mouths.

Afterwards, they slept.

The fire had died when Isobel opened her eyes. Christian was already awake, his expression playful and content. He swung his legs out of bed, careful not to disturb Jamie, who was snoring in the middle. He found his robe and Isobel followed him to the door.

'Where are you going?' she whispered.

''Tis almost dawn. A man and wife must have some privacy on their wedding night.' Christian gave a wry smile, then reached into the pocket of his robe. 'But first, I have a gift for you.'

'What, another?' She smiled.

He grinned and handed her a hunting whip. 'For whenever Jamie grows rebellious.'

It was made of engraved leather, beautifully soft and supple. She flexed the lash against her palm.

'If that end doesn't work, you can always try the other.' Christian turned the whip around. The handle was stiff, and as thick as two of her fingers. Her eyes widened.

'If he ever strays, give him a taste of that as penance, and I wager he will be content in your bed.' He winked and bent to kiss her. 'Farewell, sweet Bella.'

And then he was gone. She turned the whip in her hands, marvelling at its elasticity and strength. She eyed the man still sleeping under the coverlet and tiptoed over to him.

'Wake up, love,' she whispered, shaking his shoulder.

'What ails you?' The blue eyes were clouded with sleep.

'I want you to tell me Ramsey's jest, for I think I am qualified to hear it now. Quickly now! Tell it! For I am not in a mood to be refused!'

Celia's System

Meredith Sears

The following short piece is influenced by the mannered style of corporal punishment stories of the period between the two world wars. This is unashamed escapism into a 'golden age' of the 1930s when the England team were still fairly good at cricket and summers were always long and hot. There is always a touch of Glen Baxter to stories such as these and humour is never far away. There is certainly room in Black Lace for tales of punishment where young men are on the receiving end.

Meredith has no plans to write a Black Lace novel but has written other short stories of a similar nature.

Celia's System

*I*t had been a splendid afternoon. The evening sun threw a deep golden light over the pavilion and the reassuring murmur of friendly chatter in the distance told Celia that all was well in England and on the village green. Chislehampton Old Boys had declared at 352 for five and had pulverised the opposition – the Runcorn casuals – who had scraped a measly 198 all out. How proud she had felt as Archie made his half century! She basked in the reflected glory of her husband's prowess at the crease and smiled warmly – but not without a little smugness – as the captain of the visiting team congratulated her on picking such a stout fellow to be her nearest and dearest.

'You must be terribly pleased with his performance, my dear,' he blustered through his whiskers. 'Goodness me, how his game has come on! Last season he scraped a paltry 12 off 10 overs. Being married to you seems to have brought him on in leaps and bounds, if I may say so, my dear. Very few wives take such an active interest in their husbands' sporting endeavours. Well done, Mrs Penrose, well done.' And with that he was away to drink with his team-mates.

The game was over and the members of both teams

were dissecting the near misses and dropped catches of the afternoon's sport now that the village clock had sounded seven and the nearby public house was open. There had been a catastrophic moment when Francis Gatestone had been run out by a new boy but all was forgotten as the team captains took it in turn to bring trays of bitter to their fellow members. It was but a short walk from the bar to the green.

The game was an annual event and this was the third time Celia had enjoyed the privilege of attending the Chislehampton Old Boys' home match. The previous two years she had attended as Miss Celia Barnthorpe, fiancée to Archie Penrose, and had barely understood the lingo of what had seemed such an uneventful way to pass a summer afternoon. With marriage came respect and responsibility and Celia, always keen to keep up with what others were talking about, had taught herself the rules of this most English of games. She now knew the difference between deep fine leg and silly mid-off, could tell a googlie from a slow delivery, and was able to keep score as accurately as the umpire. It had been two years since the Jardine/Larwood debacle and, when Archie had insisted that any chaps bowling bodyline be struck off the Old Boys' team, Celia had backed her husband's decision to the hilt.

One of Archie's old schoolfriends, Reggie Pemberton, brought Celia a cream sherry. 'Can't have the dear little thing not joining in the celebrations, can we?' he said. His assembled fellow team-mates chuckled heartily as Celia graciously accepted the small glass. She smiled sweetly at her husband who was standing at ease – a picture of pride in his striped blazer – against the wooden benches on which they were all seated.

The raging heat of the afternoon had given way to a cooler, more temperate evening, and Celia found her cotton gloves and crocheted shawl a blessing now that a slight breeze was beginning to stir. She loved these long evenings; the glow of the setting sun lent a radiance to

144

her freckled skin and the light danced on her lustrous red hair which was cut in the fashionable style. She felt – and was – quite beautiful in that light; a fact which hadn't passed unnoticed to some of the members of both cricket teams. During the day's play she had caught a couple of the opposition gazing wistfully at her figure: the prominence of her neat bosom as it pressed against the cotton fabric of her summer dress; the shapely turn of her ankle and the gentle sway of her bottom as she walked to and from the ladies' enclosure of the pavilion – to fetch refreshments and powder her nose. If she were honest, she would admit that she walked back and forth to that pavilion more times than was really necessary. Celia Penrose adored the thrill of being admired in 'that' way. Rarely did she get a chance to elicit a response from so many handsome men in one place.

She sipped her sherry thoughtfully. The day's showing off had made her feel quite faint, and a substantial moistness had gathered on her silken underthings. She wanted her husband. She wanted the feel of his handsome moustache at the junction of her thighs and to feel his ample baton-hard tool sliding in and out of her dewy cleft. She was sure that if she carried on drinking sherry in front of everyone she may let slip an indiscretion. Goodness, what a thought! And her a lady, too. She tried to concentrate on practical matters: things to take her mind off her flushed state.

There was the pressing matter of clearing away the tea things inside the pavilion. At eight o'clock Mr Stone the keeper would be round to check that everything was as he had left it that morning when he unlocked the building for the day's play. She made her excuses to the gathered gentlemen, telling them she was off to attend to packing the hampers and cleaning up inside. She knew, also, her presence inhibited their manly japes and didn't want them putting on airs and graces for her benefit.

'What a perfect wife you have, Archie, old boy,' said

Francis, the team-member who had been run out. 'Could teach my Abigail a thing or two.'

'She's a real treasure, Frankie. I don't know where I'd be without her,' he agreed.

Celia blew her husband a kiss then walked off to attend to the clearing up; she could feel some fifteen pairs of eyes on her as she gracefully sashayed alongside the pavilion. She turned the corner of the green-painted wooden hut and made for the ladies' room. In doing so, she almost tripped over young Giles Outhwaite sat on the ground staring forlornly at his bat, a thick lock of light brown hair masking his handsome young face. 'Whatever are you doing round here all by yourself?' she enquired, alarmed at the boy's solitary state.

'I should not have been so impetuous,' he whined. 'I was responsible for running Francis out. How can I join in the merriment when I've played so badly? Both sides must hate me – and Francis wants to kill me, I know, I saw the look he gave me as he made the long walk back to the pav.'

Celia could see he was feeling sorry for himself and crouched down to talk to him. He looked clearly distressed and she was sure that tears were filling his eyes. 'Look at me, Giles,' she said softly. 'They don't hate you. Why, it can happen to anyone. A misjudgement is nothing to get in such a flap about. The others are in fine spirits; we won despite your mistake and the others have forgotten the incident, I assure you.'

Young Outhwaite sat against the warm wooden hut, the rays of the setting sun alighting on his cricket whites and the downy hairs which graced his strong and slender arms. He looked up at Celia through the wavy tendrils of his fringe. 'D-d'you really think so?' he asked, his eyes darting suddenly over her breasts and down to the curve of her waist.

'Why, of course,' she said. 'Why don't you go and join them?' Just then, an illicit thought crossed Celia's mind. 'Unless, of course, you would like to help me wash up and pack away the tea things?' She rested a hand lightly on his arm.

'But that's women's work,' he muttered. 'They'll think I'm even more of a cissy than they already do.'

'I don't think you're a cissy, Giles,' Celia went on. 'In fact, I think you're a very charming young man.'

'I think you're very nice. Archie is a lucky fellow to have you for a wife,' said Giles. 'Do you think, when I'm older, that I'll meet someone as nice as you? I'm so scared of girls. I never know what to say to them, let alone anything . . .' his voice trailed off as he bowed his head once more and began picking at the rubber hand-grip of his bat.

'Anything else, you mean, Giles?' said Celia, inching closer to his body. She could feel a glow of warmth coming off him and his face was quite flushed not only, she suspected, from the heat of the day, but from the persistence of desire which she was sure was coursing round his body – being in such close proximity to her soft, perfumed flesh.

'Yes. I mean – oh, I shouldn't be talking to you about such things. Your husband would think it most improper.'

'Well, yes, he might, Giles,' she continued, 'but only if he knew. I think a married lady is allowed to have one or two little secrets, don't you, otherwise life wouldn't be much fun.' Celia cast her eyes down the length of his body and almost succumbed to an attack of giddiness when she spotted the huge ridge lying across his thigh where his whites were stretched over his skin. There was only one way to deal with the situation: to take control and assist the poor chap in his plight of suffering. She also had something else in mind.

'I should very much like to help you in the kitchen,' he stuttered, then swallowed hard and looked her in the eye. He smiled then; a cheeky smile she knew to be a promising sign. Celia took his bat out of his hand and replaced it with her gloved one. She pulled him to his feet and led him into the cool shade of the hut.

Once inside, she locked the door and said, 'Now we're alone I would like to ask you one or two questions.'

He looked startled.

'Have you ever kissed a girl?'

'Yes,' he replied. 'At the pictures. We went to the Saturday matinee and I couldn't stop myself. I wanted to, I wanted to touch her breast, I don't know why. I just felt so . . .' he trailed off again and Celia was getting a little impatient with her young friend.

'Aroused?' she suggested. He nodded, his face blushing with shame.

'Would you like to practise on me?' she asked boldly. 'If you practised on me, then you wouldn't feel so nervous the next time.'

'Oh, yes please,' answered young Giles, taking a step forward and wrapping his arms around her waist. 'I want to do more than that. I want to do what your husband does, you know, when you allow him his rights.'

'You impudent young man,' declared Celia, all the while becoming more excited by the prospect of releasing his hardness from his cricket whites. 'How dare you suggest that the sacred act of love is *his* right. Why, don't you know that many ladies of modern thinking find the act so pleasurable as to exceed the capabilities of one admirer?'

At this unheard-of information from the mouth of the fair sex, Giles could barely contain his enthusiasm and he grabbed at her buttocks and breasts as if they had not a moment to lose. He looked as happy as if he'd scored a century. Celia was going to allow him unimagined delight – but it was not to be without a price. 'Patience, young Giles,' she scolded. 'You may have what you want but I can't allow my husband to go unrewarded, too. He's the captain of your team and it is my duty to

teach you how to improve your thinking so an error such
as that you committed today doesn't happen again.'

Giles looked puzzled.

Celia directed her gaze around the hut, thinking fast
all the while. Along the wall ran a row of pegs, and from
them hung a selection of scarves, team ties and belts –
articles left there by other team members when they'd
changed into their whites.

'This one, I think, will do the trick,' said Celia, testing
a particularly thick brown leather strap against her own
hand. 'Well, Outhwaite,' she began. 'How long is it since
you learnt a lesson in sportsmanship?'

'What do you mean?' he anwered, looking suddenly
scared.

'I mean, young man, are you brave enough to take
punishment for your mistakes in the game we know and
love? If you are not to make the same mistake again, you
must be given something which reminds you of your
error. Something quick, painful and administered by
someone who knows what they are doing. You are to
call me Miss Celia. And when I strike your bottom hard,
as I am about to do, you must thank me for my trouble,
do you understand me?'

Giles looked forlorn and nodded stoically. 'Can I still
be allowed to, you know, touch you?' he asked, his eyes
brimming with the tears of remorse and fear.

Celia touched his cheek softly with her gloved hand
and leant her head to one side. 'Yes, of course, my dear,'
she whispered softly. She knew he would be bruised and
sore before the sun had set but he would thank her for it
on reflection. 'Now turn around and be a good boy,' she
commanded.

He turned to face the large wooden kitchen table, still
laid with tea things. 'If you're very good, I may allow
you some angel cake and a bottle of beer.' Without
further ado, Celia reached around to the front of his
trousers and found the buttons of his fly. The trousers
were tight and she stood for a moment admiring how

the stretch of the material across his young buttocks made a tempting canvas in itself. But no, 'on the bare' was the proper way to do things, she told herself. As she undid the buttons, her hand brushed against his erection which felt full of promise. She knew he would submit to anything to be able to seek release from his turgid state. The buttons undone, she eased his whites and white cotton boxer shorts over his rump. 'Now do the decent thing,' she said.

Silently, and biting his lips in anticipation, nineteen-year-old Giles Outhwaite bent his body over the table, muttering something incoherent about 'not whacking him too hard'. Celia paid no attention and bade him 'Shhh!' She ran the leather strap through her dainty hands a couple of times before winding the buckle end around her palm to get a good grip. She rubbed his proffered arse with her cotton-gloved hands and patted him affectionately. Then, no mercy, as this lovely vision of womanhood turned into a vengeful mistress and took her wrath on his bottom. She lashed at him with vigorous enthusiasm. How glad she was that regular badminton that summer had built up her arm muscles so effectively. She watched as Giles winced and spluttered in agony. His buttocks had turned as red as a peony and she could feel the heat rising from the punished flesh.

'You won't run a fellow team-member out again will you, Outhwaite?' she barked.

'No, Miss Celia,' he cried. 'It was unforgivable of me.'

'Yes,' she said, as she brought the belt down hard once more. 'It was unforgivable, but your punishment will teach you a lesson.' After some twenty lashes of the belt she reached between his legs. His prick was ramrod straight and pushing into the table. The heat from the spanking had produced a hard-on beyond her expectations.

Such teasing was too much for him and he spun round and grabbed Celia by the hair. 'Oh Miss Celia, I must have you,' he begged, then forced his tongue into her mouth with a youthful passion. His shaking hands snaked between her legs and he tugged at the damp silky material which lightly clad his prize and reward. At the insistence of his fingers, Celia was almost powerless to resist him; almost, but not completely. His hardness dug into her belly like a baton and he writhed against her like an eel. 'Please,' he whined, 'I'm about to make a mess of your dress if you don't let me ... you know ...'

'You'll do no such thing,' she snapped, pulling herself away. 'I haven't finished with you yet.' Celia stood in the cool dark hut glowering at the impatient young cricketer, the leather strap still wound menacingly around one hand. Her other hand rested on her left hip. She breathed deeply, trying to still her breathlessness from the exertion of administering the punishment. Her neck and breasts were flushed with excitement and her heart pounded in her chest. 'You must learn patience,' she said. 'The greatest rewards come through practised effort, young Outhwaite. There is no lazy way to excellence; a chap must learn when to take the lead and when to practise a little humility. It seems, in thinking you could bound the length of the wicket and expect Francis – some thirty years your senior – to do likewise, especially when the outfield were already in possession of the ball, that your misjudgement was influenced by arrogance. In this case, I have no option but to sentence you to learning a little humility – here and now.'

Giles looked petulant. His right hand had circled his penis and he was rubbing himself up and down, desperate for release. Celia moved towards him, threw her instrument of punishment on the kitchen table, where it slithered to the floor, and once more felt between his legs. His balls were tight and swollen and he pressed himself against her. His eyes were twinkling with excitement and he licked his lips in anticipation.

'You'll stop that at once,' she ordered and, without further procrastination, took one of the Chislehampton

Old Boys' ties from a peg and stretched it firmly between her hands. 'Take your shirt and trousers off!' she commanded. 'Before I lose my temper with you.'

Giles's shaky hands fumbled with his shirt buttons then slid the garment over his tanned, young shoulders. Then he speedily undid his shoes and slipped them off, took off his socks, and stepped out of his whites. He stood buck-naked beside the table, making attempts to cover his embarrassment with his hands. Celia crooked her finger and beckoned him to come closer to her. He didn't look so cheeky now that he was naked, she thought. Swiftly, she took hold of his hands and bound them behind his back with the tie. The knots were impossible to struggle out of. Despite his wriggling protests, he was now firmly under her control.

'There,' she said, 'now you won't be able to play with yourself.' Although she was denying him pleasure, she too was desperate for his hard, youthful prick inside her. The exquisite feeling of waiting for the inevitable moment was turning into a torturous sense of longing. 'Kneel down,' she said, and he did so. The heels of her navy-coloured shoes made a sharp sound on the floor of the pavilion as she walked around him, inspecting him from all angles. She unzipped her dress from the back and let it fall to the ground. She stepped out from it and stood before him, a goddess in pale mint-green lingerie. 'Now, pull my knickers down with your teeth,' she ordered.

Almost crying with desire, young Giles Outhwaite seized the delicate satin of her French knickers in his mouth and yanked downwards. He pulled on alternate sides until they were pooled around her ankles. 'Now, lick me,' she demanded, parting her legs slightly to allow him full view of what he had never seen.

'Are you sure?' he muttered softly, his face flushing with shame at her brazen behaviour.

'Quite sure,' she said. 'Now, be a good boy and do as you're told.' Giles softly kissed the silky hair of her sex.

He licked along the outer part of her lips and blew gently on the tender flesh at the tops of her thighs. She was desperate for more diligent attention. 'Stick your tongue in there,' she said, 'and move it about. If you don't do it properly I shall beat you again.'

Giles went to his task with gusto, using his tongue to its most dextrous effect. Anything to avoid another, humiliating beating. Celia ground herself down on him, dominating him with her perfume and the rich secretions he was bringing on with his licking. She allowed herself the small pleasure of a little cry, to let him know he was performing well. She could feel him using his teeth, also, teasing at her nub and pulling at the lips of her sex. His lustrous hair fell about his face as he worked hard to satisfy her. He was a prisoner of her legs; a keen student of the art of pleasure. The delirious impulse to abandon herself to delight was building in Celia, stronger by the second. How delicious it would be to surrender to the sweet combat of the act itself. She knew he must be desperate for his own pleasure and, with his arms still tied securely behind him, would surely be aching for it by now. For a brief moment, she pictured him driven to desperate measures; dominating her, throwing her back over the table and having her roughly; holding her arms above her head, ramming into her without preamble. This wasn't possible today, though – not with the young cricketer in bondage at her behest. She was unable to stop an avalanche of impure thoughts from crashing into her mind and she took hold of his hair at that moment. She moved herself more quickly and rhythmically over his face, covering his skin with sweetly shameful secretions. 'Harder, and faster,' she begged him, feeling an electric thrill beginning to build in her legs. She twined the fingers of one hand through the thick dark locks of his hair and, with the other, pinched her nipples hard until they peaked and crested through her brassière. Then, it was coming; she was to have her moment of ultimate pleasure with the young man's face buried between her legs. He was bringing her to what she'd craved all day. She cried out his name, anointing him with the juices which were trickling out of her as she spasmed a rapturous climax.

She held his face there for the duration of her pleasure then stepped back to see him, still kneeling, his eyes imploring her to ease his plight. His penis looked huge and purple and substantial enough to fill her wanting need. 'I think you've proved that you can be patient, if you want to, Giles,' Celia said, still quite breathless but unwilling to allow her young charge to see the extent of his effect on her.

He nodded his head.

'Then what you must have is a reward of your own,' she said, untying his hands from behind his back and casting the tie aside. Once more she helped him to his feet, then sat him on one of the wooden chairs by the side of the dining table. He was still ramrod straight and his buttocks remained flushed – although not as rosy red as some ten minutes previously. His face spread into a grin as Celia straddled him and took his penis in her right hand. She was still wearing the cotton gloves. 'Tell me what you've learnt,' she whispered, beginning to slide her hand up and down the shaft, watching his expression change to one of serious concentration.

'I've learnt to be patient, to show humility and to not be so presumptuous,' he replied.

'Very good,' she said, and eased herself down on to his fleshy pole. Her cleft was warm and her vagina clenched him in an oily grasp. He exhaled violently, a look of near-horror mixed with surprise crossing his face as he realised that he was losing his virginity to the wife of the captain of his cricket team. Her feet bracing her as she sat astride the young man, and her hands planted on the back of the chair, Celia was able to rise and fall on his lap in a similar movement to that she employed when out trotting with the Chislehampton Ladies Riding School. Giles held the sides of the chair and rose up to meet her every thrust. She kissed him sweetly, running her hands over his smooth chest. She ran her fingers through his lovely hair. She said things to him that made him blush and that brought him on to the peak of his hardness. Then his young hands were all over her and he shut his eyes to block out her knowing gaze and smug smile.

'I'm not able to stop, Miss Celia,' he breathed hoarsely. 'I'm there now!' he cried, his short-clipped nails digging into her flesh as he buried his face in her bosom.

To take my delight from a newly-punished young man is what gives me my happy disposition, thought Celia as she zipped up her dress and combed her bobbed hair into shape once more. Giles had changed into his dark trousers and a sweater which bore the team crest, and was smiling to himself as he drank from the bottle of beer Celia had allowed him after their coupling. Compliant and knowing humility, he had permitted her to tie a floral apron around his waist and lead him to the pavilion kitchenette where he began his task of washing the team's cups, saucers and plates. Celia did none of the clearing away but, instead, ordered Giles to clean up every crumb, every speck of food from the wooden table. She sat regally at the head of the table, watching his bottom wiggle as he scrubbed the soap pads over the plates.

'You know, you'll make a lovely housekeeper one day,' she teased him. 'Or maybe even a ladies' maid. I could see you in a little frock, all docile and obedient.' Giles winced, but knew that he couldn't cheek her – a well-respected lady of the county. After he had finished his task, he returned to the main room just as the other team members were trooping in. Celia had unlocked the door, and was sitting down reading one of the cricket programmes from earlier in the season, a picture of wifely sweetness.

'Ah, all done, Mrs Penrose?' asked the visiting captain as he admired the pristine state of the pavilion dining table.

'I've had a little help,' she said, nodding in the direction of young Outhwaite, still sporting the floral pinny. Archie Penrose came to stand beside his wife, his hand resting lightly on her shoulder.

'Anyone seen my belt and tie?' enquired one of the team members. Archie spied the items on the floor and picked them up, caressing the leather as he did so.

'Well, my dear. I trust you've helped us out once more,' he whispered in Celia's ear, spotting young Outhwaite's downcast gaze and humbled expression. He called the young man over to him and quietly asked him, 'What have you learnt this afternoon, Outhwaite?'

'Er ... well, Mr Penrose, I've learnt to think before I make rash decisions and be patient.'

'And to learn a little humility?' he queried.

'Yes, sir,' he mumbled, looking as nervous as a deer in a trap.

'Good, good. So we can expect an improvement in your performance next match then, can we?' Archie went on.

'Absolutely, captain. No doubt about that,' he replied, unconsciously rubbing his still-smarting rump.

Later, Archie and his wife drove home to Sunray Avenue, Chislehampton, in their dark-green Armstrong Siddeley. Little was said as they meandered through the country lanes. Occasionally Archie turned to Celia and gave her an affectionate wink. 'You know, dear,' he said thoughtfully, 'I've no doubt we'll see a marked improvement in young Outhwaite's game come the next match.'

'Yes, I'm sure,' said his wife. 'Archie dear,' she continued, 'although you scored a half century today, I think you could have done even better if you had tried a little harder. I think we'll discuss it when we get home, don't you?'

Adjusting the small harness which ran between his legs and which Celia always insisted he wore, even during the friendliest of matches, Archie Penrose sighed with joy. Yes ... Celia's system had whipped his team into shape – and no mistake.

Dream Lover

Katrina Vincenzi

The next extract is from *Dream Lover*. Hard-working film producer Gemma has a chance erotic encounter with an anonymous stranger. And then another. Then she's invited to an opulent masked ball at a chateau where the guests are libertines who enjoy indulging in the finest of champagnes, the richest of caviar and the most outlandish of sexual games. Will this party reveal the identity of her mystery lover?

Katrina Vincenzi has written two other Black Lace books. The hallmarks of her work are sophistication, elegance and a love of fine things. Her first story for the series was *Virtuoso*, set in the secluded, passionate world of a once world-class solo violinist and his lover. *Odyssey* is about a search for the elusive and priceless lost treasures of Troy and the sensual deceptions of a group of people involved in uncovering their whereabouts. *Odyssey* was written after Katrina's marriage. The author is now known as Katrina Vincenzi-Thyne.

Dream Lover

*T*he costume fascinated her. It was a cat-suit, long and supple, bisected with a thick silver zip that ran from neck to crotch and then split down both legs. A tiny hood was attached to the neck. The sleek, supple leather was warm to the touch, the heavy mesh of the silver zip cool and lifeless and the contrast was strangely stirring. It had a mysterious allure that both attracted and faintly repelled her, an odd sensation that was familiar yet elusive.

The afternoon of the masked ball Gemma was to attend she spent soaking for hours in a hot bath scented with her favourite perfume, luxuriating in the steamy warmth, letting herself drift. She washed her hair and towelled it dry, letting it fall in loose waves and then massaged a rich, almond-scented cream all over her body. Looking in the mirror, she examined herself thoughtfully. Her skin was flushed a rosy pink from the bath, and her nipples were firm, jutting peaks, aroused by the touch of her hands. She let her fingers drift down the flat plane of her belly and tangle in the silvery blonde thatch of her pubic hair.

She knew then that she would wear nothing beneath the slick black leather.

It fitted perfectly, like a caressing second skin, cupping her breasts and moulding itself to her body. The mesh of the zip embraced her sex in a cool, metallic kiss that parted her inner lips and rubbed gently at her clitoris. In the mirror she saw a stranger, a ferally, fatally seductive black-leather creature who had her own familiar silvery blonde hair and dark blue eyes.

Beneath the hood, only her eyes and lips would be visible. Deliberately she exaggerated her make-up, using thick black liner and masses of mascara, and painted her lips a deep, deep red. And when the hood was in place, her hair concealed by the black leather, she was truly transformed into the stranger she had seen in the mirror.

It was a strange sensation, she reflected, as they drove to the chateau, as though by donning the disguise she had acquired something of the sleek sensuality it embodied. Unbearably conscious of her naked body beneath the supple black leather, feeling secretly decadent and faintly excited, she paid scant attention to her friends Jean-Paul and Pascaline, her attention only roused by the looming facade of the chateau. It was a soaringly elegant, impeccable Renaissance-style building with the remains of a discordantly crumbling tower to one side.

'What is that?' asked Gemma in surprise as the headlights of the car briefly illuminated the tower.

'Part of the old keep, an affectation of Leo's,' replied Jean-Paul as he brought the car to a halt and tossed the keys to a waiting servant. 'The graveyard as well . . . he's refused to restore it, strange, really.'

But as they walked up the massive stone stairs leading to the immense double doors, she forgot the tower in the new awareness of her body moving against leather and steel and knew that even her walk was slightly different, looser, faintly provocative, the gentle sway of her hips more pronounced, her body undulating under the pervasive, persuasive caress of the costume.

Pascaline and Jean-Paul, also dressed in black leather, were conversing, saying something that eluded her as the massive doors opened and then she forgot them and herself in the breathtaking spectacle before her eyes.

They were in a huge entrance hall that soared the height of the building, illuminated by a massive chandelier that shed light like tiny diamonds, drawing the fire of the brightly coloured silks and velvets, refracting the emeralds and diamonds and rubies. It was decadently opulent, a brilliant kaleidoscope of shifting shades and scents and images. A bejewelled Marie Antoinette in a dazzling confection of aquamarine silk playfully rapped Lucifer across the knuckles with her fan; an olive-skinned houri in floating gauze with a huge emerald in her bellybutton leant closer to Cardinal Richelieu; an exuberant Dionysus with a laurel wreath slipping from his temples and carrying aloft a bunch of grapes was blatantly rubbing against a nun.

A string quartet was playing from a minstrels' gallery, the stately and decorous Albinoni almost drowned by the excited chatter of hundreds of voices. She recognised the distinctive cosmopolitan cacophony of French, Italian, English, Spanish and some unusual tongue she couldn't identify ... Russian, perhaps, or some strange dialect. It was a scene both bizarre and exotic: harlequins, clowns, devils, pirates, whores and angels all captured in the shifting strobe of the chandelier.

A cloud of richly evocative Joy enveloped her as she was lavishly embraced by a Cleopatra who had no doubt mistaken her for someone else, and she quickly lost Jean-Paul and Pascaline to the shifting crowd. A waiter in formal attire offered a flute of champagne from a silver tray; she took it gingerly, brought back to earth by the expectation of the over-sweet, fizzy liquid she had learnt to detest from a hundred wrap parties.

It was a cloud of sensation, a cool frothing caress that melted in her mouth, a delicious tingling so far removed from the ordinary experience of swallowing that her senses reeled in surprise. Taittinger, perhaps, or Cristal; a wickedly expensive explosion of pure delight against the palate, a heady, bubbly swirl that left her elated yet icily sober, every sense clear and somehow sharpened. Entranced, she plucked another glass from a passing waiter and in her new, anonymous persona decided to explore.

She moved through the crowd, ostensibly looking for Jean-Paul and Pascaline, secretly rather thrilled to be alone.

Incongruous in their strict black and white formality, waiters circulated, offering champagne and an array of tempting hors d'oeuvres; mounds of caviare, glistening like grey pearls on a bed of shaved ice, surrounded by toast points, chopped eggs and spring onions arranged in the form of some exotic flower; oysters on the half-shell cushioned by pungently green seaweed and adorned with slices of lemon; delicate, tissue-thin slices of smoked salmon arranged in the scales of a leaping fish and garnished with succulent capers and black olives; prawns with a deliciously spicy dip, scallops wrapped in bacon and mussels in vinaigrette vied with more exotic confections. The mouth-watering aromas melded with the scent of exotic and expensive perfumes on hot and excited bodies.

She sipped champagne and let herself drift with the crowd towards the end of the room, eavesdropping shamelessly, secure in her disguise.

'But no one, simply no one goes to Monte Carlo anymore, it's so, so, so –'

'Utterly devastated to lose the Matisse, but at least we'd insured it for double the market value – you simply can't keep anything safe on the Riviera these days –'

'Well, one look at the Nikkei and I knew we'd made a killing –'

'So sweet of you, but they're paste, of course, the little man at the bank goes positively wild when I try to take the diamonds out of the vault, and then these boring insurance clauses –'

The conversation was almost as surreal as the surroundings, Gemma decided, as she found herself entering a huge black and white room. The floor was black, veined marble, the walls starkly white. Recessed niches held priceless Benin bronzes and the stately chords of Albinoni dissolved in the throaty smoke of slow jazz issuing from hidden speakers. In the centre of the room, on a huge block of white marble, two ebony figures, a man and woman, were posed in the act of love, their bodies highlighted by concealed spotlights.

The man seemed to glow under the hot glare of the lights, black and glistening. He was resting on one elbow, mouth poised over a dusky nipple, and his erection, a huge, dark rod, was clearly visible against the woman's thigh. The woman lay in a pose of utter abandon, legs parted and arms outstretched, a rippling mass of ebony hair snaking across the white marble surface.

It was a few moments before she realised they were real.

It was shocking, yet strangely exciting, and she felt a slow pulse begin to beat between her legs as the man moved, touching the woman's thigh, urging her legs further apart. The woman's sex was fully revealed, the dusky pink leaves of her labia swollen and glistening, the bud of her pleasure protruding like a stamen of some exotic flower.

'Performance art, darling, passé, simply ages ago,' she heard a voice murmur behind her, and then the dry response: 'Not so passé. Look carefully.'

He was touching her now, testing her arousal, one finger disappearing into the channel of her body, and Gemma felt her inner walls contract sharply, a shiver of lust spiralling straight to her groin. He inserted a second finger, and then a third, and thrust them in and out of the woman's body until he was satisfied. When he withdrew them, glistening with her body's musk, he touched them first to her lips and then to his own.

Gemma caught her breath. It was bizarrely erotic, standing alone in the press of strangers, enveloped in a perverse and anonymous prurience, a sweetly salacious complicity. They had all fallen silent now, and the atmosphere was thick and expectant. She couldn't take her eyes away from the rippling muscles of his back as the man prepared to mount the woman, mesmerised by the huge distended length of his erection as he positioned himself between her thighs.

She felt a hot tremor of excitement as he moved, sensing she would be too small to take him, and then, just as he plunged into her body there was a cool moan that might have been a woman's cry or the voice of the sax, and the room went dark. She felt the sharp intake of breath around her, as if they had all been holding their breath, rapt in the black and white carnality before their eyes.

Lights flowered over a huge, arched doorway at the far end of the room, and as if by common consent the crowd moved slowly towards it, leaving the ebony lovers in darkness. As Gemma drew nearer she realised that the low moan of the jazz and the woman were becoming overshadowed by the haunting, discordant lilt of a sitar.

The room was softly lit, pale light spilling from hundreds of intricately carved ivory balls suspended from the ceiling by chains. Crimson silk shot through with gold flowed from the walls and beneath her feet was the soft touch of an exuberantly patterned Chinese carpet in Imperial yellow. Even as she struggled to take in the huge and ornately gilded Satsuma vases, the flowing poetry of Tang horses and the milky blue and white perfection of Ming scattered in recessed niches, her eyes were drawn to the centre of the room.

On a raised dais, two women were moving languorously to the sound of the sitar. They belonged to the Orient, golden skin and jet-black hair, their nude, hairless, almost childlike bodies fluid and graceful. The hot tremor of excitement that had gripped her whilst watching the man and woman flushed into a rosy glow as

Gemma succumbed to the more diffuse, somehow more pervasive and sensual aura of the dance.

They touched each other delicately, moving to the harsh, lyrical strains of the sitar, and Gemma felt her mouth grow dry as she watched them twine and untwine together, wreathe and separate. She drained her glass and instantly a waiter appeared at her side with a fresh flute of champagne.

There was something strangely stirring in the spectacle of two women moving together, sensual rather than sexual, more enticing than exciting. The haunting strains of the sitar lent an air of dim unreality to the scene.

And then the music and lights began to fade as the two women fastened together, belly to belly, thigh to thigh, fingers weaving between their thighs in a different dance.

Gemma felt her nipples tighten and her groin grow heavy, even as they were beckoned to a further room by the low roll of drums to a shadowy space perfumed with incense.

A woman was moving through the crowd, stamping her feet in time to the drum. She was darkly exotic, dressed in gauzy, rose-coloured trousers with a ruby fixed to her navel, long dark hair free and her breasts bare. Automatically the throng parted, and soon she was alone, in the centre of the room. She jerked her hips slowly, in the rhythm of sex, thrusting and retreating, grinding and shivering, and when her arms began to tremble Gemma could feel the same hypnotic, erotic heat begin to envelop her.

The dancer's shoulders moved; her breasts shook; the muscles of her belly rippled as if in response to a probing shaft, and the rhythm of the music quickened. And then she writhed, faster and faster, and Gemma felt her own hips move unconsciously in imitation, in thrall to the music, swayed by the dancer's spell.

* * *

Watching her, the unknowing, tiny undulations of her body responding to the music, imagining her silvery blonde hair free and flowing like the Egyptian woman's, he was pleased.

'I like it,' he murmured quietly to his friend. 'I like it very much.'

'I am so pleased,' was the suave rejoinder.

It seemed as though she was being driven to climax by the voluptuous frenzy of her own body and when the music ended on a final, throbbing drumbeat the dancer uttered a sharp cry and collapsed on the floor. The tension among the crowd was almost palpable as they shifted to the next sensation. It was clear now to Gemma that they were being moved from room to room, drawn by the lights and the music into a sensual labyrinth, and she found her own arousal becoming so intense as to be almost unbearable.

Senses reeling, she lost track of her surroundings and had only a vague impression of a glass-panelled room with a steaming pool. She was dimly aware of the mounds of exotic greenery where the shrill cry of brilliantly coloured parrots blended with the jungle writhing of slick and naked bodies, but before long they spilled into a narrow corridor lined with Archaic Greek sculptures of nude kouros figures.

Hot, sweaty, aroused and bemused, Gemma knew only the impulse to escape; the over-blown, lush decadence was overwhelming, and when she saw a doorway leading outside she slipped from the crowd.

The cool night air was a relief, and she took deep, shuddering breaths, drawing the freshness into her lungs as if it could cool the heat of her arousal. She stumbled forward, found herself at the base of the crumbling tower she had seen earlier as they arrived and dimly realised that she must have traversed only one wing of the chateau.

She felt at once both over-stimulated and exhausted

and couldn't even begin to imagine the bizarre tableaux that must be taking place as the party progressed. She had the strange urge to stroke herself to climax; to find Jean-Paul and Pascaline and leave the chateau; to escape this elegant, contrived, perverse eroticism and find her way back to the tomb, back to the carved image of the hunter with his grossly enlarged phallus/spear, back to the hard packed earth floor where fantasy had become reality.

She was in a turmoil that had stripped away the comforting illusion of her disguise and knew she was far, far out of her depth.

And when the strong hands closed on her shoulders, and the harsh, faintly metallic voice reached her ears, she almost fainted in fear and relief and disbelief.

'I know what you want,' he said.

A sudden clap of thunder almost drowned his words, but she was sure she recognised the voice, the clipped consonants, the liquid vowels. Lightning flashed before them, illuminating the tower, and she wondered a little wildly if nature herself was conspiring in this strange drama.

And then she forgot to think as his hands reached between her thighs and unfastened the zip, releasing her heated sex. She twisted, tried to turn to face him, to escape him, but his hand was heavy on the back of her neck, forcing her to her knees.

She felt the tip of his penis at the base of her spine, nudging between the cleft of her buttocks, tracing the path to her secret places. He paused at the taut mouth of her anus and she shivered as a frisson of dark pleasure shot through her. And then he eased forward, parting the plump folds of her labia with slick ease, and she felt her flesh curl around him. He stopped at the entrance, just circling it with the engorged tip of his organ.

She felt the responsive quiver deep inside her, her inner muscles tensing and almost convulsing in anticipation of the pounding thrust, but he withdrew, guiding the hot length of his penis back through her engorged and aching flesh, back to the tender, secret passage, back to the base of her spine.

Again and again he repeated the stroke, sometimes slowly, sometimes fast and furious, sometimes pressing just inside, sometimes thrusting against the taut bud of her clitoris, varying the rhythm, keeping her poised on the very edge. He left a trail of burning moisture in his wake, a searing hunger, every sensation of her body centred on the lascivious stroke of his penis against her flesh.

The thunder pounding in her ears could have been the flow of her blood; when her climax finally struck, it was as though the lightning snaking across the sky had entered her body, so jarringly electric was the sensation of his full length finally thrusting home.

Her body writhed with the force of the stabbing pleasure arcing through her, stinging every nerve-ending from the tips of her fingers to her toes in thrilling awareness. She could have wept in sheer ecstasy had she not been screaming in release.

Dazed, she barely felt him withdraw. Moments later, when she finally gathered the strength to lift her head, he had gone.

It was almost midnight. Inside the chateau, the guests were gathered in the huge ballroom that was the heart of the building, a magnificently opulent Regency-style room of gilt and white marble and mirrored walls illuminated by massive chandeliers. There was no music; only an expectant hush as they absorbed the spectacular tableau in the centre of the room.

It was a huge primitivo-cubist sculpture, discordant and arresting, at least ten feet high, of a man and a woman embracing. The figures were solid marble, geometric shapes differentiated only by the heavy, triangular breasts of the female and the massive, oblong rod of the male. Both figures were white, except for the male penis, which was a shaft of distended red-veined marble, disappearing between the white thighs of the woman. It was the essence of penetration, blunt and primal, the first moment of male flesh meeting female. And despite, or perhaps because, the figures were only raw shapes, cuboid symbols, it embodied the fundamental core of sex, purely, crudely, blatantly.

Around the base of the sculpture were twelve couples, nude men and women arranged in the same pose, their bodies almost locked together. The men, poised on the brink of penetration, were all fully erect, their organs as red and distended as the massive red marble shaft of the sculpture. The women stood, thighs parted, waiting to receive them. They were motionless; but for the sheen of sweat on their brows they might almost have been mistaken for stone.

The guests, too, were still, an uneasy stillness fraught with curling anticipation as they waited for the scene to unfold. Impassive waiters moved through the crowd, silently offering flutes of champagne, pressing them into unresisting hands.

They had all passed through the sensual odyssey their host Leo had created, passed from room to room, titillated and aroused by the scents, the colours, the music, the erotic scenes enacted before them. This was the culmination. The climax. All were moved, and some a little shocked, by the stark, uncompromising sexuality of the sculpture and its human counterparts.

'Clever,' murmured one of the guests, Alexei, to Leo, who was standing beside him, a faint smile on his face. 'Brancusi?' he asked, referring to the sculpture.

'School of,' returned Leo softly. 'Ah. Now it begins.'

A massive gong struck, the first stroke of midnight. At its command, the men thrust, thick, engorged rods disappearing between the women's thighs, echoing the pure, brutal symmetry of the sculpture.

There was a strangled gasp from the crowd, as if each of them had been penetrated, pierced by the primal stab of the male organ, searched by the swollen, unthinking, driven red marble rod.

And then the men withdrew in perfect synchronicity, revealing glistening penises, rock-hard and pulsing, before they thrust again as the gong struck a second time. And though they measured time by each thrust, embodied the raw and rhythmic stroke of seconds with each thrust, the moment seemed endless.

Only the slick kiss of flesh on flesh filled the room between the resonant strokes of the clock. And the players were no longer stiff, impersonal representations; they were men and women clawing for release, dancing the primal dance to the command of the gong. When, on the stroke of twelve, they climaxed, the room seemed flooded with release, a euphoric swell of fulfilment.

A mild explosion of a hundred champagne corks popping heralded the New Year. Amidst frantic embraces and excited and exuberant cries the twelve naked couples slipped from the room.

'No balloons? No streamers? No party hats?' commented another guest, Jay Stone, who had joined Alexei and Leo on the fringes of the room. He had meant to sound sardonic, but even to his own ears his voice sounded forced and he was breathing too rapidly.

'And I was forgetting you Americans had such sophisticated tastes,' smiled Leo.

Across the room, Gabrielle de Sevigny observed her lover Leo, her arousal tempered with unease. Resplendent in evening dress, he was standing with two tall, dark men she didn't recognise, one dressed as Satan, the other ambiguous in black with a long, velvet cape.

Her body was hot and aroused, almost unbearably excited by the bizarre and erotic images Leo had created and conjured, but her mind was reeling. It was a side of him she had barely acknowledged, hardly dared to suspect; an ice-cold, calculating, sensual connoisseur whose dark depths had barely been exposed by the blatant tableaux.

This was, for Leo, she sensed, a mere bagatelle, a pretty device to amuse and entertain, no more.

And if the thought frightened her, it aroused her even more.

She looked down at her dress, suddenly dissatisfied with her costume. She had wanted something erotically suggestive, something sexy. Briefly she had toyed with the notion of appearing as the Marquise de Pompadour, mistress of Louis XV, or even Catherine the Great, the notoriously whorish monarch, but discarded them both as clichés. And the costumes were too voluminous, too concealing. Finally, after much deliberation, she had decided to dress as a twenties-style flapper, hoping to lure him with the irresistible, irrepressible, flirtatiously light-hearted decadence of the period.

She was wearing a shimmering knee-length silver tube of iridescent beads that caught the light, saucily slit to the waist on one side where a black garter-belt could be glimpsed whenever she moved. Her stockings were sheer black silk, her heels high, stiletto points. Diamonds dripped from her ears, flashed on her wrists and glittered on the twenties-style headband adorning her brow.

She knew she looked beautiful, sexy, desirable; and she knew now that it wasn't enough. Perhaps it never had been.

Still, she made her way over to Leo with an expression of cool boredom on her face, even though her heart was pounding.

'Gabrielle, my dear,' Leo welcomed her, kissing both her cheeks. It was no more than a traditional, polite greeting between acquaintances; yet the mere brush of his lips against her skin made her blood heat and thicken.

'Let me present my friends, Alexei Racine, Jay Stone.' Conventional murmurs, then, 'What did you think of my little divertissement?' he asked, eyes glowing like coals.

'It was,' she shrugged elegantly, 'amusing. Yes, very

amusing. I had no idea you were so interested in ...
sculpture.'

'One of my ruling passions,' he replied easily. 'Would
you like to see more?'

The heat was still in his eyes. She recognised the look
with relief. 'Yes, yes, I would,' she said, barely managing
to conceal a frisson of pleasure as he ran his hand down
the naked skin of her arm and cupped her elbow.

'Jay? Alexei? You'll excuse me? This way, my dear.'

He led her out of the ballroom, past a series of retiring
rooms sumptuously decorated in blue, white and gold
in the manner of Louis XV, then through a long mirrored
hallway of gilt and crystal chandeliers into a series of
interconnecting rooms so lavish and opulent that she
found herself holding her breath.

They passed through a small door concealed by a
Gobelins tapestry and she found herself on a dimly lit,
narrow stone staircase. Leo led the way silently until
they emerged into a long, low-ceilinged room with a
faintly sloping floor. A massive forest of huge stone
columns supported the roof. It was cool and faintly
sinister and Gabrielle shivered.

'What is this place?' she asked Leo, her voice echoing.

'Part of the old keep,' he replied, moving towards a
large wooden door reinforced with metal bands. 'I
thought about converting it to a wine cellar, but the
servants are superstitious.' He made a vague gesture to
his left.

Narrowing her eyes, she saw, between the interstices
of the columns, a series of rusting metal grilles.

'The dungeons,' he explained casually. 'And this,' he
said, opening the heavy wooden door, 'was the torture
chamber.'

He urged her into the room with a palm on the small
of her back. It was dark, and she could see nothing. And
then a match scraped and a torch on the wall beside her
flared into life.

It was a scene from some surreal hell. Contorted,

174

writhing black metal forms, tortured and tortuous, swarmed along the walls, some vaguely human, others simply menacing shapes.

'Modern, of course,' Leo said. 'One of the few pieces I've commissioned.'

Her eyes were fixed on a human face, eyes closed and head flung back, the mouth a contorted rictus that might have been agony, might even have been ecstasy.

'But it captures the spirit, I think.'

There were knives and manacles, whips and chains, strange and bizarre-looking shapes she couldn't name. Her eyes were drawn to a female nude, the nipples pierced with tiny darts.

'A rather playful little piece in some ways. I feel sure he was influenced by Tinguely and Saint-Phalle.'

The torchlight flickered and it seemed to her as though the figures began to shift slightly, to move, to redefine themselves. What she had first perceived as a spear thrusting into the distorted flesh of some grotesque belly became an enormous, distended male organ rutting through the folds of female flesh. Pincers clawing at a woman's breast transformed themselves into clutching fingers. The tortured savagery of the piece became somehow subtly infused with a deep, dark eroticism.

'Well, what do you think? Do you like it?'

'I think,' said Gabrielle softly, 'I think it frightens me.' She had intended to lie, but it was impossible to dissemble in the face of such a powerfully brutal work.

'Excellent,' murmured Leo. 'Excellent.'

He placed his hands on her shoulders and turned her face to him. She relaxed slightly, relieved to turn her back on the writhing, metal mass, and anticipated his kiss, the warming touch of his lips on hers.

Instead, he tugged on the glittering band on her brow, dragging it down to cover her eyes. Instinctively she stiffened and tried to reach up, but he captured both her wrists in one hand.

'As you may have guessed,' he said smoothly, 'I am

particularly intrigued by the physical aspect of sculpture, the translation of flesh to stone or bronze, the contrast . . . which is always enhanced, I think, by . . .'

The words washed over her, meaning nothing. Deprived of sight, deprived of movement by the iron clasp of his hand, it seemed as though all her senses had suddenly sharpened in response. The acrid smell of smoke from the torch seemed stronger, the expensive perfume of his aftershave more pungent. She could feel her skin prickling as he found the zipper at the back of her dress, and the sound of it slithering to the floor was unnaturally loud.

With one hand around her waist he lifted her free of the shimmering silver folds and carried her a few steps until she felt the cool, twisted metal at her back. His erection was hard against her thigh; any moment now, she knew, she would feel the hot length of him probing her sex.

Instead, he lifted her higher and there was a harsh, metallic click as something closed over one wrist and then the other. He let her go and, as she felt for the floor, she became aware of the harsh brush of metal on the inside of her thighs.

He stood back to admire the effect. Her arms were stretched above her head, one wrist clasped by a black manacle, the other trapped in the fanged jaw of a skull. Against the rough black metal her skin shone a warm, pearly white, the milky flow of flesh interrupted by the dark plume of her pubic hair, the massive black penis-spear between her legs and the black garters and stockings.

It was more than lewd, he decided. There was something almost obscene in the pose. Perhaps it was the glittering band that obscured her eyes. If only her hair were a different colour . . . Gabrielle's raven black hair dissolved too readily against the dark metal . . . a blonde would be better, masses of silvery blonde . . .

176

'Leo, what is this?' asked Gabrielle, a faint tremor in her voice.

'This, Gabrielle? It's called "The Torment",' he replied. 'Let me show you.'

She felt his finger slip between the lips of her sex. She was tight and dry, any arousal chilled by the menacing sculpture, and his touch was intrusive, almost painful. The quick thrum of his fingers chafed her clitoris, a rapid stroke from the stem to the tip repeated again and again until the first burning irritation began to dissolve as she heated and moistened. She felt her lower lips begin to swell in response, grow plump and slick.

His touch was hard, almost too hard, a thick, stabbing pressure that quickly roused the pulsating between her legs. She felt the delicate tissues swell and suffuse as the heat of arousal enveloped her sex, a fiery heat that followed the path of his finger.

All sensation spiralled to the hungry flesh between her legs, the quick stab of his fingers. She forgot the twisted black mass behind her, the unseen points digging into her shoulders and back, the cool metal at the top of her thighs; she forgot even to breathe as the flickering heat pooled and swelled.

She felt the first incandescent ripple deep in her belly, the first singing surge as her body gathered itself for climax, and the muscles in her legs began to tremble.

Immediately he changed the rhythm, moving his finger gently, exploring the swollen pink flesh around her clitoris, denying her the final rough, orgasmic stroke. She felt it throb and pulse as he skirted it delicately, swirling his finger around its protective flesh, a cunning, subtle stimulation.

Even as she began to flow with his new rhythm, relax to the rosy flush that replaced the burning heat, find the dreamy, languorous warmth, he changed his stroke, flicking his finger rapidly against the tip of her clitoris in a quick staccato beat.

Cleverly, mercilessly, repeatedly he brought her to the

edge of orgasm and then denied her the final, cleansing explosion until the pleasure changed to a deep, physical ache and the sweet humid heaviness became a clawing need.

He made her body heat, then cooled it, startled and then soothed it, conjured the sweeping red mist that suffused her senses and then banished it before it could envelop her. And he did it again and again and again, moving to her breasts when she was about to climax from his hand against her sex, sucking them and biting them into hard, aching points, drawing all her body's focus to her nipples and then moving back to thrust his tongue deep inside her.

Even as her body succumbed to madness, she realised, finally, the purpose of his paradoxical lovemaking, how surely and cleverly he had led her to this dark, demonic dissolution where nothing mattered but release.

Her whole body was swollen, nipples and labia inflamed and engorged, the hot, flickering tide swelling and subsiding and then rising again as he used his mouth, his hands and his cock to drive her to frenzy and then refuse her climax.

His penis searched for her, circling the wet, aching void, then pushed inside, just the tip, reminding the melting inner tissues of his hot, hard length before withdrawing, circling, then nudging in again, never to full length, never pulsing against the rippling muscles that ached for friction.

Writhing helplessly, she felt the harsh, metal, impaling sting against her back, her shoulders, her buttocks, and knew that she was grinding against the tortured metal hell of the sculpture on the wall. The sensation was almost a relief, a counterpoint to the excruciating, excoriating, agonising need that consumed her.

She was burningly distended; her inner lips were tumid and swollen, her nipples hard points, aching with need, a shivering, raw, animal need for release, an overpowering, atavistic need that transcended any known sensation. She felt the thick length of his penis enter her again, then withdraw quickly.

She screamed then, a primal cry of fury and frustration that echoed through the room and blended incongruously with the low sound of Leo's laughter.

'Excellent, Gabrielle, excellent. You begin to understand the essence of the piece.'

The Sins of the Flesh

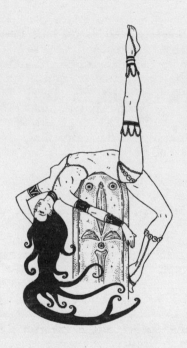

Cleo Cordell

Cleo Cordell has been writing for Black Lace since the imprint was first launched. A specialist in tales of Gothic fantasy and the darker reaches of the sexual imagination, the following story is no exception. Seances were all the rage among the more bohemian thinkers of the Victorian age. *Sins of the Flesh* takes the central character, Flora, into a world of erotic paranormal experience and depraved behaviour. The enigmatic psychic, Joseph Hoffman, is in charge of the proceedings. Is he a genuine medium, or is it all a sham?

Cleo's first Black Lace book was *The Captive Flesh*, which caused controversy with its harem setting and graphic descriptions of sexual punishment. Its sequel is *The Senses Bejewelled*. Her other books are *Juliet Rising*, set in a strict academy for ladies during the eighteenth century; *Velvet Claws*, set in Africa during the time of nineteenth-century exploration; *Crimson Buccaneer*, which tells the story of a Spanish woman who turns to piracy for revenge; *Path of the Tiger*, set in India during the days of the Raj; and *Opal Darkness*, a story of forbidden love between siblings Sidonie and Francis set in the latter part of the nineteenth century.

The Sins of the Flesh

*I*t was a little before midnight when the hansom drew to a halt outside the great wrought-iron gates of Christchurch cemetery. Flora Brennan alighted first, then stood by while her mistress paid the driver. Annaline was resplendent in velvet and furs, a warm hat topping her elaborate coiffure. Although Flora too was swathed against the cold she shivered in the night air.

This is wrong. We should not be here, she thought. Only trouble can come of this.

As if to echo Flora's thoughts the driver said to Annaline, 'I'll wait for you, if you wish it, ma'am. 'T'aint safe for gentlefolk to be abroad in these parts.'

'We'll do very well, thank you, cabby. The dead can't harm us,' Annaline answered in her well-bred, clipped voice, already striding purposefully towards the gates.

Flora hung back reluctantly. A gust of wind blew a lock of her hair into her eyes. She tied the ribbons of her bonnet more securely, glad of the moment's delay.

The cabby grinned down at her. 'The gentry has some strange fancies, don't they ducks?' he said in a piercing whisper, his eyes inclining heavenwards. 'You wouldn't get me in that place, not after what I've heard. Lights burning in the small hours and 'orrible shrieks at all hours of the day. Fair gives me the creeps.' He peered at her more closely. 'You look scared. You can wait in 'ere with me if you like. I know ways to put a pretty girl like you at ease.'

At his clumsy attempt to make advances Flora lifted her chin. 'I'll thank you to mind your manners,' she said pertly. 'And you're mistaken. I'm not afraid of anything.'

The cabby shrugged. 'Hoity-toity. Well don't say I didn't warn yer.' He tipped the edge of the horse whip to his hat brim and urged the horse forward.

Flora hurried to catch up with Annaline. As she brushed past the open gates, her skirt caught on a loop of cast iron. She tugged at it impatiently, the rusting hinges creaking as the gate moved. The noise grated on her strained nerves. Oh how she wished now that Annaline had told the cabby to wait. The dark empty road and shadowed fields that bordered it on both sides looked desolate in the moonlight.

'Do come along, Flora,' Annaline called out, pausing for a moment. 'We shall be the last to arrive at this rate.'

'I'm coming. I'm coming,' Flora murmured under her breath.

As Flora drew near, Annaline set off again down the wide, tree-lined pathway, her heavy silken skirts brushing aside the papery leaves. Frost rimed the grass beside the path and in the moonlight the tombstones looked like polished bone. The cold air stung Flora's nostrils. Inside the woollen gloves her fingers were cramped with the chill. By now she ought to be tucked into her own warm bed. This clandestine creeping around in the graveyards was madness. If Annaline's father ever got to hear about it there'd be the very Devil to pay.

'I wish that invitation had never arrived,' she burst out. 'Oh, Miss Annaline do let's go back.'

Annaline tossed her head and kept on walking. 'Go back to the house if you want to, but you needn't think that I'll come with you. I don't intend to miss this chance. Do you realise what a privilege it is to be asked along to one of Joseph Hoffman's private meetings? He is very much in demand.'

Flora gritted her teeth. She knew that her strong-willed mistress was as good as her word. It was Anna-line's penchant for flouting convention which had begun this whole thing. Her passionate interest in psychical investigation would have been just another fad had she not been introduced to the enigmatic and mysterious Joseph Hoffman.

Flora let out her breath on a sigh. This Mr Hoffman with his so-called psychic powers was probably just another penny braggart, though an unusually handsome one by all accounts. He also seemed to have a high sense of the dramatic, hence the siting for his meetings. Her own good sense told her to have nothing to do with his sort. She was sorely tempted to go back to the road and hail another hansom, but it was impossible to let Anna-line go to the meeting unchaperoned.

Annaline looked over her shoulder, her lips parting in a tremulous smile. Her expression now was less certain. The blue eyes, set wide apart in the pale oval of her face, were sparkling in the moonlight. 'Dearest Flora. I knew you wouldn't let me down. I know you have misgivings but I beg you, indulge me in this. Once you meet Joseph, you'll understand.'

Reluctantly, Flora smiled in turn. She felt her resist-ance melting away. Annaline had always been able to talk her round. They were more like sisters than mistress and lady's companion, being almost of an age and having grown up together.

As they fell into step, Annaline began speaking about Joseph Hoffman, who was reputed to have studied at an institute for psychical investigation in Paris. His creden-tials, apparently, were impeccable. 'I feel sure that tonight will be a special experience; I feel it.' She wrung her hands with sudden impatience. Despite the cold there was a fine sheen of sweat on her top lip. 'We'd best hurry. They must not start without me.'

The trees cast long shadows across the pathway in front of them. Some of the older tombstones leaned drunkenly, sticking out at angles like pegged teeth. Here and there a grander tomb was topped by a stone angel or marble statue. The brief conversation with Annaline had diverted Flora's attention from their surroundings, but now she felt herself affected once again by the brooding atmosphere of the place. As they passed through a stone archway, she caught the faint glimmer of a light in the near distance.

'We're almost there,' Annaline said. She lifted a gloved hand and pointed. 'There. See?' The ruined abbey. A splendid confection for a mausoleum, is it not?'

Emerging from the spreading cover of an ancient yew tree, Flora saw the jagged silhouette. Outlined in silver against the indigo sky, it seemed to loom upon them.

Suddenly a tall figure appeared on the path in front of them. One second the path was clear, the next Joseph Hoffman was there – as if he had simply formed from the ether.

'My dear young ladies. Well met. Allow me to accompany you to the place of our meeting.' His accent was pronounced. And his voice deep, rather husky.

Annaline had given a shocked little gasp when Joseph appeared so suddenly. Now she smiled nervously and extended her hand for his kiss. 'Mr Hoffman. You took us quite by surprise. It's ... it's a pleasure to see you again. Allow me to introduce Flora, my companion.'

As Joseph Hoffman turned, Flora found herself pinned by deep-set, dark eyes. For a moment she glimpsed something avid in his regard, then it was gone.

Joseph affected a shallow, courtly bow. 'Flora. Delighted to make your acquaintance.'

Flora could not speak for the sudden dryness in her throat. Nothing had prepared her for her reaction to this man. Annaline had mentioned that Joseph was handsome, but the word was patently inadequate. The man was stunning. Her mind balked at the word beautiful, for it sounded too feminine, and there was nothing of softness or tenderness about Joseph Hoffman. Yet he was, in a strange, wild way – beautiful.

Thick dark hair, swept straight back from a lofty brow, flowed over his shoulders. It was so black as to have a bluish sheen and gleamed softly, like satin. His face was hard, chiselled, and with something of savagery in its planes and hollows. But his mouth seemed to belie the harshness of his nature. It was large and sensual, the sculpted lips darkly coloured, like burgundy wine. He wore a caped greatcoat, which reached to his calves. Around his neck was an outmoded white stock, the spotless linen providing a single stylish contrast to the overriding darkness of his ensemble.

'It is always a delight to meet open-minded souls,' Joseph said, still holding her gaze. 'You will be most welcome at the meeting. I think I can promise you something special.'

Flora could not help herself. She stared at Joseph openly, the blood thumping in her ears. A moment of extended time opened between them. It was as if some thread connected her to him. Why could she not move or look away? It seemed as if he held her attention by a simple exertion of his will.

Joseph's mouth curved in a cool smile and she found herself compelled to lift her arm and offer him her hand. He took it in a firm grip. In a movement too rapid for her to assimilate, he lifted aside the woollen cuff and pressed his lips to the tender flesh on the inside of her wrist. For a moment only, his hot, firm mouth moved over the skin as if questing for her pulse. The edges of his teeth grazed her flesh and there came a brief flare of sensation as his tongue probed at the underlying sinews.

Flora almost cried out. A dart of desire, white hot in its intensity, penetrated deep into her belly. There was an answering pulse between her legs and a flow of liquid warmth from her quim. She had never felt anything like it before. When Joseph released her hand, she swayed drunkenly and took a step backwards to steady herself.

Annaline did not appear to notice her state. Flora fought to recover her composure as Joseph murmured some pleasantry and Annaline laughed. They began moving towards the meeting place. Flora fell in step with them. Her legs felt like water. Beside her, Joseph was an all encompassing presence. It was something more than physical; something both frightening and intriguing.

'Ah, here we are. I see that our number is complete,' Joseph said as they approached the entrance to the abbey, passing on the way an avenue of granite slabs.

Inside the arched doorway, which was imposing in scale and somehow oppressive, stood a group of men and women. Greetings were exchanged and introductions made. Annaline seemed to know most of the people there. With lanterns held aloft they all proceeded into the ruined nave.

Overhead clouds scudded across the moon. Light and shadow fell by turns on the aisles where lay the white marble sarcophagi. Ivy clotted the crumbling pillars and scrambled up the exposed buttresses. Frost lay over everything like a thick dusting of sugar. Those gathered together were silent. Waiting.

Flora was tense with anticipation. She seemed to feel the expectancy of them all as something tangible. Their thoughts lay upon the very air, spreading above them in a smoke-like haze. Surely Joseph had done something more than awaken her physical senses when he kissed her wrist. Some subtle, inner sense, hitherto dormant, had been quickened into life.

'Let us begin, ladies and gentlemen,' Joseph announced, his voice deep and compelling. He spread his arms to indicate that they should form a circle. 'Some of you have brought rugs. Spread them on the grass. Those who have none can share. Each lady sit next to a gentleman, if you please. The male and female energies must be in balance.'

Not you, Flora. You sit alone. Flora was aware of the unspoken words inside her head as Joseph impressed his will upon her.

She moved to take her place on the rug which he spread for her himself. Some of the women cast sidelong glances at her. There was envy in their faces, but she paid them no heed. Joseph's voice spread oiled tendrils into her mind. A honeyed warmth spread through her limbs.

How could her body be such a stranger to her? She clenched her thighs, trying to ease the pressure in her belly and the growing moistness of her quim. Inside her stays her breasts felt swollen. The nipples had puckered and hardened into firm little buds. At her slightest movement, they rubbed quite maddeningly against the starched cotton of her chemise.

'Pass these candles around,' Joseph said. 'Light them and place one in front of each of you. Now. Begin to relax. To let the things of this world pass out of the sphere of your thoughts.'

Flora lit a candle with shaking fingers. She sat staring at the golden flame but it was impossible to do as he asked. There was no physical connection between herself and Joseph, yet she felt him with every fibre of her being. The entire surface of her skin felt bruised and tender. Her drawers were quite damp now where they pressed against her swollen quim. And the pulsing in the base of her belly was heavier, more insistent. Oh what was happening to her?

'Flora?' Annaline hissed beside her, groping for her hand. 'My dear. Are you quite well? You are very pale.'

'I'm – well enough,' Flora managed to say. 'This is all – so strange, that is all.'

'It is odd, the first time, but there's nothing to be afraid of as long as you do exactly as you're told.' Annaline's lips curved in a secret smile in which there was a wealth of knowledge. 'Joseph is in complete control. Put your trust in him. Didn't I tell you that he was special?'

Flora opened her mouth to speak when the gentleman who sat next to Annaline hissed reprovingly, 'My dear young woman, I really think we should concentrate on the matter in hand, rather than exchange gossip.' He was a severe-looking man of mature years with a pinched face, made remarkable by a set of luxurious whiskers.

'I beg your pardon, sir,' Annaline said in a low voice.

'Silence now,' Joseph rapped. 'We shall begin. All of you, close your eyes.'

Except you, Flora. I have something special planned for you. Flora caught her breath as Joseph smiled, his dark eyes boring into her. Her cheeks burned. He knew. He knew exactly how she felt. She closed her eyes, seeking escape. But there was no escape from his will.

Into her mind there came an image – of Joseph crooking his finger and beckoning for her to come to him. Flora saw herself falling to her knees at his feet. At his command, she unbuttoned his trousers and reached into his open fly. His tumescent cock sprang free. It was thick and veiny, the skin partly drawn back from the flaring tip. A silvery drop of lubricant seeped from the slitted mouth of his glans. The bush that surrounded the root of his cock was dark and silky. His balls were firm and potent, heavy with sap. Flora's mouth watered. Her hands itched to cup the hairy sacs and palm their liquid weight. She saw herself stretching her neck forward, extending her tongue to scoop up the drop of pre-come. The lewdness of the image aroused her further. Oh, God. If he ordered it she would suck and mouth and lick his glorious member. Pleasure him in front of everyone, until the creamy sperm spurted into her mouth. Under the influence of that seething will, she was powerless to disobey. The image faded abruptly.

Flora's eyes flew open as she bit back a cry. She felt empty, her body scorched and dry. It was all she could do to remain sitting upright, for, in that moment of complete withdrawal something had been made plain to her. Whatever sexual favours Joseph would demand of her they would be darker, more exciting, and more dangerous than anything she could ever imagine.

And what was worse was the fact that she knew she would not be able to resist him. Having once been aroused to fever pitch, she yearned for that intoxication again.

'You have put aside all thoughts of the outside world now, my friends,' Joseph said. 'Let us all now reach for that quiet space within. We must still the clamouring of our minds, and hold ourselves ready for whatever may enter.'

In the silence there was only the sound of deep breathing. The darkness around the group was as dense and textured as velvet. Long moments passed. Now and then Joseph gave out instructions. The members of the circle seemed spellbound by his voice. Flora couldn't have said exactly when she became aware of the change taking place, but it seemed to her that there was a thickening on the air.

In the centre of the circle came a shimmering disturbance, like the glittering motes in a child's snowstorm. There was a faint smell of musk and salt.

'He comes, Flora,' Joseph said. 'Born from the sexual energy radiated by those gathered here together. Watch and marvel.'

The saline smell grew stronger. It was something primeval, amniotic. Flora was frozen by dread. What was happening? And why did no one else react? She glanced at Annaline for help, just as Annaline gave a soft moan. Her mistress's cheeks were hectic with colour, her lips compressed over her teeth. With a shock Flora realised that the severe gentleman with the whiskers had one hand under Annaline's skirts, while the other was busy between his own thighs. Arching her back, Annaline threw back her head and gave a long, ecstatic sigh of pleasure.

Joseph gave a husky laugh. 'Oh, don't worry about her. Your mistress will wake unharmed, having only the barest recollection of this night's work, though she'll remember the pleasure.'

Shaken to the core, Flora saw that the same or similar acts were in progress all around the circle. Directly opposite, a woman threw herself backwards, her hopped skirt gaping to reveal a froth of petticoats and wide-spread thighs. The man beside her leant over and thrust his hand into the open crotch of her drawers, his fingers seeking her moist centre. To one side, a youngish man had unbuttoned the flap of his trousers. He worked his erect member up and down with loving slowness. The plum-like glans was engorged and shiny. Beside him, an elderly woman grunted with eagerness as she tore the buttons from her bodice in her haste to open it. Everyone wore the same glazed expression.

In the centre of the circle, the glittering motes of light seemed to draw together. Taking shape now on the backdrop of darkness was an elongated figure, blacker still than the night which had birthed it. The dark shape grew gradually paler, as if leaching the whiteness of the marble sarcophagi into itself. The musky smell of it flowed towards her.

Flora moaned with terror and covered her face with her hands as the apparition solidified. She could not bear to look at the creature which Joseph had called into being.

'Lower your hands,' Joseph ordered coolly. 'You need not be afraid.'

Flora peered through the bars of her fingers. A naked man stood before her, fearful only in his perfection. A pearly lambency outlined the well-shaped limbs, the wide, muscled chest and lean hips. His face was angelic. His hair, very dark, fell straight in a drenching wave to below his shoulders. Apart from the smudge of hair at the base of his belly, his body was hairless. Against the milk whiteness of his skin, the blackness at head and groin was shocking. But more shocking still was the heavy phallus which jutted upwards at such an angle that it almost rested against the flat belly.

A dark sexuality leaked from the phantom. Flora felt caught up in the silken web of its desire. As it registered her interest, one slender hand brushed against the rigid stem. The cock leapt and throbbed with a life of its own. Its lips formed a single word, 'Now.'

'Patience,' Joseph said to it. 'She is not yet ready.' He stretched out his hand to Flora. 'Come here.'

Flora rose to her feet unsteadily. She was bound between revulsion and fascination, yet it seemed that the larger part of her will was made subject to the demands of her flesh. The touch of Joseph's hand on her arm was like a brand as he led her towards a marble sarcophagus. The phantom kept pace with them, the big cock bobbing up and down. She could not take her eyes from it, nor help imagining how it would feel to have the huge thing pushed into her.

Joseph threw his head back and laughed with delight. 'How quickly you become a wanton. Do you see yet, Flora, that I only hold up a mirror to your true self?'

All around them, partly clothed figures writhed in every sexual position imaginable. Male buttocks thrust lustily between spread female thighs; heads dipped to sup at the founts of Venus; fingers sought eager orifices. A sense of fatalism settled over Flora. How could she fight this powerful man who seemed to know everything about her? Her deepest, most secret lusts had been exposed.

'There is freedom to be found in embracing the darkness within yourself,' Joseph said as he laid her down. 'But I will not force you. Give me the word now, and I will stop.'

He curved his body over hers, his face inches from her own. If only he would kiss her then, she could still believe that it was his will alone that had forced all of this upon her. She dug her hands into his back, urging him on, but he made no further move towards her.

'I beg you,' she croaked. 'Be kind now.'

'Kindness is such a little thing. It will not be nearly enough to slake your thirst. Why do you continue to delude yourself?'

Ah, God. Did he have no pity? She was a red wound of need, but he must make her bleed still more. Damn him. How could he know so much? She screwed her eyes shut, a tear squeezing from under her lashes.

'You want it all then?' he said, his breath hot on her cheek. 'Everything I can give you? And that is very much indeed. Be assured that I will show you no mercy.'

'I don't care. I want . . . I want . . .'

'Of course you do,' he murmured, tender now. 'It's not so hard to ask, is it? The sins of the flesh are there for the taking, such trophies are there for those who are brave enough to demand them.'

Flora surged beneath him. There was nothing in the world but this moment. Then Joseph's mouth claimed hers. The kiss was hard, demanding. She opened her mouth, accepting the tongue, loving the muscular probing. He tasted sweet and faintly metallic. A renewed shock of wanting speared her. Her womb pulsed with a dull ache.

Joseph's smell made her senses swim: cologne, hair oil, and something else which was essentially him alone. He grasped her breast, massaging it beneath his palm, then began unbuttoning the front of her bodice. His fingers pushed into the opening and brushed the lace of her chemise. Oh dear God, he was going to undress her. She had expected him to simply raise her skirts and push himself inside her. With a muffled sound of protest she raised her hands, grappling with Joseph's fingers. 'Must you uncover me?'

Joseph's teeth flashed in the moonlight as he grinned wolfishly. 'Too late for modesty of any kind. Far too late.'

He pulled open her bodice and pressed his mouth to the prominent bulge of her breasts, then dug his fingers into her chemise and eased the heavy globes free of her stays. Supported by the boned garments, her breasts offered themselves up eagerly. The heat prickled all over Flora's skin as he rubbed and pinched at her nipples. No man had ever touched her in such an intimate and proprietorial way.

Little shocks of sensation flowed down her body, finding an echo in the clamouring flesh between her thighs. Joseph buried his face in her cleavage, his questing tongue making wet circles on the exposed flesh. Grasping a breast in each hand, he squeezed gently, forcing the engorged nipples out still further. When his mouth closed over one jutting teat, Flora almost fainted with the pleasure of it.

She tossed her head from side to side, giving herself up gladly to the sweetly pulling demands of his lips and teeth. The pins flew from her hair and it tumbled across the white marble in silky waves. She was faintly aware of the phantom watching nearby, but it was Joseph who demanded her complete attention.

Suddenly there came a low cry of eagerness, very close to her ear. A shadow passed over her face. Lewd images bloomed in her mind. She saw herself in a forest, naked but for her lightly laced stays. She had been thrown belly down over a log, her wrists secured with twine. Her breasts hung down, the nipples brushing against the coarse tangle of brambles. It seemed awful that the prickled soreness sent a starburst of pleasure through her breasts. But far worse was the way her buttocks were thrust out, her thighs dragged widely apart. Her exposed and pouting vulva looked shockingly red. The labia were swollen ridges, her vagina shiny and wet. In the shadowed valley of her buttocks she could see the tight brown rose of her anus. The phantom made flesh stood beside her, a bunch of birch twigs in its hand. It raised it and brought it down again and again on her unprotected sex.

Flora cried out, aroused still further by the scene she was witnessing. In the here and now, Joseph continued to kiss her and fondle her breasts. She felt the warm heaviness of him, the weight of his lower body between her parted legs.

Then cold, invasive hands were thrust beneath her skirt, pushing aside her petticoats in their urgency to touch her skin. Somehow the entity had become invisible. Its form had flattened and insinuated itself between Joseph's body and her own. The demanding, alien presence was all over her, its sexual odour hot in her nostrils. She began to struggle, arching her back, trying to pull away, but the exploring hands were insistent. Joseph calmed her, gentling her with lips and tongue.

There was a strong odour of musk and salt. The pictures in her mind became more obscene. An unholy, syrupy voice whispered in her ear. 'Enjoy.'

The phantom's cold fingers slid up her thigh, found the gap in her drawers and entered her cleft. She felt it tugging exploratively at her pubic bush. It delved inward, parting her folds to find the firm, hooded swelling. Taking her pulsing bud between finger and thumb, it began working it back and forth like a tiny cock. At the same time a rough, cat-like tongue rasped at her anus, circling the orifice wetly.

Flora moaned, the sound vibrating deep into Joseph's throat. She could hold herself back no longer. The waves of her first climax were sweet and penetrating, but the tension within her did not ease.

While the invisible spirit was still at work on her, Joseph ran his hands down her body and began gathering up her skirts. She opened her thighs wide and felt his hard cock as he pressed against one linen-clad thigh. Joseph's touch was warm, while the spirit's caresses were cool.

It was a matchless sensation to feel the domed head of

Joseph's cock press against her vaginal entrance, while the invisible wet tongue lathed her cleft. She clutched urgently at Joseph's shoulders, desperate to be penetrated by him.

'Give it to me. Your cock,' she said, glorying in using the language of a street-walker.

He slid into her, filling her completely with his hard male flesh. Flora lifted her thighs, tipping up her hips so that he could plunge more deeply into her.

She felt consumed by the pleasure of having Joseph inside her. The rhythm of his thrusts, the heated traction of their joined bodies, eclipsed even the potent images in her head. Then, incredibly, she felt the phantom's big, cold cock nudging at her anus. Ah, no. Not that! It was impossible. She would tear. But the icy glans pushed through the ring of muscle, easing her open slowly. She did not tear. The feeling of being stretched was delicious. As the phallus plundered her, feeding into her measure by measure, Flora threshed and chewed at her bottom lip.

Ah God. Surely she could not bear this forced pleasure. She began sweating with shame, even while the erotic tension within her built to new heights. This was the ultimate intrusion. She had become simply a receptacle, a thing of raw nerve endings and quivering flesh. The thrusting cocks duelled within her, rubbing against each other, separated only by hot, silken membrane between bowel and vagina.

Then Joseph moaned loudly, the first sound he had made. Flora found herself catching the dark thread of his pleasure and feeding upon it. He mouthed at her neck, his teeth scraping the delicate flesh as he ploughed into her taut quim. Flora's sensitised nipples rubbed against his chest. Her pubis mashed against the base of his belly, where the hair was soaked with her buttery juices.

With each inward stroke, the root of Joseph's cock brushed her erect bud. She screamed and her legs scissored wildly as she came, her muscular inner walls squeezing him. At almost the same second he climaxed in great tearing spurts, the semen bathing her womb. Flora's orgasm went on and on. She was dimly aware of the second cock drawing partway out of her, of something icy cold jetting deliciously into her rectum. Then she lost consciousness.

When she came back to herself she was lying on the marble tomb, her skirts pulled down to cover her legs and her bodice buttoned up high to the neck. There was no sign of the phantom or of Joseph. She felt light-headed and strangely energised. Pushing herself upright, she looked around.

All the candles had gone out and the nave of the abbey was illuminated by the grainy light of early morning. A thick mist shrouded everything. Annaline stood a little way off, looking rather bewildered. She was fully dressed, as were the other men and women. Some of them were grouped around Joseph, shaking his hand and complimenting him on a successful evening.

No one seemed to have realised that Flora was missing, but she knew that it would not be long before Annaline began looking for her. Hurriedly she reached for her cloak and bonnet which lay beside the tomb.

Everything seemed so normal. Was it possible that Joseph Hoffman was, after all, simply a master illusionist? But if that was so, what was she doing lying on the tomb? She could not delude herself. All of it had been real. Besides, there was the residual soreness between her thighs and the soft glow of remembered pleasure. When she walked across to the others, a trickle of something warm ran down the inside of her leg.

'Well Flora, dear. Was that not thrilling?' Annaline said, smoothing her gloves along her fingers. 'I told you that Joseph possesses a rare talent.'

'Indeed,' Flora murmured, not daring to look at Joseph. He had committed the ultimate act of intimacy, that of understanding her completely. Oh, if only she could leave this place without speaking to him or meeting his eye. He was far too wise, his powers too dark and dangerous. the whole experience had been so devastating. No one must ever know to what depraved depths she had fallen. When Annaline took her leave of Joseph, Flora hung back, careful to avoid him.

But as she and Annaline began making their way out of the abbey, something he had said rose into her thoughts. *The sins of the flesh are there for the taking, such trophies are there for those who are brave enough to demand them.* She felt the strength of Joseph's will, reaching out to her even as the distance lengthened between them. The voice in her head was arrogant and full of conviction. *Farewell, until the next time. You are more demanding than you know, Flora. This is only the beginning.*

And though she fought against the knowledge, she knew he was right.

The Big Class

Angel Strand

Cia, a young woman of Anglo-Italian parentage, is on her way back to England after being given notice from her job in Italy. En route she becomes embroiled in a complex web of sexual adventures. It's the latter part of the 1930s and everyone seems to have a political agenda, not least Giordano, the gorgeous Italian communist with whom she has fallen in love. In a time of such uncertainty, Cia finds a great comfort in the physical pleasures she shares with her Italian lover.

Angel Strand has written two Black Lace books: *The Big Class*, from which this extract is taken, and *La Basquaise*, which is set in France in the 1920s and tells the story of a young woman caught up in a world of sexual blackmail when all she wants is to enjoy the company of artists, hedonists and intellectuals.

The Big Class

Cia and Giordano staggered out into the dark night air. Their friend, Tellino, stood in the doorway, swaying, and watched them to the gate where Giordano waved the torch to signal goodbye.

For a while they didn't speak. Up above, the stars were so close they seemed like a sparkling blanket. The moon was waxing and low in the sky. Below their feet the earth of the track was soft and dark.

The village lights became visible down below as they rounded the mountain. There were only one or two lights. It was very late.

With her gaze on the village, Cia missed her footing and almost fell. Giordano caught her. There was no real danger but he fussed over her as if there were. He took her hand and didn't let go.

Cia felt so happy with her hand resting in his, she thought she might feel happier than she ever had before. The strength of her feelings for him was as mysterious as the night. Why? She had no idea.

When they were almost home, Giordano said, 'Let's go down by the lake.'

He didn't wait for her to say yes. He led her through the edge of the forest to the lake shore. The water lapped on the small strip of beach. He let go of her hand and stared out into the darkness of the water. Somewhere, the wild call of a bird sounded through the night. Giordano hardly seemed aware that he had company.

Cia had the luxury of being able to look at him without being seen. What did she mean to him?

Suddenly, he turned. 'It's late,' he said. 'Let's go in.'

His face was close enough to touch. She was mesmerised by his lips, and her own parted involuntarily.

He looked so vulnerable in that second before their lips met. She responded hungrily; she wanted him so much. They kissed for a long, long time. She touched his hair and then his shoulders for the first time. She felt his hands on her back and she nestled in his arms as he held her tight. There was such an energy about him, she thought she would levitate. Every inch of her wanted him, and she knew his body was hungry for her. It was taut, stretched to the limits of control. She felt she had to tell him that she wanted him. He wanted to hear it, didn't he?

But when she opened her mouth, he put a finger on her lips and stopped her. He led her inside the house to the foot of the stairs.

'Go to bed, Cia,' he said.

It was very difficult not to argue, but some absurd propriety told her to accept his will this time. As she was walking up the stairs, her whole body wanted to turn around and run to him, take him by the hand, lead him up to bed and undress him. But she couldn't. She wouldn't.

Sleep eluded her. She lay naked under the covers in the small bed and listened. Eventually, she heard a chair creak. He was in the kitchen. The chair had creaked, that was all. Would she hear his footsteps on the stair? She willed it. She waited but he didn't come.

The moon was just bright enough to read the white clock-face. When she had been in bed an hour she was still so aroused she could no more sleep than fly to that moon.

She found herself suddenly thinking about her grandma as she looked at the waning sphere. She remembered the summer in Cowes. Sometimes they went down to the gazebo and sat in the dark, with the moon, and chatted.

What shall I do, grandma? she said to the air. 'Grandma, what shall I do? Shall I go downstairs?'

'Of course. What are you waiting for?'

It wasn't exactly a voice that said it. It was more like a spirit removing some prejudice and clearing the way for herself to say it.

She got up quickly, slipped on her robe and Chinese slippers, and combed her hair. It shone glossily dark against her pale skin.

Giordano was not in the study. She went downstairs. He was not in the boat room. She took a deep breath and went into the kitchen – but he was not there either. The back door was open.

Outside there was a chill in the air. She stood at the edge of the yellow pool of light from the kitchen lamp. She could see nothing close. Far away, a slice of light that must have been on the other side of the lake disappeared into blackness. The last of the world had gone to bed.

'Giordano?' she called softly. In reply she heard a splashing sound and a voice. She stepped out into the darkness towards it. 'Giordano?'

'I'm here,' he shouted.

Her eyes got used to the darkness very quickly and she saw his head. The rest of him was underwater.

'I couldn't sleep,' she said, feeling she had to offer some excuse for being outside.

'What's the matter?' he called.

She opened her mouth to tell a lie; something a little girl might say when she is frightened of the bogeyman. But nothing came out. The truth was she was lustful.

Her sex was swollen and her breasts felt ready to burst from her clothes. Her sex dripped on to her thighs. She was a fuckable, fuck-wanting, grown-up woman.

She kicked off her Chinese slippers. She peeled the robe back off her shoulders and let it fall. She stood on the shoreline in the moonlight like some goddess released from a tree. The air on her naked body felt delicious. She exulted in her nakedness.

She waded into the cold, dark water. It shocked her skin and took her breath. She waded until the water was breast-high and then she swam, swift and strong, towards him.

It wasn't deep. Giordano was standing on the bottom. She clung to him like a gentle octopus and wrapped herself around him. She pressed her sex against him and kissed his wet face. She circled him, kissing everything. Finally, his lips – red and open and wet – met hers.

He wrestled with the octopus and tamed her enough to wade out of the water with her white body attached to his, sucking him sweetly. On shore, the water ran down their naked bodies and dripped around their feet. He put her down on her back on a bed of pine needles, and took his towel and rubbed her skin to take away the chill. The friction sent pain mingling with desire through her.

Then he took her breast in his mouth, and whatever was left of her self-control fled under the soft assault of his lips while his hands held her ribs in their strong embrace. She could feel his sex lose its chill, then harden and grow hot next to her body as he kissed her damp belly. The touch of his soft lips acted like the gentlest of levers, somehow prizing her legs apart. His fingers reached inside her opening cunt and searched. She moved on his hand, pushing her clitoris into the softness of his wrist where his pulse beat. The honey inside her poured all over him.

In the hiatus between his hand melting away and his sex penetrating her, Cia heard an animal rustle in the forest somewhere and the tiny waves on the lake lapping at the dark shore.

When he entered her, she enclosed him like a glove and wriggled unconsciously to eat his pelvic bone with her clitoris. There was no escape; only surrender to the pressure and pleasure of his body.

She gasped as she began to come. His groans filled her ears and she felt him come as she came and came and came.

When she awoke she was in the big bed, with the light of dawn on her face. Giordano was looking at her intently, studying every contour. His sex was hard against her hip. She rolled against him. She raised herself, climbed on top of him, and dropped on to the erection like a siren riding a wave. She fucked him hard, gripping his torso and grinding on to him. She was completely uninhibited, and she pushed wildly into his belly, her thrusts puncturing his calm. His head jerked back and she triumphed. She rode him. She dismissed everything from her awakening mind but the feel of him in the dawn.

Orgasm was not instant. She settled in a slow rhythm, like a song without words, knowing something of power. She squeezed the muscles of her vagina. It wasn't easy, but she put all her concentration into it. Slowly her reward emerged, beginning deep in her womb, then becoming a spasm.

Now it was unstoppable. He grasped her hands and held tight until the inevitable took them over and flooded every cell of their bodies. As they came they were gourmands at each other's mouth.

Her emotions were pierced so thoroughly, Cia began to cry, and she hid from Giordano in his neck. But he felt her tears and kissed them away, then held her head to his chest and enclosed her safely.

When it seemed right to get up, he took her down to the lake and washed her all over – every little part of her. She shivered. Her teeth chattered. And then her stomach gave a great unladylike rumble. So they prepared their breakfast together and everything tasted fantastic.

'I must finish my work today,' said Giordano, placing his drained coffee cup on the table.

His words felt like a knife cutting into Cia's cocoon. She kissed him goodbye and stood up until he had gone upstairs. Then she went outside to retrieve her wrap and slippers and took them upstairs, passing him in his study on her way to the bedroom. This time he reached out a hand and drew her to him for the softest kiss. It was hard to part.

The day was interminable. Cia went to the village and bought some fish for their dinner. She walked determinedly past the bar, deciding she didn't care to know if she had money enough to leave. She rushed back to the house just to be near Giordano, and she listened to the clicking of the typewriter upstairs. Every key seemed to beat on her body somewhere. Her sex, her heart and her abdomen all came in for the gentlest of beatings and she imagined all kinds of wonderful things. He was a marvellous lover. Marriage was good for making men better lovers. This one also had the pull of being a dedicated man; a hero perhaps. Tellino thought so. All day long, scenes of the hero of the Italian communist movement, his head on her breast and his soul groaning helplessly as he came inside her, lent a magic to the chores.

She marinated the fish. She rinsed out her best underwear and hung the wisps of silk out on his washing line between two trees. She picked wild, exquisitely coloured flowers and arranged them in a vase in the kitchen. They looked beautiful. Everything looked beautiful. She felt beautiful. In the afternoon she slept, lulled into dreams by the clicking typewriter.

She was awoken by him calling her name.

'Get that, Cia, will you?' he called.

Mingling with the typing sounds was a light knocking on the back door. She crept, sleepily, to the edge of the big bed and looked down, sticking her head right out of the open window. Auburn was standing there, carrying a parcel and a suitcase.

'I'll be down in a minute,' called Cia.

Auburn nodded.

Cia ran down, wrapped in her robe.

'I've brought you a present,' said Auburn. 'And I've come to say goodbye.'

Cia took the parcel Auburn handed to her. 'What is it? Shall I open it or is it for Giordano?' she asked.

'It's for you,' she said. 'Open it when you are bored.'

Cia placed the mysterious parcel on the table. 'He's working,' she said, 'but I'm sure he can break off just for one minute to say goodbye. Where are you going?'

'To Holland first. Then America perhaps.'

Cia ran upstairs and fetched Giordano. She felt a twang of ridiculous jealousy as she watched him hug the tiny woman.

A few moments later, Giordano was back at work, and Cia was watching Auburn take the route down to the train tracks. Then she took the scissors out of the kitchen drawer. Well, she was a little bored.

Inside was a length of printed red silk. There were geese and grasses on it. On closer examination, Cia saw that the scenes were all different, and in between each there was a yard of plain red. The first scene was a lone goose sitting in the branches of a tree. The next depicted three geese on the shore of a lake, and on the next a whole flock were floating on the lake. On the next they were flying across it. Each scene unfurled as she handled it. On the last, the goose was gone.

There was more than enough for a dress, a coat, or an evening pyjama. She began to think about it. To cut it would take some nerve – there was something very powerful about the images. She wished she could know more about it. On impulse, she ran out of the house and down the path to the point where she could see the train tracks. But there was no sign of Auburn.

When Giordano finished work, he helped her with the cooking and they ate a lazy dinner. Afterwards they sat together against a tree and he held her waist in a gesture of unselfconscious ownership.

'What are your obsessions, Cia?' he asked.

She wanted to say 'you' but she dare not. It didn't sound right.

'Think about it,' he said.

She took a long while to think. Too long.

'Come on. There's something wild about you, Cia. You could have grand obsessions.'

She thought she might tell him about designing clothes. What was that, if not an obsession? All that money she had spent in Florence! You were obsessed, surely, if you were that uncontrolled. But she decided against it. She was still a little in awe of his seriousness. What was something as trivial as designing clothes to someone like him?

He was doodling on her knee with a finger, bored with waiting for her to answer. He pushed up the fabric of her dress, first up one thigh, then the other. His touch was like the breath of a bird. Her thighs parted involuntarily.

He kissed her legs. 'Let's go inside,' he said.

He led her upstairs to the big bed and pulled her down on to it, still clothed. He kissed her passionately, then pushed up her dress and bit playfully at her clothed sex, teasing a release of powerful feelings from her. He chewed at her for a long time, taking her to the realm of sex, where anything was possible. His tongue reached in her knicker leg and licked at her. He pulled apart the press-studs and dipped his tongue deep into the folds of her cunt, easing her clitoris out. With the tip of his tongue he flicked rhythmically.

She opened her eyes and watched his head with a love

in her heart that might rip her open if she let it. Why did he affect her so deeply? Was this love? Could it be? Is this how it happened? With the wrong man? He was someone else's. He was supposed to be a temporary ... all the reasons why not skittered through her mind. But they were powerless with this man. She had never felt so deeply before.

She stretched back and heard the rip of one tiny stitch at her armpit. Her head fell over the side of the bed. She pushed her sex into his face. His tongue entered, right inside, then he encircled her with a gentle arm, bringing her back on to the bed so he could kiss her mouth. She tasted the cool saltiness of her own sex on his lips, and she pushed her sex on to his hand, seeking his wrist again. She found it. She knew she was going to come on his hand – her whole day had been waiting for this moment. Now the moment was here and she could not stop herself. She pushed; she opened. She swallowed his fingers in her sex. She rammed his arm. She gripped his bicep between her two hands and held it.

For one blind moment, his arm was a disembodied instrument of pleasure, its sole function to give her orgasms. She took her bliss.

He lay still, his hand inside her. After a moment, he stroked her head with the other and she sat up, emptying herself of him.

She curled her legs under her and looked at him. His sex was stiff and straight as an arrow, jutting from his hair. His abdomen was flat and muscular, and at his waist there was a slight curve where it was beginning to thicken. The muscle definition on his torso was delectable, accentuated in the last of the evening light that gently fell through the open shutters. The small amount of hair on his chest was wet with sweat. He raised his abused arm and put it under his head. Something about the way he did that aroused her so much that she ached.

She felt vulnerable under his scrutiny. She fixed her eyes on the bodice of her crumpled dress.

He raised her chin. His eyes looked gentle and she had the feeling he understood her. She kissed him full on the lips.

In the back of her mind she knew that she could refuse him, make him wait. She had had her pleasure. What did it matter if he had his or not? She could be a petulant, spoilt cat if she so chose. But she chose to please him instead. She enclosed his stiff sex in her hand like a rudder, and she steered him into deep water.

Beyond his writhing body, she could see that the lake, the trees and the mountains in the distance were all still and calm. All was peace. But here his passion was exploding. He reached for her and feebly tried to undo the buttons of her damp dress. He couldn't do it. He was too much overcome. She pulled the dress over her head for him, then she sat naked and watched his face change to an expression of pure joy. He lunged at her nipples and bit, sending a deep throb of desire right through her.

He kissed her belly, licking the sweat. 'Are you ready again?' he murmured.

She thought it was sweet that he asked. She heard his words as if from a distance. She smiled, assenting.

He took her body in his firm grasp and used it with determined and extreme passion. He drove all thought from her mind.

She opened her legs more and more as he fucked her. She felt as though she was opening them as wide as the window, as the lake, as the darkening sky. She felt the passion beating through his skin, filling her. Everything that she was – all her beauty, her womanhood, all of her – was with him there at that moment, fucking. Orgasm overtook her like nightfall.

The next day Giordano had to go off and drive trains. Cia felt desperate, as if she had been grafted on to him and was now being pulled off. She prepared his breakfast like a *hausfrau* in a Nazi fantasy, complete with an apron she found in a kitchen drawer. He kissed her passionately with lips tasting of coffee and hurried away. She watched him until he was out of sight. He would be gone a full 24 hours – this was the shift required of him.

With his disappearance she suddenly became self-conscious. What was she doing here? She walked back into the house, past the boat to the kitchen. She automatically went to wash up. But there was no need to wash up. He was gone – damn the dishes. What was the point? What was the point of anything if she was without the constant nearness of him, the smell of him, the sound of his voice? What the hell was she going to do until he returned? The prospect was so bleak, she went back to sleep.

She awoke refreshed, with a sense of purpose regained. Not only did she wash up but she cleaned the kitchen because it was his kitchen, their kitchen, their life. She was possessed of a certainty that she wanted to be absolutely his in everything she did.

When she finished, she took the carbon copy of his communist news-sheet and went to sit down by the lake to read it. She adored every word: the list of Fascist lies, the truths about Germany. She felt so proud that he was hers – today, here, now. There was no need for anything else, she told herself. No need for her to do anything but be his.

But it was different when night fell. The dark corners in the house disturbed her. She needed something else to occupy her mind. And then she remembered the silk. It was lying in its package on a paint-splattered chair in the boat room. It felt heavenly as she touched it. She suddenly wanted to feel this silk over her whole body. A great sense of excitement made her heart beat faster as she climbed the stairs. She took off her linen dress and her camiknickers. She took the red silk out and brushed it against her face. She draped it about her white body and let it fall, red, over her thighs. Her hair on her sex made a little bulge, rustling against the silkiness. She draped the fabric up, around her neck. Geese flew between her breasts. It was fabulous on her skin. She lay down with it covering her. It was enough to just lie and feel.

As she lay, inspiration came. In her mind she saw ways to cut and use the silk, ways to respect it while making it hers. She imagined in such detail that she knew she had to draw.

She got up, found a box of scrap paper beside Giordano's desk and took a whole pile out. She drew for hours at his desk. She skipped dinner. It was one o'clock when she had to stop because her muscles were stiff. She fell into bed and slept.

When she heard him arrive home the following lunchtime Cia felt a wave of self-conscious excitement.

'Where are you?' he called.

'Upstairs,' she replied, and she gathered her drawings together.

He smelled of work. His clothes felt rough under her hands as he hugged and kissed her passionately. Eventually he held her at arm's length and saw her drawings on the desk.

'What have you been doing?' he asked. His brown eyes were alight with curiosity. She showed him. 'These drawings look lovely to me,' he said. 'You have a talent, don't you?'

'Maybe,' she mumbled.

'Don't be so self-effacing. You must develop this work. You must believe in yourself.'

She loved him for saying that. 'You're not just being kind?' she asked.

'No.' He shook his head. 'Why would I bother to do that?'

She believed him – he wouldn't patronise her. She was overjoyed that he didn't think her obsession trivial.

She watched him as he turned on the water for a bath. As he started undressing, she ran to him.

'Let me do that,' she said.

He laughed a little nervously. But he let his arms fall to his sides and acquiesced.

She peeled his work clothes away from his body. Each opening revealed the delight of him. At his collar her fingers shook as she undid each button. She calmed herself and resisted the urge to kiss him. She felt strange, as if by this act of service and self-control she gained power. He lifted his hand to undo his cuffs but she stopped him firmly and did it herself. When his torso was bare she undid his trousers and slipped them to the floor. She knelt before him and took them off. She reached up his legs to pull down his underwear and he took hold of her arms and lifted her up.

'What are you doing to me, Cia?' he growled.

'I want to serve you,' she whispered. She was trembling. She could feel his hard sex against her belly.

'I don't want you to,' he said. 'I don't want to be served. No one should serve.'

'You want something,' Cia responded, pressing her belly on to his arousal.

'I want a bath,' he said. Cia recoiled. 'And then I want you.' He lifted her chin and gave her a peck on the lips. Then he climbed into the bath.

She wanted to watch his body become clean; watch him soap up and stroke away the tiredness. But a great desire to respect his privacy overtook her lust and without a word she slipped away.

She went into the bedroom and unbuttoned her dress. It rustled around her thighs as it fell. She took off her best underwear and picked up the red silk. It felt heavenly in her hands. As she wrapped herself up, the geese flew around her body.

She began at her ankles, winding herself a skirt. She wound it tightly, wanting its constraint. Round and round her waist she wound it, then up between her breasts, leaving them bare. She wound it round her neck. She draped it over her head and round her shoulders. She held the surplus over her arm. She felt like a handmaiden or a slave. She straightened her back and took tiny steps towards the bathroom. A train flowed from her arm. She stepped around the screen. Silently she looked at him.

He was under the water, rinsing his hair. He emerged through a wall of water and stared at her, blinking away the water. 'Madonna!' he cried softly.

He jumped out of the bath and went for her. The water on his skin soaked through the silk and on to her skin as he held her and kissed her. His sex was hard against the fabric. The silk fell away from her head and tightened at her neck as his embrace pulled it. She gasped for air and he unwound it.

'Are you mad, Cia? Are you going to make me mad?'

She raised her face to him. Her neck stung. He kissed her flesh. He stood back from her and unwrapped her. Bit by bit her body was exposed. On her white flesh there were red weals where the silk had imprisoned her.

'Look at you!' he exclaimed.

She looked down at her body and touched the redness between her breasts. Then she looked at him; a long slow look. She was thinking, I am yours, wholly yours, do anything you wish to me. I have wounded myself for you. Devour me.

She didn't dare speak.

He took her hand and led her to the big bed. She scooped the red silk off the floor and trailed it behind her. When she lay down on the bed she draped it across her waist, cutting herself in two. His fingers played with it as he touched her skin and she felt once more that there was a silent understanding between them. He knew that she was his devotee and that he had incredible power over her. What would he do with it? Danger made her tremble.

He wrapped the silk across her breasts and bit her nipples with only his lips, leaving mouth shapes on the fabric. She relinquished her mind to the exquisite pleasure of being bitten. His lips toyed with her wrapped breasts for a long time and when he stopped the fabric floated on them.

Their kisses lasted an age. She took the fabric and dropped its folds across his body. She wound the end over his back and between his buttocks, and then she pulled it between his legs so that it pulled his balls. He growled as he too was lost to pleasure.

She quickly wound the silk across his hips, covering his cock, then across his chest, and arms, immobilising him. He lay back, his eyes closed and his face contorted.

She could see a patch of darkness seep on to the silk where the tip of his trapped cock creamed. She touched it. She pressed hard. He thrust his hips upward and opened his eyes. He went to grab for her, but his arms were constrained and he fell back and watched her, his brown eyes full of thunder.

She put her hand up into the skirt that the fabric had made around his hips and teased his inner thigh and his sex. She manipulated him for a long time.

He struggled to shake the fabric loose enough so that he could get out of it and then he took her roughly by the shoulders and pulled her his way. His lips on hers were hard and demanding.

'Turn over,' he breathed.

She lay flat on her belly on the soft bed, with her arse feeling huge and beautiful, waiting to cushion his fuck and get it all inside her. She opened her legs a little and the air breathed on her sex. She turned her head to look at him. She decided to play coquette and damn him. She raised her arse and wiggled it a little, like a tail.

He slipped his hand under her waist and pulled her up like a doll so she was on all fours. She felt his legs between her knees, then felt his body pressing at her arse and his fingers on her clitoris.

She gasped as an orgasm began even then. He spread her sex wide and penetrated her. She hung on him like a fruit on a bough and he thrust. As her own orgasm overtook her, shook her and detached her, she felt him come.

He held her tightly afterwards and told her she was beautiful. She kept quiet. She kissed him. He squeezed her so tight she could hardly breathe and then he stroked her hair and she lay still. Gradually his hand grew still and she listened to him breathing. She loved every breath he took.

The Houseshare

Pat O'Brien

Assuming an alias or alter ego is always fun, until you're caught out – then things get tricky. This is exactly what happens to Tine – the central female character in the next extract, taken from a contemporary Black Lace novel called *The Houseshare*. New technology features prominently in the book and anyone who is familiar with the Internet will understand terms like IRC. Internet Relay Chat is a way of conversing with others who are unlikely to know your real identity. When attractive computer whizz-kid, Rupe, moves into Tine's house and begins talking to her on IRC, things become complicated, highly charged and set to change both their lives. The chosen excerpt is from about half-way through the book. After a period of living alone, Tine has opened her house to guests. It's summer, and the heat seems to be getting to everyone.

Pat O'Brien is a prolific writer of erotic material with the accent on technology. *The Houseshare* is her only Black Lace novel. She also teaches erotic writing.

The Houseshare

*T*ine was hot from the kitchen. She had a cool shower and slipped on a strappy black summer shift, then raced back to the kitchen. She drew the banana bread from the oven and left it to cool on a wire rack. Rupe had already stacked china, serviettes and silverware on the table in the dining-room, and was on the patio playing with the cat. Sharon had returned home and was poised in the wide doorway with her back towards Tine. She was wearing, as far as Tine could make out, absolutely nothing but a string around her waist. The men had not yet noticed Sharon and Tine paused, her breath held, waiting for their reaction when they did.

It was Rupe who looked up first. His eyes widened and then moved firmly back to the cat as he muttered a greeting. Jerry, the gardener, was transfixed when he saw her. He stared in open admiration, his eyes sweeping Sharon with naked lust. It was sufficient for her to sway down to the patio to his side and pat him lightly on the bum.

Tine collected a flute of champagne and wandered over to the pair, anxious to prevent their degeneration into open sex-play. She was relieved to note that the 'string' Sharon wore was a sun-suit of sorts: a white

fabric all-in-one with a halter top and thong bottom.
From the front it was daring enough, barely covering her
breasts which threatened to bounce out of the sides, the
legs cut high to the waist. All that held it in place were
strings around the neck and waist, and the thong string
rising between her bum-cheeks to tie with the waistband.

It seemed that her close proximity merely served to
provoke the pair, rather than dissuade them from action.
Jerry took the gleaming tongs from the barbecue tools
and traced them up Sharon's stomach, then under her
breast, to catch her nipple in the pincers. The long handle
allowed him to angle the tool downwards so his hand
brushed Sharon's vee. He tucked his little finger under
the material covering her mound.

Tine could see his movements worming under the
fabric and the slight tilt of Sharon's hips as she urged
them forward to enjoy the tickling. She was aware that
her complicity was a repeat of the previous encounter,
and that Rupe was again present. Despite her misgivings
she was held to the spot, her excitement already mounting. She was so close to Sharon she could hear the blonde
woman's quickened breathing and smell her perfume.

Tine tore her eyes from Sharon long enough to cast a
glance at Rupe. He smiled enigmatically and fluttered
his fingers around the glass. She realised that he was
going to stay and watch. Effectively, he was telling her
to get on with it. It added to her excitement and she
swayed slightly, touching Sharon's shoulder briefly. The
violet eyes sought hers and held them in a bright gaze.
Then the woman leant towards Tine and softly kissed
her, her lips opening slightly and her tongue flicking.

Tine had never kissed a woman before and, despite
the permissions implicit in Rupe's behaviour, felt a
moment's doubt before she was lost in the sensation.
Sharon's mouth was gentle and wide, her tongue softly
insistent. Tine let the mouth move over hers, savouring
the moment, then parted her lips. Sharon's tongue-tip
slipped along Tine's soft inner lips, tracing the line of

222

her teeth. Sharon cocked her head slightly and positioned her open mouth firmly on Tine's, slowly pushing with her tongue.

When Tine reciprocated it was with the same, slow motion. The women edged to face each other, leaning but not touching, to prolong the kiss. When they drew apart they stood gazing at each other, Sharon licking her lips, Tine catching her lower lips between her teeth to enjoy the sensation of the sharp bite on the swollen flesh.

Jerry had moved behind Sharon, his eyes wide, and peered over her shoulder at Tine. He was barely in control, excited by the women's contact. His hands crept around the blonde woman's hips and tucked under the thong, pulling her back towards him so he could rest the length of his erection between her bum-cheeks. He rode, sliding along the crevasse, in tiny lifting movements. His hardness was still trapped beneath his shiny running shorts but the silky fabric served to increase the friction, and his pleasure.

Abandoned by the tongs, Sharon's nipples were sharp exclamations under the white fabric. Tine, barely able to control her movements, brought her hands to the blonde's waist and slid them softly upwards until her thumbs crept beneath the fabric and tucked under Sharon's breasts. She urged the slightly elastic material inwards until the pale orbs were exposed, the stuff of the garment trapped between them. Releasing her hold, she picked up her discarded, half-full flute and poured the pale champagne on the naked mounds. Sharon gasped as the liquid trickled over her, then trembled when Tine drew her fingertips softly up from under her breasts to circle her nipples.

Fascinated by the smooth, soft texture, Tine felt a moment's retrospective jealousy. This is what men felt when they touched a woman: the velvet give of flesh, the rounded lend to the palm and the hard, excited tips. She felt powerful and overcome with a sensual curiosity.

Her lips sunk to trace Sharon's teat, feeling the little ridges, tasting the sheen of champagne and the woman's own perspiration. She hefted the globes in her palms, enjoying the weight and give of them, then buried her face in the valley between, pressing the mounds into her cheeks and inhaling deeply.

Tine felt she could meld with the soft, fragrant flesh for a long time. A part of her noted Sharon's increasing arousal, and that of Jerry who was leaning hard into Sharon so he could peer over her shoulder to watch Tine. His hands still worked softly on her mound, and the blonde had her head tilted back on to his shoulder, her long neck exposed, eyes closed. Sharon's length was open and available.

Tine pulled reluctantly from Sharon's breasts and, placing her hands softly on the swanlike neck, eased them slowly downwards. She floated over the swollen nipples and brushed along Sharon's fluttering stomach. Jerry stilled, his hands easing slightly to allow Tine access when her fingers met his over the fabric. Through the material Tine traced Sharon's mound, its gentle hummock, then the vee beneath. She pushed so the fabric caught and grew swiftly damp in the cleft, outlining the vulva.

Then Tine knelt on the hard flagstone and forced her tongue into the crease of the damp cloth. She tasted Sharon, her sweetish musk, through the barrier and felt heady. A strange, wondering hunger rose through her, followed by impatience. She placed her hands between Sharon's thighs and they parted. Tine plucked the material aside to reveal the blonde's wispy mons, swollen pudenda and clitoral nub.

Jerry, not able to see her from his angle, had all but withdrawn his hands, surrendering space, but Tine trapped his fingers. She urged his fingertips into position so they held Sharon's folds apart for Tine's view. She stared for a long moment then leant forward, her tongue extended, and swept the length of Sharon's crease with long, slow laps, like a child with an ice-cream. Soon her laps became more demanding and her tongue pushed deeper, riding hard amongst the damp folds and pressing against the nub to force back Sharon's clitoral hood.

Sharon groaned. Her hands sought and locked Tine's head, forcing it hard against her as she ground wetly into Tine's face. The older woman obliged by crouching further underneath, feeling the urgency of Sharon's excited pressure.

Jerry, no longer able to control himself, caught Sharon on a backsweep and, holding her firmly, freed his prick from the loose running shorts, and urged it into her. Tine watched for a moment, then reached to cup his balls and massaged them softly, fascinated with the explicit view she received of his slippery penetration and the pull and release of Sharon's flesh around Jerry's shaft.

Tine tilted her head, laying the bridge of her nose firmly against Sharon's clitoris. Needing a hand to balance her awkward angle, she relied on Jerry to control the choreography. He responded to the different feeling tracing along the out-slide of his cock and slowed. Tine eased back, caught Sharon's clitoris gently between her teeth, and sucked softly. Her hand urged Jerry forward, squeezing to set the tempo, then releasing him as his own driving need took hold.

She refused to release her teeth, and Sharon's hands forced Tine's head hard against her. As Sharon came she felt Tine bite hard and the painful, dull flow joined with and heightened her throbbing. Sharon barely noticed Jerry's climax until she felt his wet withdrawal and, freed, she joined him, slumping to sit on the hard flagstone. The three gazed at each other.

Tine felt at a great distance, confused by her recent intimacy with Sharon. It seemed inconceivable that it had actually happened, and she witnessed the same bewilderment in Sharon's eyes. Both expected that there would be no repeat. It seemed a singular libidinous act. Jerry appeared an even more remote part of the triad, and in Tine's eyes was now back to being the gardener. She resolved to try to keep her distance in the future, erecting a barrier to prevent further such interplay. While she did not regret the experience, it seemed alien, thrilling only for its rarity.

Sharon reached out a hand which Tine grasped. It was a friendly act, one of consent, endorsing the recent experience and taming the boundaries.

It was Rupe who surprised Tine most. He lifted her to her feet with exquisite gentleness, enfolded her in his arms and held her tightly for a moment. She leant into him gratefully, aware that his act was one of support. His lips brushed her forehead and he slipped away. There was no hint of an erection but she noted a damp sheen on his cotton shorts.

It seems, she thought wryly, that I am the only one who did not come.

Rupe needed time alone. He had watched the scene, at first alarmed then roused to fever-pitch when Tine's tongue sought and caressed Sharon's sex. He had been so entranced that he did not take account of his own hardening, except to absently slip a soothing palm to his shaft. He was amazed at his empathy. Jerry had seemed merely a passer-by to the action, which had all centred on Sharon. Tine was the protagonist. He had urged Tine on in his mind, almost proud when Sharon shuddered to climax. He felt generous, and when Tine sat on the hard flagstone he all but applauded, except his hand was busy easing him to stillness.

Tine had looked so pale and confused, somehow lonely and very small, that he had been driven to hold her. She had seemed grateful for his reassurance and he knew, even whilst slightly bewildered by what had happened and why, that the attraction between them had heightened. A bond was forged, a trusting closeness. He left to shower and change, walking silently with Sharon into the house and up the stairs. They did not say anything, merely exchanging puzzled looks, then he continued to the attic while she entered her room.

Jerry settled back to normality with disconcerting swiftness. He was soon shoving at the coals with a steel prod, and demanding the meat for cooking. Tine sluiced her face at the kitchen sink to wash away the evidence of her recent involvement, smiling at the taste still in her mouth, then carried the chicken to the patio.

She poured more champagne for herself and Jerry, and settled on a lounger to watch him jiggle the chicken breasts expertly on the grill, occasionally spooning marinade on to the cooking flesh. It was still very hot, although the long shadows had started to cloak the lawn with cool evening promise. A part of Tine's mind still reviewed the earlier sex-play, but it was a distant picture. Given the excitement of the houseshare so far, it merely seemed a prelude to something more profound.

Tine recognised that through her recent fantasies, her voyeurism and her manipulation, she had rediscovered her libido, but had thus far failed to experience her own fulfilment. She felt frustrated and uncertain, displaced and a little afraid that she had erected a barrier to prevent her own, real involvement. Perhaps she was absorbed in some mind-world, a fantasy without responsibility. She felt concerned that, were she to actually surrender her control in sex-play, it would fail when compared with her fantasies. While she could clearly recall the soft feel and taste of Sharon she knew that some part of her had kept aloof. Waiting for what, she wondered – waiting for Rupe?

When her other guests, Stevie and Demmy, appeared, Tine was startled. She had forgotten they were there, but was sure they had not witnessed the patio scene. She swiftly placed the salad bowls on the dining-room table, put the garlic bread in the oven to heat for ten minutes and laid the fruit salad and banana bread on the sideboard.

The air was full of aromas: the smoke from the barbecue overlaid with oak, the charcoal, hot honey scents of the cooking chicken and the warm scent of the banana bread seeping through the house. Tine made her way to the lounge and placed Beethoven's *Piano Concerto No. 5 'Emperor'* in the CD deck. Returning, it was easy to judge from Demmy's expression that the music was not to her taste, nor that of Stevie. However, it lifted Tine's heart when Rupe reappeared, his expression rapt and approving.

He had changed into his vest and cut-off jeans. Anticipating the demand, he also flourished two more bottles of Piper Heidsieck. The party began well, with Tine retrieving the garlic bread to add its own pungency to the dining-room, and Jerry's insistence that people collect meat from the barbecue.

Sharon entered amidst a flurry of hungry diners and was quick to join in, seemingly uncertain whether to flourish the glass or a plate. She wore another sun-suit, a black halter-neck, with shorts; soft swirling shorts. As she twirled, the material floated up to leave no one in doubt of the absence of underwear.

Demmy had not encountered Sharon before and was spellbound, the turquoise of her eyes deepening in admiration. Stevie seemed more aloof but was still unable to resist staring. They all settled companionably on the patio, each finding a perch on the terraced edge or at the table, and silence fell while the meal was consumed. They worked their way through the barbecued food and dessert, finishing the champagne and two bottles of Chablis, before Jerry announced he was tired of the 'witches' piss' and was going to drink beer.

He had stocked up when he fetched the coals and, retrieving a six-pack from the kitchen, tossed cans to anyone who wanted one. The strands of conversation wound around Tine as she settled comfortably into a lounger.

Sharon was quizzing Demmy and Stevie on Silky

Lizzie's, eventually soliciting an invitation from Stevie and a sulk from the younger woman, who seemed to feel left out. Demmy had found a seat at Sharon's feet and stared up adoringly, like a small, love-struck spaniel. Rupe chatted about motorbikes with Stevie when he learnt she owned a Kawasaki. Jerry kept his peace, his bright eyes roving the company, settling butterfly glances here and there.

Long after the meal was finished and they had soaked up the excess alcohol in their systems with banana bread, Tine rose to collect the debris and take it into the kitchen. She got as far as the dining-room door before she was blocked by Stevie, who marshalled Demmy, Jerry and Sharon and marched them, laden with dishes, into the kitchen to wash up.

Re-emerging, Tine found Rupe slumped in her lounger and so she settled into its neighbour. Despite the long day and the stress she felt alert. The meal had helped and the champagne had added its own zest. Tine was slightly drunk, and Rupe seemed not far behind her. It emerged that Stevie played guitar and produced one, amid good-natured catcalls and derision. She soothed the group with a medley of African lullabies. Demmy was the surprise. She had a fine, deep voice and a range to rival any country singer. She competently dealt with a selection from k d lang and got the party to sing along with a medley of Irish songs.

Tine fell silent amidst the voices, her contentment sweet. Her angst and lusts had faded and her conviction had returned that opening up the house to tenants had been a perfect idea. The good-natured joshing, warm companionableness and ease which seemed to flow through the small gathering seemed very sincere.

It was hot, in spite of the cool shield of black night. Dazed by champagne and lulled by the murmuring conversation around her, Tine felt an urge to seek the cooler environment of her study, with its high ceiling and open windows promising a less oppressive temperature.

As if some invisible hand had gestured, the group started to disband. Stevie gathered Tine in a firm hug, thanked her for the party and dropped a small kiss on her lips.

Demmy muttered, 'Oh yeah, thanks,' and trailed after Stevie, demanding a space on her bedroom floor for the night.

Sharon and Jerry moved across the patio and rounded the corner of the house with small, farewell waves. Tine wondered where they would go in the dead of night, and shuddered to guess. As if in echo, Rupe voiced her thoughts aloud as he followed her to the base of the stairwell.

'Probably the graveyard,' Tine laughed. 'After all she is the Oddball.' She continued up the stairs, leaving Rupe to stand for a moment with a small, disturbed frown on his face. He shrugged, reaching the landing as Tine disappeared into her study and the door swung shut. He stood, his hand poised to knock, still thinking deeply. Then he shook his head and continued to the attic.

Tine logged on to Internet Relay Chat. She kept pushing at the heavy fall of her hair, to ease it from her sweating nape. Eventually she rose in irritation and sought a hair-clasp in her bedroom, winding the chestnut fall into a loose topknot. She felt agitated. A thought nagged at her but slid away every time she seemed to grasp it.

Returning her attention to the screen, she found it blank. She felt disappointed because she had thought that Rupe would log on, as had happened on previous evenings. After a few minutes she joined her old channel #midlife but, disinclined to talk, she simply watched the screen scroll with the conversation of the chatting group. She checked to see if Rupe was around.

Rupe, she thought, who would tell her Internet persona, Astyr, all about the party and the revellers. Suddenly Tine shot to attention in her chair, her mind whirling. He had never called Sharon 'Oddball' outside of IRC. She felt aghast at her blunder.

It was some time before she realised that she had curled up, her feet on the chair, hugging her knees hard. 'Damn, damn, damn!' her mind repeated. A paranoia cloaked her. Of course he had not logged on. Right this minute he would be angrily stuffing clothes into a bag to leave, calling her a scheming bitch. He would be wondering at her shallow amusement as he had laid himself bare, his generous self-exposure in response to her cock-teasing, pathetic seduction.

A voice reasoned that perhaps her comment had passed over him, or that he would convince himself that he had, in fact, used the term 'oddball' with Tine. They had talked a lot outside of IRC. Even if he was puzzled he would, perhaps, give her the benefit of the doubt. If not then she would face his contemptuous rejection and the icy coldness of his glare as he left the house to find a more trustworthy place to live.

Tine chastised herself. She barely restrained her urge to race to him and face him with the truth, risking his censure in the chance that she could convince him of her own dismay at the situation. No, he would see it as an attempt to crawl out from under her gaffe and would be even more hostile.

Perhaps she could disappear. Feeling guilty and self-serving, she swiftly examined this option. She had told him the previous night that she was thinking of rejoining IRC. Why not, but as the tamer persona 'Leeter', her previous character? She could simply kill Astyr, log off now and never appear as her again. If she actually sought Rupe, calling herself Leeter, it would be honest. She would let him know she was actively looking for him, having returned at last to the chat arena. The question of Astyr would simply be open-ended. Guilt upon guilt.

As the options jumbled in her head her screen flickered and then it was too late:

Rupe>   Busy? I see you are on #midlife.

Tine could not kill Astyr now. If he had realised her mistake, and she tried to disappear, it would compound the deception. He had approached her and she would have to face it out. His words were not threatening and she could not guess whether he had noticed her slip, or not.

Astyr>   No, I am actually just lurking . . . not joining
          in.
Rupe>   #glade?

Tine mistyped her exit from #midlife three times, her fingers trembling on the keys. Eventually she managed to join #glade.

Rupe>   Hi. I am glad I found you here. Mind you, I
          sort of expected it.
Astyr>   Tell me.

It seemed to Tine that he was suspicious and uncertain, hinting that he was aware of something amiss but not wishing to confront her. Her heart lifted a little at his next words.

Rupe>   Nothing really. We had a party, it was great.
          I guess it just seems an anticlimax to be here.
          I don't mean that you're an anticlimax! I
          simply anticipated something different. I
          feel disturbed. Something is bothering me
          but I just can't place it.
Astyr>   Want to talk it out?
Rupe>   No not really, but I do think it's about time

we talked about you. You are a little mysterious, you know?

Tine's heart sunk. He was suspicious. If she could
show herself to be someone other than Tine, he might be
satisfied. Perhaps then she could abandon the Astyr
persona. It would involve her in a much more elaborate
lie, forcing her to create another Astyr in some other city,
with another life, just to placate Rupe. Suddenly sick of
all the lies, drained in the heat and nauseous in the
aftermath of her panic, she went blank. The idea of
seeking somewhere cool seemed overpoweringly
important. At that moment, more so than Rupe.

Astyr>   Fine, but right now I am sick with the heat.
           I absolutely have to find a cold place to be. I
           shall return in half an hour. Then we can
           talk.

Tine logged off. Feeling slightly faint, she staggered
down the stairs and through the dark kitchen, where she
yanked open the refrigerator door. She grasped the top
shelf, arms straight, her body a taut line as she leant into
the cold air. Breathing deeply through her mouth, she
quelled her nausea and felt her heartbeat slow to an
easier pace. The soft material of her shift clung to her,
glued by perspiration, and the cool, refrigerated air
soaked through her hot dampness.

With her eyes closed she did not notice that she was
no longer alone until she sensed, rather than felt, a
presence close behind her. Rupe's voice was low, traced
with pain, and held a much deeper, stranger element.
His breath brushed her ear.

'Astyr . . . you crossed over. Now who are you going
to be?'

Tine grappled feebly with his question, before deciding
it was irrelevant. What was important was the nearness

of the man behind her, the reality of his breath; soft coffee-fragrant clouds, wisping and misting in the refrigerated air.

She played his voice in her mind, seeking the strange, tight undertone. Reproach? Yes, but the tone was deeper. Beneath his words she could sense his desire. He still wanted her and was available to her. He was guileless and uncertain but still generous enough to withhold judgement. She was swept with a humility, knowing that if she pursued him now it would be on his terms – without barriers. Lowering her guard and giving her trust was a risk but, in all honour, she could do no less. Even this rationalisation was irrelevant. Rupe was mere inches from her and she had no intention of walking away. It would be impossible to drift from the golden cage they had been building over the past days. The time was right.

Tine released her hold on the shelf and stood up. She turned towards Rupe, searching his face. In the calm, pale light his eyes were translucent, a watchful green; still uncertain. Hers were dark, wide and vulnerable.

'What's in a name?' she whispered.

They stood, stripped of pretence, facing each other at last on an equal base. She felt him a stranger, but somehow familiar, and knew the inevitability of their pairing. He seemed vulnerable, his arms loose at his sides and his chest bared.

Tine felt empowered. It felt so natural to raise her hand to touch Rupe's face, trace her fingers over his temple and along his cheek. She felt the slight, rough stubble of his evening beard contrast with his silken, soft lips. His mouth twitched in an involuntary hiss, as he suddenly breathed again.

When Tine caressed his chin, Rupe tilted his head back, exposing the pulse in his neck. She pressed her fingers softly into his throbbing vein, delighting in his blood-rhythm. Her eyes swept over his chest, anticipating so much to explore. She felt an impatience at war with the languor which flooded her. Her hand dropped and her palm came to rest over Rupe's heart.

His chest was lightly cloaked in sweat, the effect of the heat of the evening. Tine leant forward and dipped her tongue in the cup of his collar-bone. He tasted of salty ferns and smelt gently musky. She swept her tongue upwards until she pushed at his pulse, her tip probing his vein, her mouth seeking the hot throb of his blood. His groan vibrated through her swollen lips and he eased his head to hers. Tine swiftly caught his lower lip between hers, holding his flesh as if to savour his desire.

She swayed to him, at last meeting his firm flesh as his hands spanned her waist. His hold was too tight, betraying his barely contained lust, and his heart pounded beneath her palm. His mouth was a harsh demand on hers. They fed. Their hunger and thirst seemed unquenchable as each plundered the other's mouth. They paused only when Rupe crushed her to him with arms of iron, jamming her face into his neck as he, likewise, buried in hers.

She leant into him, glorying in his strength and the depth of his passion. She flowed perfectly along his hard contours, rubbing against the thick, silky pelt of his chest through the thin fabric of her shift. His neck was hot and yielding against her mouth and his shaft was a hard rod trapped against her mound through his tracksuit pants. Tine's dress rode up in the rough embrace and her naked thighs pressed against him.

Rupe drew away and held her firmly from him, his thumbs twisting beneath the thin straps of her dress. He drew his palms over her shoulders, pulling the straps with him until the neckline fell away. The material slid fluidly over the slope of Tine's breasts, meeting some resistance at her nipples, then settled at her waist.

Rupe stared, his eyes roaming over Tine's breasts, then settled at the thrusting tips. He eased her back against the refrigerator. A shelf cut below her shoulder-blades, the cold metal harsh but not painful. His hands cupped her small bosom, weighing her breasts softly before he brought his mouth to cover her pert nubs. Rupe suckled at Tine, his lips pursing and working each nipple in turn. He supped liked a starving child, with strong, wet and noisy demand until her areolae puckered and hurt. Tine crushed his head to her, thrilling to the ache as she encouraged his hunger.

Lust tendrilled in her, forking like small lightning shafts, and she moaned and shifted trying to force his head down. He seemed immovable, then stared full into her face, grasped the fabric of her shift and tugged. The material swathed over Tine's hips and thighs before settling in a soft, dark puddle around her feet. Apart from a lacy scrap of panties, Tine now stood naked before Rupe in the silvering, refrigerated glow. Her face was shadowed, framed by a cascade of auburn hair, plucked through with coppered threads. Tine appeared carved, a marble statue, her hips thrust slightly forward for balance.

Rupe caught the light, his face strong-lit planes and his lips swollen and red. He had moved slightly back from Tine to release her clothes, but his hands remained at her waist. His eyes were intent on the tiny lace barrier embracing her hips. He sunk to his knees before her and encircled her thighs, his face pressed to her stomach. Then he rubbed like a cat against her soft flesh, inhaling deeply. He felt her tremble, shift her hands to frame his head and twine her fingers in his hair.

Rupe recognised Tine's need. An explicit memory rose of her bending at the front door, her blushing pudenda open to his view. He linked the image to the taste and texture of rose-flavoured Turkish delight. Then he recalled Tine worshipping at Sharon's blonde altar.

He rose swiftly and, clasping Tine's waist, swung her to sit on the edge of the thick, wooden table with her legs splayed. She lay back and pillowed her head on crossed arms. She could now see down her length, viewing the uplifted mounds of her breasts, the taut curve of her belly and the dark presence of Rupe urging the lace panties from her. He tussled with them, then groaned, and tore them from her. He held the flimsy fabric to his face and inhaled deeply as he stared between her thighs. At last he bent and sucked her swollen lobes.

The strain on Tine's back was excruciating and she felt she could not hold the position long without support for her legs, so she brought her heels to rest on the edge of the block. She was then spread more widely for Rupe's noisy feasting. When at last he drew back, he stared for what seemed a long time, his eyes shifting in minute exploration of her wet and shining lower lips.

Rupe felt vulnerable. The ache in his groin was a strident demand, urging for release. Almost absently, he loosed the string of his tracksuit bottom, slipped the fabric over the tip of his bulging, upright penis and kicked the fallen garment from his feet. His slick, purpling bulb waved proudly atop his quivering shaft as it lined up with the sloping landscape of Tine's furred mound.

Despite his own need, Rupe was not yet visually sated. He gently pressured Tine's thighs further apart until her delicate, damp vulva parted before his gaze. With one finger he traced over her clitoris, its hood pulling back to reveal the tiny, rubbery focus within. He dipped among her warm folds and continued his exploration until he found deeper access. He slowly slid his finger in and twisted it as if to examine the length and width of her, then added another finger, then another, until she was full and stretched.

Almost as a backdrop he became aware of Tine's whimper and her urgent push on his hand. She was drenched and swollen, wide open under his ministration and now vocal in her demand. It seemed that, although he penetrated her with three fingers, she was still hungry and writhing with an urgent need.

Rupe turned and reached into the refrigerator, seeking a surrogate. He worked himself close between Tine's thighs to hold her wide to his view, allowing the refrigerator light to fall boldly over her. His one hand gently nursed inside her, his other drew a courgette along the soft flesh at the top of her inner thigh.

As he eased the cold, green-veined substitute inside her, Tine's muscles clenched hungrily, surrounding the icy cold intrusion to welcome its invasion. She gasped, puzzled, and rose to her elbows to stare in fascination as Rupe directed the chilled rod into her. After the cold came a numb delight and, peering at the hilt of the manipulated green object, Tine felt a relaxing of barriers and an intimate bonding with the man who stood between her knees.

Rupe watched Tine's vaginal ring tug softly at the courgette as he withdrew it, her elastic flesh stretched and pursing around the mottled girth. He felt as if he was watching Tine's intimacy with another man, a usurper, and the mental image of another penis caused his grip to falter on the now warming vegetable. His wrist brushed his own erection with an electric thrill. His own need was becoming more urgent. He glanced at Tine's face, her eyes staring down, viewing his manipulation. There was a fascination in her expression, not repugnance but excitement at the intruder.

When she raised her eyes to meet Rupe's, her gaze was wide and lucid, her lips almost impossibly swollen and her excitement blazing across her face. He urged the courgette from her and drew it, glistening with her juices, under his nose like an exquisite Havana cigar. He slid his tongue along its length, then leaned over and eased it across her lips, leaving a viscous trail of her own pomegranate sap for her to lick and savour.

At last Rupe gave in to his need. His heavy erection curved out from him, stretching towards the soft cushion of Tine's sex. He edged closer, stilling her hips with firm hands. His eyes never left her face as his rod pressed at her entrance, its tip seeking permission to enter.

Tine widened herself as much as she could to assist his penetration. He paused a moment, then slid slowly into her velvet embrace, hearing his own groan of pent-up pleasure echoed in hers. Buried to his hilt, he stopped and stared at Tine, his expressions changing between triumph and humility. When Rupe started to thrust, Tine shed her remaining reserves and her cry was one of freedom and surrender.

Deep inside her, merging with the rampant physical tide, was a welling of exhilaration. She felt her naked lust and boiling needs explode in her conjunction with Rupe. She made animal cries and her throat, unaccustomed to the strange language, growled around them. She mewled and whimpered as she found her release. Her senses pulsed, absorbing Rupe and spreading the delight of his pitching member to her limbs; her muscles burned with effort as she ground her hips and bucked against him.

At last she reached the vortex of sensation, the deep pleasure whirling and throbbing through her. Rupe rode the final distance as Tine's clenching intensified. Her muscles sucked him to release, drinking from his flesh in thirsty demand, creating a vacuum that was almost painful. He felt as if his root was being torn and he ebbed in her strong grip as he found exquisite release inside her.

As their harsh breathing abated, Tine reached out to Rupe. She craved closeness in the aftermath of pleasure, the mingling of scents and the press of warm, intimate flesh. He eased himself limply from her and she shifted lengthways along the table so he could join her there. He slid one arm under her neck, resting his head close to her cheek.

Tine lay quietly beside him, her eyes soft, her face and neck rosily flushed. In surrender she was peaceful, her fears flown. She had been able to relinquish control, not merely submitting to Rupe but joining him with abandon. She felt very close to him and, as he eased himself up to rest on one elbow at her side, she recognised the perfect torpor of afterglow; the intimacy following untrammelled lust. Her hand traced softly along his chest and waist as she felt a great languor overcoming her.

As she drifted into sleep she could sense him trying to shut the refrigerator door with his foot. She felt a mild alarm when he failed the first time and a series of cracks and thuds alerted her to the avalanche of contents to the floor, then the silver light blinked out and the kitchen dropped into the soft grey of early dawn. Tine's last sense was of smell, the sweetish odour of spilt milk almost overlaying the heady musk of sex.

Ace of Hearts

Lisette Allen

The year is 1816. The wealthy elite of England, led by the ageing Prince Regent and his friends, are enjoying an era of hedonistic pursuits. Parties, balls, sexual dalliances and scandal are the order of the day and gambling dominates every gathering. In such a world, trickery and competence at fencing are useful skills to acquire and Marisa Brooke is a young lady who excels at both. Love and fortune are more easily lost than won, however, and Marisa has to use all her skill and cunning when drawn into dealings with her nemesis, the handsome Lord Delsingham, who is no stranger to the *en garde!*

All of Lisette Allen's Black Lace stories have historical settings. In addition to *Ace of Hearts*, from which the following extract is taken, she has written four others. *Elena's Conquest*, her first novel, is set in Britain just after the Norman invasion and features the dark Lord Aimery who is keen to slake his lust with Saxon women; *The Amulet* is set during the height of the Roman occupation of Britain; *Nicole's Revenge* is set in France in 1792 – a time of passion and revolution; and *Nadja's Quest* is the story of one woman's search for love and adventure in the court of Empress Catherine the Great of Russia – a notoriously decadent female. The sequel to *Elena's Conquest* is due for publication in November 1997 and is titled *Elena's Destiny*.

Ace of Hearts

*O*ne afternoon, when her friends John and Lucy had driven into Crayhampton for household supplies, Marisa felt a sudden urge to take her rapiers out and feel their familiar suppleness in her hands once more. It was late August, and although the heat of summer still lingered, the sky was dark and lowering with the promise of heavy rain later. Shivering a little, Marisa lit a candle against the unaccustomed afternoon gloom and went up to her bedchamber, where she swiftly changed into tight buckskin breeches and a man's silk shirt that felt cool and free against her warm breasts. She pulled her loose blonde curls back into a black velvet ribbon, and slipped her silk-stockinged calves into the soft, leather top boots that she'd had specially made for her in Bedford Row. In the easy garb of a man, she immediately felt more confident, more in charge. Picking up her father's pistol from her bedside table, she took her candle in the other hand and hurried up the narrow flight of stairs to the gun-room.

This was a spare, masculine room, with a high ceiling and tall windows. The floor was of bare wood, while the whitewashed walls were adorned with nothing but rows of metal hooks for the storing of old-fashioned weaponry and harness. There were no other furnishings except for the gun cabinets, a big oak table in the centre of the room, and an old carved settle set beneath the window. The air was redolent with the distinctive aromas of smoke-stained panelling and oil and gunpowder. Carefully she set down her flickering candle on the oak table, glad of its light because the sky was now almost black and the heavy raindrops were already beginning to beat against the leaded windowpanes.

Eagerly she unlocked the case that contained her precious rapiers and examined them critically, balancing the familiar metallic weight in her hand. She tried a few delicate moves, letting the blade become part of her again, feeling her supple body seem to come to life as the blade danced in the shadows. Carefully she balanced her weight on her slender hips, feeling her wrist sinews tingling as she straightened her arm, imagining that her tutor was there watching her and murmuring curt words of encouragement. 'Speed and accuracy, Miss Brooke.'

'There's no replacement for speed and accuracy!' she laughed aloud, throwing her weight onto her left foot to make a straight thrust. 'Prepare for the *en garde*!'

And then, above the drumming sound of the raindrops against the window-panes, she suddenly heard something else, the sound of a door opening and shutting quietly somewhere down below. A shiver of alarm trickled like ice down her spine, and then, to her horror, she heard the sound of footsteps, slow, steady, deliberate, climbing up the narrow stairs to the gun-room. Marisa stood transfixed, the fine hairs prickling at the back of her neck. Someone was coming up here. And that someone was neither Lucy nor John, because she would have recognised their footsteps immediately. Whoever it was was getting nearer now; the big oak door was slowly opening. With a little sob, she quickly positioned herself with her foil outstretched, her arm poised, ready.

The door opened wide, and Lord James Delsingham

stood there, filling the doorway. His brows arched, just a little, when he saw her in her man's garb with her blade held ready. Then he murmured, 'Well, Ganymede. I'm glad you're so pleased to see me. Is this how you usually welcome your guests?'

Marisa caught her breath, conscious that her outstretched arm was beginning to tremble. 'Guests are invited,' she said in a low voice. 'Who let you in?'

'Nobody. I let myself in; the door was unlocked, you see. You really should be more careful, Ganymede.' He wandered over to where the other foil lay on the oak table and picked it up thoughtfully. 'A trifle overlong, aren't they? And the hilt is somewhat heavy; however, that's a matter of opinion. You play with these toys?'

After her earlier shock at his intrusion, Marisa found herself growing more and more enraged at his calm possessiveness. 'Try me and see if I play, Lord Delsingham.'

He turned to face her. He was wearing a loose but superbly cut grey coat over his ruffled silk shirt; his close-fitting nankeen breeches were tucked into glossy black hessians, and he looked effortlessly graceful. His cropped hair was black from the rain, emphasizing his dangerous good looks. She felt a little weak, because she'd forgotten how physically devastating he was; six foot of hard-packed muscle and bone that made her own slender feminine frame seem quite diminutive. He responded to her fevered challenge by saying carelessly, 'You're serious? I must warn you: I have some skill in fencing.'

'No, I must warn you, my lord,' she said through gritted teeth. 'So do I.'

He stroked the blade he was holding carefully, feeling its edge with the ball of his thumb. 'Well,' he said, 'since you're obviously not going to put your rapier down until someone disarms you, I suppose I'd better oblige.' And he eased off his coat, unwittingly displaying his tall, wide-shouldered frame to perfection. Marisa hated him, wondering if he'd done it deliberately to weaken her, then realised that he'd done it quite unselfconsciously, because he was without any kind of peacock, male arrogance. Staring at him without realising it, she suddenly caught the laughing mockery in his eyes as he waited for her to recollect herself, and she felt the blind rage spill through her again. Carefully she rolled up her shirt sleeves, then she hissed venomously, 'Prepare for the *en garde*, my lord!' and their swords flashed in brief, hostile salute.

Delsingham was good; she realised that quickly. She'd hoped his size would be a disadvantage, but he was surprisingly speedy and graceful for so tall a man. But she was good too, well taught, with quick reactions and plenty of courage, and her much smaller size enabled her to move deftly to avoid his blade. Even so, after a few moments she was brought to realise that she had perhaps met her match, and he didn't seem to be even trying particularly hard, damn him! She lunged forward suddenly on her right foot, delivering a lightning thrust in tierce that she hoped would catch him unawares, but he parried and countered with a scuffling of blades, saying, 'A good try, Ganymede. But it's too well known a trick; try something different. And remember to play from your wrist, not your shoulder.'

Marisa gritted her teeth, her breathing by now coming quick and hard. She could see the sinewy muscles of Delsingham's forearm rippling in readiness, could sense the wily, skilled strength that informed every shift of his glittering blade, and suddenly she wanted more than anything in life to beat him, to humiliate him. Swiftly shifting her balance, she attempted a flanconnade, but just at that moment Delsingham disengaged, giving way with the point of his blade, so that Marisa's foil spun glittering from her grip and landed with a clatter on the bare floorboards.

Marisa hissed out an oath as she grabbed for her fallen blade. Delsingham leaned calmly against the big oak table, examining his hilt, and saying, 'Gently, now, my dear. Your flanconnade was premature, you know. Try a little more subtlety next time. You really are quite a capable opponent – for a woman, that is.'

Marisa lifted her reclaimed rapier threateningly. By now her hair was falling from its ribbon, and she could feel the perspiration wet on her palms. 'Damn you, Delsingham, don't patronise me.'

'Patronise you? I wouldn't dare. Play on, my dear.'

Marisa gasped another oath and lunged again, clumsily. Her hilt was slippery with sweat, and as her foible was raked by Delsingham's forte, she realised, in a flash of instinctive alarm, that the protective button had slipped from her point, so that her blade was naked, lethal. Delsingham saw it too. Parrying with cool precision, he took a step backwards and said quickly,

'Draw back your blade, Marisa. Your point is uncovered.'

But Marisa was wild with rage and humiliation. Crying out, 'What does it matter, when I've come nowhere near you anyway?' she began to press him steadily backwards towards the door, intoxicated with her advantage at last, feinting and thrusting with her arm muscles stiff and outstretched. She saw a flicker of real concern cross his hard face as he slowly gave way, concentrating solely on his defence against her whipping, deadly blade. She saw the light perspiration sheening his clean-shaven jaw, saw the play of the powerful muscles beneath his thin silk shirt as their blades grated and jarred.

'Come to your senses, Marisa,' he snapped, as the point of her blade caught at his shirt just below his armpit and a ragged tear exposed his gleaming, muscle-padded ribcage. Marisa paused, breathing hard, secretly aghast at the dangerous folly she was indulging in. Another half inch and she'd have caught his flesh, drawn blood. And she was endangering herself, because now she could see that he was no longer lazily detached, but was cold, angry, purposeful. Suddenly he whipped up his point deliberately against her forte so that his own protective button flew off. He said between gritted teeth, 'So we're playing that kind of game, are we?' and there was a dazzling glitter of steel and a sliding of his booted feet sideways as his blade caught in the thin silk of her shirt and split the fabric from shoulder to waist, so that her left breast was completely exposed. 'A hit,' he said.

Marisa drew in a deep, shuddering breath, feeling the cool air kissing her pink nipple as it protruded shockingly from the torn fabric. 'You – you could have killed me,' she gasped.

Delsingham smiled, a dangerous, lupine smile. 'Oh, no,' he said softly. 'If I wanted to kill you, then I would, believe me. Are you ready to disarm yet?'

'No, damn you!'

'Very well. If this is how you want to play, then so be it.'

Their blades clashed once more. His point glittered in the shadowy candlelight, slithering lethally down her forte. Marisa wrenched it free with a little sob of indrawn breath, but not before he'd caught at her billowing sleeve with his blade and ripped it almost away. Her upper half virtually naked, she gritted her teeth and lunged forward on her right foot, delivering a lightning thrust in carte. There was a scuffle of blades and she lunged again, her point catching in his loose shirt just an inch above his breeches. She whipped it away, slicing a foot-long scar through the silk, so she could see the flat, hard muscle of his belly tensing as he moved. He swore softly under his breath as they disengaged, and, with his blade lowered and his eyes all the time on Marisa, he deliberately ripped away the last remnants of his torn shirt. Marisa watched him, breathing hard, feeling her heart thudding against her ribs, and not just with exertion. He was magnificent, this beautiful, half-naked male animal who stood before her in the darkening gun room. Her whole world seemed to have narrowed down to a breathtaking vision of those wide, powerful shoulders that tapered enticingly down to his sinuous hips. Inevitably her eyes flickered towards the all too evident bulge of masculinity at his groin, confined into a hard, challenging knot by the tightness of his breeches, and she felt quite faint.

By now her own shirt was in tatters from Delsingham's subtle play, and damp with perspiration. Her upper body was all but naked now, like his. She could feel his eyes on her breasts as they thrust out high and provocative from between the remnants of her slashed shirt. Beneath his dark, purposeful gaze she could feel their pink crests stiffening involuntarily, but the sight didn't put him off his stroke, damn him, as his own body put her off hers. Apparently quite impervious to her near-nudity, he was moving again already, and their swords rang together with wrist-bruising ferocity, scraping fiercely before the inevitable disengagement. Delsingham was beginning now to press the attack, but still Marisa fought on more and more wildly, her slim wrist numb from the jarring blows, until she knew with despair that she was tiring, making mistakes. She was also more than a little distracted by the sight of Delsingham's naked torso, and by the sight of his powerful muscles sliding and coiling beneath his perspiration-sheened skin. She backed up further, her eyes on his dangerously exposed blade, knowing with despair that the wall was only a few feet behind her. Already she could smell the musky, virile heat of her opponent's body as he relentlessly pressed on with his attack. No escape. The end must be near, she thought desperately.

He made a sudden feint, and she parried a fraction of a second too late. It was what he'd been waiting for, and his point flashed in under her guard. She tried to counter his attack, but he was bearing her wrist irresistibly upwards until she thought that the delicate bones would snap with the strain, and then, in blind despair, she felt her foil spin away from her aching hand and heard it land with a sickening crash on the floorboards.

She leant back against the wall to steady herself, her legs trembling and her fists clenched, trying to conceal her wild panting. Delsingham was still advancing on her slowly, his sword outstretched. He seemed to tower above her, and his body looked lithe and dangerous.

'The disarm, I think, Miss Brooke. You concede victory?' he said softly.

Her blue eyes blazed up at him. 'No. You took advantage of me. You cheated.'

'How?' he frowned, tossing his blade with a clatter to the floor. He was only inches away from her now. Her eyes were on a level with his chest, and as she gazed helplessly at the enticing curves of gleaming male muscle, the fierce desire licked at her stomach, dragging away the last of her strength. 'By – by distracting me,' she retorted helplessly.

He laughed. He leant slightly forward, resting his hands against the oak-panelled wall on either side of her head so that his wrists were just above her shoulders, while his slate-hard eyes devoured the sight of her small, pouting breasts as they rose and fell rapidly beneath the tattered remnants of her shirt. 'Am I to take it, then, that you don't consider yourself to be a distraction, Miss Brooke?'

Feeling quite faint with wanting him, scarcely able to stand, she tossed back her blonde head defiantly. 'Obviously I'm not a distraction,' she snapped back sharply, 'as you seem able to disregard me quite easily, for weeks on end.'

His grin showed his even white teeth. 'So you've missed me, sweet Marisa?'

'Of course not.'

There was a silence. 'I've missed you,' he said.

She caught her breath. 'What?'

'I've missed you,' he repeated. He was gazing down at her; she could see the golden sparks dancing in his intense grey eyes. 'Oh, my dear, how delicious you are when you're angry.'

And before she could think of escaping, he'd cupped her face gently in his hands, and bent his head to kiss her. His mouth was firm and warm and strong as it persuaded her tremulous lips to part. Then he drew his tongue lightly, caressingly along the line of their parting, and took possession of her, his teeth nipping gently at her silken inner lip, his tongue moving wickedly to ravish her moist inner place with cool masculine intent. Marisa shuddered, feeling her own tongue entwining helplessly with his as his hands slipped round her shoulders, pulling her firmly against him so that her breasts were pressed against his naked chest. She could feel the hardness at his loins nudging with increasing urgency against her slender hips as she arched with instinctive longing towards him.

As if sensing her surrender, he gave a low sigh of triumph, and Marisa froze suddenly. How dare he! How dare he leave her for weeks, without a word, to go and visit the woman they said he was going to marry, only to return, and think he could take her, casually repossess her, just as if she was nothing, just some slut of a backstreet girl whom he could carelessly discard until he felt the need to sate his restless loins on her again. No one treated her, Marisa Brooke, like that – no one.

Well, there wasn't much time to prove her point. Delsingham's breathing was growing heavier, slower as he pressed intimate kisses against her face and throat. His hand had slid from her shoulder to fondle her breast, rubbing at the nipple, and sending shivering darts of longing down to her abdomen. Fighting back her own betraying lust, Marisa stretched her hand behind his back, reaching towards the oak table on which her father's pistol lay. She fumbled for a moment or two, her senses in disarray from his caresses, but at last her fingers fastened round its familiar cold smoothness. She lifted it up, and flexed her wrist to press the pistol's muzzle against his naked back.

His mouth moved away from her throat in stark surprise at the kiss of cold metal against his ribs. 'Marisa?'

'Get away from me,' she said.

He twisted a little, then saw the pistol and laughed. 'Sweet Marisa, what joke is this? You want a duel with pistols now?'

'No,' she replied evenly. She drew the pistol close to her body and pointed it steadily at his chest. 'I want to remind you that this is my house and my property, Delsingham, and I'm not some cheap little doxy you can come to visit whenever you can't think of anyone else to sate your lust on.'

He put his hand out defensively. 'Marisa – '

She cocked the pistol. 'I'm warning you, my lord. I know how to use this toy. Another useful lesson my father taught me.' She fingered the pistol thoughtfully. 'An unfair advantage, strictly speaking, but as you're twice as heavy and powerful as I am, I think I deserve a little assistance, don't you?'

His body was poised and still. 'What are you going to do with me?' he said quietly, watching the gun.

Marisa shrugged. 'I suppose I could just ask you to leave. And yet . . .' Her blue eyes glinted wickedly. 'I'd like you to know how it feels, I think. How it feels to be used, as if you were just some cheap, impulsive purchase, and then discarded without a thought.'

And then, as she paused, she heard the voices down below. Lucy and John were back. Her wide blue eyes gleamed maliciously: oh, perfect timing. Keeping her gun pointed on Delsingham, she backed towards the doorway to call out to them, and immediately they came up the stairs, still chattering and laughing together. When they saw Marisa's state of undress, and saw Delsingham pinned against the wall, they fell silent, and

Lucy's eyes grew suddenly hot with lust as they alighted on his superb torso.

'Lucy,' said Marisa silkily, 'as you see, we have a surprise visitor. He wasn't invited, Lucy. So we're going to teach him a little lesson, about manners.'

Lucy licked her lips. 'Beautiful,' she murmured, still gazing at Delsingham, her eyes flickering from his starkly muscled chest down to the skintight breeches that covered his well-muscled thighs. 'Quite beautiful. What are we going to do with him, Marisa?'

Marisa gestured to the corner of the gun-room, where the leather harness and belts that were used to store the old weaponry were slung on iron hooks. 'You're going to tie him up, so he can't move. John, help her.' Delsingham made an involuntary move towards the door, but Marisa levelled the gun at him. 'Oh, no,' she said softly. 'You're not going anywhere, my lord.'

Delsingham's face was still as Lucy and John advanced towards him, but he remained silent. Marisa felt herself quicken with excitement as she watched them spread-eagle his arms, and carefully secure each of his wrists to the wall by twisting the supple leather harness around the hooks until the sinews of his shoulders stood out like steel cords. With a surge of power she saw that his arousal had, if anything, increased; the bulge of his genitals against the tight crotch of his breeches was unmistakable.

Still levelling the gun at him, she said steadily, 'I'm going to make you beg me for release, Delsingham. You're a bit too used to people begging you for the favour of your rather splendid cock, my lord, but now you can feel what it's like to wait in humble silence, to be tormented until you can't stand it any more.'

He said nothing but just watched her, a pinioned, silent prisoner who nevertheless dominated the shadowy room with his breathtaking male beauty. Lucy couldn't drag her eyes from him, but John was watching Marisa, his hot eyes feasting on her naked breasts and her loose blonde hair curling round her slender shoulders as she lounged casually on the window seat with her pistol in her hand. Outside, the rain was drumming down coldly against the leaded glass panes, but in here the warm air was tense and expectant.

Marisa was conscious of an insistent beat of excitement throbbing at her own loins. She wasn't quite sure what was going to happen yet, but she knew it was going to be good. And then Lucy came sidling up to her. 'Please. Oh, please, Marisa. I've got an idea.' She whispered carefully in Marisa's ear so Delsingham couldn't hear, and Marisa smiled grimly. 'Go ahead,' she said. 'Do whatever you like.'

Delsingham knew. He could tell, she knew, what he was in for. He kept himself very still in his bonds, but she saw a muscle pulse in his lean jaw. Her eyes slid downwards to the delicious knot of male flesh at his groin, somehow obscenely prominent against the backdrop of his slender, snakelike male hips. The greatest humiliation for him would be that he would enjoy everything they did to him. Lucy would make quite sure of that.

Marisa settled herself back against the window ledge, her booted legs slightly apart, her arms folded across her naked breasts. There was no need for the gun now, because he was trapped. The rain beat down outside as the afternoon light faded, and the solitary candle guttered warningly. The room was filled with the pungent scents of oak, resin, and gunpowder, and the strong musk of heated sexual arousal.

Lucy knew what to do only too well. She sidled across to the spreadeagled man, pulling coquettishly at her own tight bodice and slipping out her full breasts to cup them lusciously in her hands. As she drew near to Delsingham Marisa saw a tremor run through his lean, pinioned frame. Lucy, mimicking the enticements of a Covent Garden flower girl to perfection, jiggled her breasts inches from his face and simpered, 'Well, my fine gent.

You're a handsome specimen and no mistake. Like the look of my rosy teats, do you? Like a taste?' She rubbed her breasts mockingly against the hard wall of his chest until her nipples hardened with excitement. He shuddered involuntarily, his eyes half closed, and Lucy, seeing it, laughed. 'I think you do like me, my lord. Let's see what's happening to your beautiful cock, shall we? But first, I think you'd like to take a better look at me.' And with a mischievous smile, she slithered completely out of her dress, letting it rustle to the floor, and stood there clad only in her laced white corset and her silk stockings.

Lucy was plump but shapely. The corset, which was cunningly stiffened with buckram to push her full breasts up and apart, was laced tightly down the front, and came to a point just above the enticing dark curls of her pubic hair. Her thighs were round and creamy above her garters, and her bare bottom-cheeks below the tightly waisted corset were deliciously dimpled. Marisa heard John's grunt of excitement from the shadows as Lucy paraded slowly before the helpless Lord Delsingham, the heels of her little laced-up ankle boots clacking on the floorboards.

'Like what you see?' taunted Lucy to her prisoner. 'Like to stick your cock up me, would you?' Still Delsingham was silent. With a wicked chuckle, Lucy dropped to her knees and began to work at the placket of his breeches. Then she gave a gasp of delight.

His penis sprang out fully erect, and Marisa, watching, fought hard against the desperate renewal of desire between her thighs at the sight of that long, thick member, duskily pulsing with power. Lucy stepped back, breathless with excitement at the sight of the superbly built man standing there pinioned, his arms stretched wide and taut as his lengthy, purple-tipped shaft thrust up helplessly from the hair-roughened pouch of his testicles. Ready for the taking, thought

Marisa, wildly imagining that beautiful length of flesh sliding deep within her own melting core.

Lucy, regaining her breath, gave a gurgle of delight. 'Oh, it's beautiful! So long, so thick. Let me taste you and lick you; let me feel your mighty cock in my mouth.' And Delsingham closed his eyes as Lucy's vigorous pink tongue darted out and encircled him. Marisa watched, eyes narrowed, as Lucy slid her full lips avidly over the throbbing muscle of his penis and slid up and down the silky rod with little crooning noises, her hands caressing his flat, taut belly and his seed-filled balls.

Then John, who had been standing silently in the shadows with his fists clenched at his sides and his breath coming in ragged bursts, suddenly moved. Marisa, a little dizzy from the sight of Lucy pleasuring Delsingham's shaft, was about to shout to him, to order him back, but then she realised what he intended, and she went very still.

John had knelt behind Lucy and was grunting as he clumsily pulled his thick penis out of his rough breeches. He pumped it quickly into fulness, and then, while Lucy continued to caress Delsingham avidly with her mouth, John grabbed her plump bottom-cheeks where they flared out beneath her tight corset, pulling them apart and thrusting blindly between her thighs until his cock was anointed with the creamy nectar that flowed between her pink sex-lips. Then, pulling back with a groan, his purple member moving and thrusting with a life of its own, he began to prod blindly at the dark cleft between her buttocks, until the glistening tip of his penis found the tiny pink rosebud of her secret entrance and slipped eagerly up into that tightly collared hole.

Lucy cried out in delight as John tenderly started to ravish her, carefully sliding his thick shaft deeper and deeper between her fiercely clenching bottom-cheeks. In a frenzy of delight, she licked and mouthed avidly at Delsingham's straining phallus, grunting out her pleasure in time to John's manly thrusts. By now Delsingham's head was pressed back helplessly against the wall, and his thin, sensual mouth was compressed against the onslaught of rapture as Lucy's wicked tongue snaked up and down the lengthy, rigid shaft of flesh that jutted fiercely from his loins.

Marisa felt faint as she watched them. In the shadowy candlelight, she could see Delsingham's beautiful silken cock sliding in and out of Lucy's greedy mouth; she could see John's muscular, hairy buttocks pounding away at Lucy's rear, his ballocks swaying against her as the fat, purple stem of his cock eagerly pleasured the gasping Lucy. Marisa longed to join in. Her breasts were painfully tight, the nipples tugging like fiery cords at her abdomen, while the moisture seeped wantonly from her swollen labia. She wanted Delsingham's beautiful, captive body so much; she wanted to kiss his agonised face, to take his cock into her aching core, and run her hands over his straining, sinewed torso, to feel the glory of his orgasm exploding all through his beautiful body.

But there was no time. John was shouting out hoarsely now, reaching round to fumble with Lucy's heavy breasts as he pumped faster and faster. Lucy, with a cry of joy, wriggled back against him, relishing every inch of his glistening fat rod as it penetrated her so deliciously. At the same time she continued to rub at Delsingham's saliva-slick penis with eager hands and fingers, and Marisa saw her prisoner go helplessly rigid as his magnificent penis spasmed into orgasm, sending milky jets of semen gushing over Lucy's plump breasts. Lucy, in the throes of climax herself, rubbed frenziedly against his twitching glans, delighting in the floods of hot seed spilling across her engorged nipples, clutching at his tight, thick testicles as the dark pleasure convulsed his powerful body. John, too, was spent at last, and they were all still. Delsingham, his arms still pinioned high to the wall, stood with his head bowed, while Lucy subsided with a contented sigh to the floor, and John knelt beside her, slowly lapping their prisoner's copious semen off her now soft pink nipples with his long, rough tongue.

Marisa felt suddenly tired and drained. The solitary candle had gone out, and outside it was almost dark, with lowering clouds obscuring the last of the daylight. Walking slowly across the room, she said flatly, 'That's all for now, Lucy, John. You can go.' They nodded their heads and scurried off, pulling their clothes around them as they went, their faces still flushed with exertion. As their footsteps faded away down the stairs, Marisa moved across to Delsingham and began to unstrap his wrists. She concentrated steadfastly on her task, avoiding his gaze, and avoiding too the sight of his now-soft phallus as it hung, still thick and lengthy even in detumescence, against the silken-haired skin of his inner thigh.

'You can go too,' she said shortly as the last of his bonds came free.

He began to rub his wrists gently, bringing back the circulation. Marisa trembled, realising that even now, now that she'd humiliated him, she still wanted him as badly as ever. She'd hoped to make him appear lustful and degraded and stupid as her two servants played with him, but instead he'd been magnificent, and the memory of his hard, silken penis spasming with a life of its own across Lucy's swollen breasts still made her feel faint with longing. She wanted to stroke him into arousal again, wanted to take him for herself, to feel his virile shaft tenderly caressing her, filling her, urging her into the realms of sweet, sensual delight she knew he was so superbly capable of providing.

A fantasy. She'd driven him away now for good, and wasn't that what she wanted? She went slowly to pick up the rapiers and started putting them away in their case. 'You heard me,' she repeated tersely, not looking at him. 'You can go.'

But he was walking up behind her. She could hear the soft fall of his leather boots on the floorboards as he came nearer. He put his hand on the rapier case, and said, quite calmly, 'Why, Marisa?'

She twisted round sharply at his words. 'Why what?'

'Why all that charade?' he said softly, his eyes assessing her. 'Why do you hate me so much, when I thought we were friends?'

She laughed scornfully, planting her hands on her slender hips. 'Friends? I thought you would have described me more as some kind of free whore. Someone you could just come to when you felt like a quick bit of fun. Well, you can't! And maybe the memory of that,' and she nodded sharply at the discarded leather straps on the floor, 'will remind you that you can't just go off to visit the woman you're going to marry and then come back to me!'

'The woman I'm going to marry?' he said. 'What do you mean?'

Marisa caught her breath. 'And now you're trying to deny it. How truly pitiful. I mean Lady Henrietta, of course, who I believe is taking the waters in Bath.'

Delsingham gripped her shoulders, his fingers burning her flesh through the tattered remnants of her shirt. His breeches, still unfastened, were clinging by some miracle to his lean hips; his exposed genitals in their nest of soft dark hair were a threatening reminder of his all too potent masculinity, though he himself seemed calmly indifferent to his nakedness. 'Who told you', he said, in a dangerously quiet voice, 'that I was going to marry Lady Henrietta?'

Marisa tried furiously to twist away from his strong grasp, but failed. 'What does it matter who told me, you bully?'

His fingers tightened painfully around her narrow shoulders; his dark eyes burned her. 'It matters,' he said, 'because it's a lie. There was talk, once, of an alliance between her family and mine, but I never took it any further. I'm not engaged to marry anyone, Marisa.'

She gazed up at him, stunned. 'Then – where have you been all this time?'

'Minding my own business,' he said curtly, 'but I can see that I should have been here, minding yours. What's all this I hear about your dangerous exploits?'

'How do you know?'

'I have my methods,' he replied grimly.

Again she tried to struggle free of him. 'I don't see that any of it matters to you, Lord Delsingham.'

He shook her. 'It matters because you matter to me, Marisa, damn you! Maddening as you are, I find you quite, quite irresistible, as you can see all too clearly for yourself.'

Her eyes dropped once more to his groin, and widened. Her heart was hammering wildly, but she did her best to sneer up at him coldly in response. 'I can see that your powers of recuperation are quite remarkable, my lord, but so are those of a rutting stag. Am I supposed to be impressed?'

'No,' he said, his eyes narrow slits, his voice husky with restrained desire. 'No, but you're supposed to kiss me, damn you.'

'And you,' she replied angrily, 'are supposed to ask me.'

His breath was coming short and hard now: she could see the hot desire burning in his dark gaze. His hands slipped to her breasts, cupping them, twisting at her throbbing nipples. 'When', he said slowly, his eyes glinting, 'did you ever have any time for men who asked you, Marisa?'

She gasped as the fierce arousal leapt through her body at his touch. 'Never,' she said, with a sudden, tiny ripple of laughter. 'Oh, never,' and with a growl of masculine victory he started to cover her face and breasts with burning kisses.

'A hit?' he said softly.

'Oh, yes,' she murmured breathlessly. 'A veritable hit,

my lord . . .' And she sighed aloud with delight as his tongue circled and flicked at her tight pink nipples.

He drew himself away, just for a moment, in order to lay her carefully back against the big oak table, pillowing her hips and shoulders with cushions he pulled almost savagely from the window seat. Then, desperate for the renewal of his touch, Marisa helped him to ease her buckskin breeches from her hips, slipping them completely away so that he could pull her slender thighs wide apart as they dangled over the edge of the table. She knew that her lush, crinkled feminine flesh was already honeyed with moisture. He ran his fingers teasingly through the pale down of her pubic mound, and let the ball of his thumb separate her darkly engorged labia, spreading them like petals and pushing up gently into her yearning sex with his fingers until she cried out and almost climaxed against him. He let his hand slide away, keeping her teetering deliciously on the brink, straining in exquisite torture, and desperately she reached out to feel for his beautiful, thick penis, guiding its solid length towards her churning hips. He laughed gently, saying, 'Patience, little one,' but Marisa had forgotten the meaning of patience, and as he carefully parted her sex lips and slid the swollen head of his dark shaft into her honeyed passage, she clasped him to her, thrusting her yearning breasts against his warm, wet mouth and clamping her hands round the firm globes of his buttocks, gasping with joy as she felt that beautiful, solid shaft of male flesh slowly driving into her. She arched frantically up to meet him and, sensing that she was well past the point of no return, he reached down carefully with one hand to savour her glistening clitoris as it thrust out hungrily from her parted flesh folds, while continuing to drive his lengthy penis deep within her, and pleasuring her into such a wanton frenzy of lust that her splayed thighs trembled and jerked. She clasped him to her, feeling all that delicious length ravishing her, again and again, until nothing else existed but the sweet, hard pleasure of his penis. She cried out his name, engulfed by the white hot explosion that was rippling out in great, sensual waves from her very core.

He drove himself powerfully into her as he too reached his climax. She stroked his heaving shoulders as he lay against her breast, feeling her womb still pulsing slowly and sweetly around him.

Afterwards he kissed her very tenderly and helped her to her feet. She leaned dizzily against the table, trying to push her disordered blonde curls back from her face. Her hand strayed to the discarded rapiers. 'I rather think', she said a little distractedly, 'that you were the victor in that particular bout, Lord Delsingham.'

BLACK LACE NEW BOOKS

Published in May

AVENGING ANGELS
Roxanne Carr

Disillusioned by the chauvinistic attitude of men in the idyllic summer resort of Tierra del Sol, tour guide Karen puts her fledgling skills as a dominatrix to the test. Pleasantly surprised by the results, Karen opens a bar – Angels – where women can realise their most erotic fantasies. However, the one man Karen really wants – Riccardo Baddeiras – the owner of a rival bar and brother of her business partner Maria, refuses to be drawn into her web of submission. Quite clearly, Karen will have to fine-tune her skills.

ISBN 0 352 33147 X

THE LION LOVER
Mercedes Kelly

It's the 1920s. When young doctor Mathilde Valentine becomes a medic in a mission in Kenya she soon finds out all is not what it seems. For one thing, McKinnon, the handsome missionary, has been married twice – and both of his wives have mysteriously disappeared. Mathilde falls for a rugged game warden but ignores his warnings that she might be in danger. Abducted and sold into slavery, she finds herself in the weird and wonderful harem of an Arabian sultan and discovers the truth about the two Mrs McKinnons. Will she regain her freedom?

ISBN 0 352 33162 3

PAST PASSIONS
An Anthology of Erotic Writing by Women
Edited by Kerri Sharp
£6.99

This is the second of the two larger format Black Lace anthologies – *Modern Love* being the first. While *Modern Love* is a selection of extracts from contemporary Black Lace novels, *Past Passions* is an inspired collection of excerpts taken from tales set in a variety of countries, cultures and centuries giving the reader the added pleasure of detail essential in the creating of historical settings.

ISBN 0 352 33159 3

Published in June

JASMINE BLOSSOMS
Sylvie Ouellette

When Joanna is sent on a business trip to Japan, she expects nothing unusual. She soon finds that her sensuality is put to the test as enigmatic messages are followed by singular encounters with strangers who seem to know her every desire. She is constantly aroused but never entirely sated. As she gradually gives in to the magic of Japan – its people and its ways – she learns that she is becoming involved in a case of mistaken identity, erotic intrigue and mysterious seduction.

ISBN 0 352 33157 7

PANDORA'S BOX 2
An Anthology of Erotic Writing by Women
Edited by Kerri Sharp
£5.99

This is the second of the Pandora's Box anthologies of erotic writing by women. The book includes extracts from the best-selling and most popular titles of the Black Lace series, as well as four completely new stories. *Pandora's Box 2* is a celebration of four years of this revolutionary imprint. The diversity of the material is a testament to the many facets of the female imagination. This is unashamed erotic indulgence for women.

ISBN 0 352 33151 8

To be published in July

COUNTRY MATTERS
Tesni Morgan

When Lorna inherits a country estate, she thinks she is set for a life of pastoral bliss and restfulness. She's wrong. Her closest neighbour, a ruthless businessman and a darkly handsome architect all have their own reasons for wanting to possess her, body and soul. When Lorna discovers that paganism is thriving in the village, the intrigue can only escalate.

ISBN 0 352 33174 7

GINGER ROOT
Robyn Russell

As the summer temperatures soar, art gallery director Eden finds it harder and harder to stick to her self-imposed celibacy. She starts to fantasise about the attractive young artists who visit the gallery, among them a rugged but sensitive sculptor whom she sets out to seduce. It's going to be an exciting summer of surprises and steamy encounters.

ISBN 0 352 33152 6

If you would like a complete list of plot summaries of Black Lace titles, please fill out the questionnaire overleaf or send a stamped addressed envelope to:-

Black Lace, 332 Ladbroke Grove, London W10 5AH

BLACK LACE BACKLIST

All books are priced £4.99 unless another price is given.

------✂------------------

Please send me the books I have ticked above.

Name   ....

Address   ....

            ....

            ....

            .... Post Code   ....

Send to: **Cash Sales, Black Lace Books, 332 Ladbroke Grove, London W10 5AH.**

Please enclose a cheque or postal order, made payable to **Virgin Publishing Ltd**, to the value of the books you have ordered plus postage and packing costs as follows:

UK and BFPO – £1.00 for the first book, 50p for each subsequent book.

Overseas (including Republic of Ireland) – £2.00 for the first book, £1.00 each subsequent book.

If you would prefer to pay by VISA or ACCESS/ MASTERCARD, please write your card number and expiry date here:

....

Please allow up to 28 days for delivery.

Signature   ....

------✂------------------

WE NEED YOUR HELP ...
to plan the future of women's erotic fiction –

– and no stamp required!

Yours are the only opinions that matter.

Black Lace is the first series of books devoted to erotic fiction by women for women.

We intend to keep providing the best-written, sexiest books you can buy. And we'd appreciate your help and valued opinion of the books so far. Tell us what you want to read.

THE BLACK LACE QUESTIONNAIRE

SECTION ONE: ABOUT YOU

1.1 Sex (*we presume you are female, but so as not to discriminate*)
    Are you?
        Male   ☐
        Female   ☐

1.2 Age
        under 21   ☐   21–30   ☐
        31–40   ☐   41–50   ☐
        51–60   ☐   over 60   ☐

1.3 At what age did you leave full-time education?
        still in education ☐   16 or younger ☐
        17–19   ☐   20 or older   ☐

1.4 Occupation _____

1.5 Annual household income
    under £10,000 ☐ £10–£20,000 ☐
    £20–£30,000 ☐ £30–£40,000 ☐
    over £40,000 ☐

1.6 We are perfectly happy for you to remain anonymous;
    but if you would like to receive information on other
    publications available, please insert your name and
    address

    _____

    _____

    _____

    _____

SECTION TWO: ABOUT BUYING BLACK LACE BOOKS

2.1 How did you acquire this copy of *Pandora's Box 2*?
    I bought it myself ☐ My partner bought it ☐
    I borrowed/found it ☐

2.2 How did you find out about Black Lace books?
    I saw them in a shop ☐
    I saw them advertised in a magazine ☐
    I saw the London Underground posters ☐
    I read about them in _____
    Other _____

2.3 Please tick the following statements you agree with:
    I would be less embarrassed about buying Black
    Lace books if the cover pictures were less explicit ☐
    I think that in general the pictures on Black
    Lace books are about right ☐
    I think Black Lace cover pictures should be as
    explicit as possible ☐

2.4 Would you read a Black Lace book in a public place – on
    a train for instance?
    Yes ☐ No ☐

SECTION THREE: ABOUT THIS BLACK LACE BOOK

3.1 Do you think the sex content in this book is:
    Too much ☐   About right ☐
    Not enough ☐

3.2 Do you think the writing style in this book is:
    Too unreal/escapist ☐   About right ☐
    Too down to earth ☐

3.3 Do you think the story in this book is:
    Too complicated ☐   About right ☐
    Too boring/simple ☐

3.4 Do you think the cover of this book is:
    Too explicit ☐   About right ☐
    Not explicit enough ☐

Here's a space for any other comments:

SECTION FOUR: ABOUT OTHER BLACK LACE BOOKS

4.1 How many Black Lace books have you read? ☐

4.2 If more than one, which one did you prefer?

4.3 Why?

SECTION FIVE: ABOUT YOUR IDEAL EROTIC NOVEL

We want to publish the books you want to read – so this is your chance to tell us exactly what your ideal erotic novel would be like.

5.1   Using a scale of 1 to 5 (1 = no interest at all, 5 = your ideal), please rate the following possible settings for an erotic novel:

Medieval/barbarian/sword 'n' sorcery ☐
Renaissance/Elizabethan/Restoration ☐
Victorian/Edwardian ☐
1920s & 1930s – the Jazz Age ☐
Present day ☐
Future/Science Fiction ☐

5.2   Using the same scale of 1 to 5, please rate the following themes you may find in an erotic novel:

Submissive male/dominant female ☐
Submissive female/dominant male ☐
Lesbianism ☐
Bondage/fetishism ☐
Romantic love ☐
Experimental sex e.g. anal/watersports/sex toys ☐
Gay male sex ☐
Group sex ☐

Using the same scale of 1 to 5, please rate the following styles in which an erotic novel could be written:

Realistic, down to earth, set in real life ☐
Escapist fantasy, but just about believable ☐
Completely unreal, impressionistic, dreamlike ☐

5.3   Would you prefer your ideal erotic novel to be written from the viewpoint of the main male characters or the main female characters?

Male ☐   Female ☐
Both ☐

5.4 What would your ideal Black Lace heroine be like? Tick as many as you like:

Dominant	☐	Glamorous	☐
Extroverted	☐	Contemporary	☐
Independent	☐	Bisexual	☐
Adventurous	☐	Naïve	☐
Intellectual	☐	Introverted	☐
Professional	☐	Kinky	☐
Submissive	☐	Anything else?	☐
Ordinary	☐	_____	

5.5 What would your ideal male lead character be like? Again, tick as many as you like:

Rugged	☐		
Athletic	☐	Caring	☐
Sophisticated	☐	Cruel	☐
Retiring	☐	Debonair	☐
Outdoor-type	☐	Naïve	☐
Executive-type	☐	Intellectual	☐
Ordinary	☐	Professional	☐
Kinky	☐	Romantic	☐
Hunky	☐		
Sexually dominant	☐	Anything else?	☐
Sexually submissive	☐	_____	

5.6 Is there one particular setting or subject matter that your ideal erotic novel would contain?

_____

SECTION SIX: LAST WORDS

6.1 What do you like best about Black Lace books?

_____

6.2 What do you most dislike about Black Lace books?

_____

6.3 In what way, if any, would you like to change Black Lace covers?

_____

6.4   Here's a space for any other comments:

_____

_____

_____

_____

_____

Thank you for completing this questionnaire. Now tear it out of the book – carefully! – put it in an envelope and send it to:

Black Lace
FREEPOST
London
W10 5BR

No stamp is required if you are resident in the U.K.